THE AGE OF OLYMPUS

ALSO BY GAVIN SCOTT AND AVAILABLE FROM TITAN BOOKS

The Age of Treachery
The Age of Exodus (April 2018)

GAVIN SCOTT

THE AGE OF OLYMPUS

A DUNCAN FORRESTER MYSTERY

TITAN BOOKS

The Age of Olympus
Print edition ISBN: 9781783297825
E-book edition ISBN: 9781783297832

Published by Titan Books
A division of Titan Publishing Group Ltd
144 Southwark Street, London SE1 0UP

First edition: April 2017
10 9 8 7 6 5 4 3 2 1

© 2017 Gavin Scott

A CIP catalogue record for this title is available from the British Library.

Printed in the USA.

TO MORRISON HENRY JACKSON

1

SUNSET OVER ATHENS

"We held them off for a week up there back in 1944," said the press attaché, pointing up to the Acropolis.

"The Germans?" said Sophie.

"No, dear lady," said the attaché, a pop-eyed man with a military moustache, "the Greeks."

Sophie glanced at Forrester, puzzled. "I thought the British were on the same side as the Greeks," she said.

"We were on the same side as the *Greeks*, yes," said the attaché. "But not the *communists*."

They were inching their way along Aeolos Street, which runs west from Stadium Street to the foot of the Acropolis, and every few yards the car had to slow down to avoid old ladies spilling into the roadway offering hot chestnuts, green-dyed cakes, black market cigarettes, candles decorated with pictures of the Virgin Mary, transfers of the crucified Christ to stick on your arm, and fireworks with which to celebrate Holy Week, 1946. Forrester had flown to Athens because, to his amazement, the Empire Council for Archaeology had finally given him the funds for his expedition to Crete. But it turned out there were people in the Greek capital who wanted to see him before he set off for the island, and the press attaché from the British Embassy had been waiting for them at the airport in a Lagonda, which must have been in use before Archduke Ferdinand went to Sarajevo. Possibly *when* the Archduke went to Sarajevo.

"During the war, of course," said Forrester, "the communists were some of the best fighters. And we were all on the same side." Every other house, Forrester noted, now seemed to be daubed with red communist slogans.

"That was then," said the attaché, whose name was Lancaster, "but ever since the Germans left, the Reds have been trying to take over. Came as close as dammit just after I arrived, too, in forty-four. Hence the fight outside the Parthenon."

"Which I imagine would have been a very good defensive position," said Forrester.

"That's my point, old chap," said Lancaster. "Made you realise why the Greeks put the Acropolis there in the first place. It looks magnificent – but it's all about power."

Countess Sophie Arnfeldt-Laurvig's eyes met Forrester's in a secret smile. They were both savouring the delight of being together again after their brief, dangerous encounter in Norway. When Forrester had asked her if she wanted to come with him in the Cretan expedition he had held his breath, wondering whether he had misread what had passed between them during those tense, tender and almost fatal hours at Bjornsfjord, but to his profound relief she had responded to his invitation immediately. After four years of balancing the demands of supporting the Norwegian resistance and protecting the tenants on her estates from the German occupiers, she was eager to escape, and when they had met at London Airport it was as if they had never parted. During the flight to Athens she had clasped his hand tightly in hers, and though they had said little, it seemed that little needed saying. The war was over and they were back together again. It was enough.

Now they were being driven through what was left of the old Turkish bazaar, past alleys full of toymakers, shoemakers and coppersmiths, like something out of the Middle Ages. There was even a row of shops whose windows were entirely filled with buttons. Sophie smiled. "I must go to those shops," she said. "In Norway, for some reason, it was impossible during the occupation to readily obtain any buttons." Her English, lightly accented and perfectly pronounced, was composed of a slightly old-fashioned vocabulary once provided to the nobility of Europe through well-qualified governesses.

"Say again?" asked Lancaster. "Hard to hear through this din."

Which was an understatement. The Greeks, Forrester had always felt, had a unique passion for noise. Radios blared from every open window, the street was loud with conversations being carried on at the top of voices, seconded by church bells, crowing cockerels, the clanging of trams and the roar of internal combustion engines. A motorcycle passed them with a deafening boom.

"Look at his exhausts," said Lancaster, his fingers

drumming the steering wheel. "I'm pretty certain that not only are those not silencers – they're actually *amplifiers*." The attaché's Christian name was Osbert, which Forrester remembered reading somewhere, during the war.

Lancaster turned to Sophie. "So what was it you wanted to shop for, Countess?"

"Buttons," said Sophie.

"Buttons tomorrow," said Lancaster decisively. "*Sunset* tonight," and swerved the car violently into the kerb beside a ramshackle taverna whose sign was almost hidden under a canopy of vines. "Hop out and grab a table."

Moments later they were looking over the shoulder of the proprietor, an unshaven man in a shirt that looked as if it had not been washed since the German invasion, as he poured liberal doses of yellow retsina into well-chipped drinking glasses.

"It's only going to last two minutes," said Lancaster, "so keep your eyes open."

Obediently, Sophie and Forrester fixed their eyes on the Acropolis.

"Watch how the last rays of the sun leave this hideous city in blessed darkness and just light up the hilltop."

Sure enough, as post-war Athens vanished into the dusk, the marble of the Parthenon and the Propylaea began to gleam as if with an inner fire, and behind them Mount Hymettus turned rose-red.

"It's perfect," said Sophie. And it was. It was like a stage set, complete with lighting, which had been arranged for their delight two and a half thousand years before.

"Your health," said Lancaster, raising his battered glass – and then paused and held up his hand in warning. "Have you alerted the countess to what this stuff tastes like, Forrester?"

"The wine has hints of pine resin," said Forrester to Sophie.

"For which read emphatic overtones of the best turpentine," said Lancaster.

Forrester smiled. "But you might come to enjoy it." He clinked his glass against hers, and Lancaster's, and as they drank, the sunset reached its climax. Sophie looked at Forrester, her eyes bright with merriment.

"My admiration for the ancient Greeks is very much increased," she said, "if they built their civilisation while drinking muck like this."

"They say this was the hour that Socrates took the hemlock," said Lancaster, his long fingers caressing his silky moustache, "so you may be witnessing the last thing the old boy ever saw." They watched in silence as darkness reclaimed the great temple, thinking of the snub-nosed, henpecked philosopher who had paid the price for questioning the gods four hundred years before the birth of Christ.

"Tell me more about your run-in with the communists," said Forrester. "Some of them were probably chaps I fought alongside during the war."

"Doubtless some of them were splendid fellows," said Lancaster, "but we couldn't let them turn the cradle of civilisation into a Soviet People's Republic." He swallowed some more wine, and grimaced. "Not without an election anyway, which they seemed to want to avoid. So, there was much fighting in the streets, embassy under siege, British peacekeeping force outnumbered, machine guns, mortars, bombs, all that kind of thing. And then in the middle of the battle who turns up but Winston Churchill? In a Royal Navy cruiser, naturally. Horribly dangerous, but he was in his element, of course. Insisted on holding a press conference while hostilities were still in progress – in the embassy garden, of all places."

"What was wrong with the embassy garden?" asked Sophie.

"Nothing in itself, but you came into it down a set of steps, and I knew that as soon as Winnie clapped eyes on them he'd stop at the top and strike a heroic pose for the photographers. They were all waiting eagerly among the rose bushes down below. And here was the problem – the top of the steps was the one place in the garden where a sniper in one of the surrounding houses could take you out. I explained this to Winnie and he promised to keep moving, but I knew perfectly well he wouldn't be able to resist temptation, and sure enough, as soon as he comes out of the embassy he adopts one of his bulldog stances and the flashbulbs start going off and he wouldn't move till they'd stopped taking pictures. I was sure the end had come."

"What did you do?" asked Sophie.

"Pushed him down the steps," said Lancaster. "Not a very elegant solution, but sure enough, at that very moment there was a rifle crack and a handful of plaster flew out of the embassy wall right where he'd been."

"I hope he was grateful," said Sophie. Forrester grinned.

"Knowing his probable reaction to having his moment of glory spoiled," said Lancaster, "I said the ambassador did it."

Sophie grinned, there was a pause, and Forrester knew they were about to discover the reason why Lancaster had given them a lift from the airport.

"Anyway," said the press attaché, "I wanted to fill you in on the situation before you meet up with everybody."

"Everybody?" said Forrester. "A reception committee?"

"No, no," said Lancaster, refilling their glasses. His and Forrester's anyway: Sophie's remained largely untouched. "It's just that there happen to be a lot of people you know in town at present. Paddy Fermor, for a start."

Patrick Leigh Fermor had been in charge of the operation in Crete in which British commandos had captured a German general and spirited him away to Egypt. It was while performing his diversionary role that Forrester had found, in the Gorge of Acharius, the cave he was coming back to excavate. He grinned as he heard Leigh Fermor's name.

"What's Paddy doing here? Last I heard he was in London looking for a job."

"Well, he's found one here, lecturing on British culture to the Greeks on behalf of the British Council."

Forrester laughed. "I wonder what the Greeks make of that," he said.

"They lap it up," said Lancaster, "because all he really does is tell them war stories, and there's nothing they like better than a war hero telling his tale. Xan Fielding's backing him up, and we hope you will too."

"If it helps," said Forrester.

"Every little thing helps," said Lancaster. "The fact is we're in a precarious position here, and so is Greece. The fighting's over for the time being, but it could start up at any moment. The communists are putting together an army and when the time comes, they'll strike. Tito's backing them from Yugoslavia."

"So the Iron Curtain could fall over Greece too?" said Sophie.

"It could indeed," said Lancaster, and fixed his pop-eyed gaze on Forrester. "And that's where your old friend General Alexandros comes into it. We're a bit worried about him."

"He's not a communist," said Forrester. "I know that for a fact."

After the Germans invaded Greece in 1941, Forrester and Aristotle Alexandros had spent weeks together, planning guerrilla operations while hiding out in a cave near Mount Olympus, and they had talked about every subject under the sun, including the Soviet Union. "He's the most rational man I've ever met. One of the best read, too. He saw through Marx as a teenager."

"But after you parted he spent the rest of the war fighting the Nazis *alongside* the communists," said Lancaster, "and that makes him a suspect now as far as the Greek Army is concerned. They're all royalists, you know."

"But he's the best strategist in Greece," said Forrester. "Best tactician too. Don't tell me the regular army's put him on ice."

"That's exactly what they've done," said Lancaster.

"And he's getting bored and impatient. The communists want to put him in charge of ELAS."

"ELAS?"

"Their strike force. The so-called Greek People's Liberation Army."

"But surely he wouldn't—"

"The present regime's pretty rotten. Too many people who cosied up to the Germans. He might think he could use ELAS to take over, clean house and start again with a fresh slate."

Forrester was silent for a moment. It was all too plausible. And if Aristotle Alexandros joined the communist army, they would win. Stalin's campaign to control Europe would be one step closer to fulfilment.

"What do you want me to do?" he asked.

"Just talk to Alexandros, find out what you can about his thinking. Then let us know."

"I'm very fond of him," said Forrester. "I'm not going to sell him down the river."

"Wouldn't dream of asking you to, old boy," said the attaché. "Just sound him out about whether he's going to join ELAS, that's all."

"If we come across each other."

"Oh, you'll come across each other," said Lancaster. "This is Greece. Besides, there's a party tonight at the Regent-Archbishop's, and I've wangled you both an invitation."

"I had hoped to have a quiet dinner with Sophie," said Forrester.

"I know," said Lancaster, with patently insincere sympathy, "but I also know we can rely on you to be a good scout, old man. They speak very highly of you at the War Office, and the same can't be said for most academics, I can tell you."

2

HIS BEATITUDE

They walked through the warm evening air along Kifissia Street, which ran from Syntagma Square alongside the Old Royal Palace, its grounds now known as the National Garden. The topiary bushes and winding paths, Forrester knew, concealed the hastily buried bodies of the victims of the failed communist uprising in 1944, but he did not mention this to Sophie, determined not to disturb her pleasure in exchanging the cold austerity of Scandinavia for the balm of the Mediterranean.

Opposite the gardens were the pompous, wedding-cake buildings of the Egyptian Legation, the French Embassy, the Greek Foreign Office and the Ministry of War, but the edifice to which they were headed, Skaramangar House, residence of His Beatitude the Orthodox Archbishop and Regent of Greece, surpassed them all in opulent vulgarity.

"You'll recognise it quite easily," Lancaster had told them when he gave them directions. "It's built in a style

I call 'Hollywood Balkan'." Forrester placed the name then: before he became a press attaché, Osbert Lancaster had published several very funny books about, of all things, architectural history, inventing names for pompous styles and skewering them in spare, elegant cartoons. "Make sure you look out for the debased Byzantine capitals," he had advised as they parted. Sophie looked at Forrester, puzzled.

"Debased?" she said. "Doesn't that mean—"

"I think in this case it's a technical term," said Forrester. "But we *are* in Athens. You never can tell." The Archbishop's door opened and a liveried footman ushered them into a vast and crowded room. As he took their names they stopped, astonished at the spectacle before them.

Massive oak beams rested on squat pillars (topped, as promised, by the gilded shapes of the debased Byzantine capitals) from which hung baroquely ecclesiastical candelabra illuminating a sea of guests resplendent in dinner jackets, heavily braided uniforms and elegant evening gowns. Waiters glided around the room offering *spanakopita*, *saganaki* and *tiropitas*. A huge log roared in a fireplace so immense it reminded Forrester of Xanadu in *Citizen Kane*, which he and Barbara had seen the night before he parachuted into Sardinia.

Beside the fireplace, in a chair that might once have served a medieval warlord, sat Archbishop Damaskinos, robed and bearded with all the magnificence of Byzantium itself. Even seated, he looked huge: at least six foot six, seventeen stone if he was a pound, and adding to that already imposing appearance were a tall black headpiece

like an upside-down top hat and a silver-knobbed staff
of office, clutched in a large, meaty hand, its sausage-
like fingers thick with wiry black hair. On his feet were
stout black boots, which again reminded Forrester of an
image from the cinema. It was a moment before he had
it: the massive footwear sported by Boris Karloff as
Frankenstein's monster. Suppressing the lese-majesty of
the image, and watched closely by the two splendidly
uniformed Greek soldiers behind His Beatitude's chair, in
their traditional flounced skirts, pom-pommed shoes and
red sock-like berets, Forrester bowed low.

"Welcome to Greece, Dr. Forrester," said the Archbishop
in thickly accented English. "May you and your countrymen
help bring us the peace for which we hunger."

"I hope very much that that is possible, Regent," said
Forrester. Damaskinos was currently regent of Greece
because King George II was still in exile in London.
During the war the king had been supported by the Allies
as the country's legitimate ruler, driven from power by
the Nazis. But *before* the Axis invasion he'd been hand in
glove with a semi-fascist dictator who had persecuted not
just communists but anyone he considered liberal. Even
the works of Plato, Thucydides and Xenophon had been
banned. As a result of King George's support for this fairly
loathsome regime, it was not just the communists who
never wanted to see him again.

As a result, to avoid setting off a firestorm after German
troops withdrew, the Allies had persuaded King George to
stay in London until a vote could be held about whether

he was allowed to return, and in the meantime Archbishop Damaskinos was officially Head of State. But tonight His Beatitude did not apparently want to discuss politics; he wanted to defend his religion. Some disparaging remark about either himself or the Greek Orthodox faith, Forrester guessed, must have appeared in the British press.

"You British disapprove of Greek Christians," said the Archbishop. "You regard us as insincere."

"I'm not sure—" began Forrester. Sophie suppressed a smile, and Forrester realised His Beatitude had mistaken him for someone else.

"You think of us as worldly, as lacking a sincere belief in our maker," said the Archbishop.

"No, Your Beatitude —"

"You think we are too close to the old pagan ways."

"Why would people be thinking such things, Your Beatitude?" asked Sophie, innocently. Deflected, the Archbishop seemed to notice her for the first time, and his face suddenly lit up with mischief.

"Perhaps because it is true," he said, instantly switching his position. "You see, dear lady, it was much easier to turn the old gods into saints than to try to abolish them."

"So much easier," said Sophie. "We did it in Norway with Thor and Odin. And I see you have a kouros yourself. A beautiful kouros." The Archbishop beamed with pride and followed her gaze towards the niche in the wall at the far end of the room in which stood a four-foot-tall statue of a handsome, naked young man, his shoulders square, his head erect, his lips curved in a mysterious smile. Several people were gathered around it.

"Do you think he is the god?" asked the Archbishop. "Or an acolyte?"

"I think he is both," said Sophie. "I think he is perhaps the god in man." The Archbishop looked at her appreciatively.

"That is exactly what I think myself, dear lady," he said. "You may touch him if you like." He noted Sophie's surprise. "As my other guests are doing." And indeed, several members of the party were laying their palms flat on the head of the kouros, one after another, their eyes closed as if in prayer.

"They say that if you think of heaven when you touch him, God will ensure you a safe passage there. Which god and which heaven I leave for you to choose." Abruptly, as if remembering his real purpose, he turned his attention back to Forrester. "What you British forget," he said, "is that the Greek people love their church. They may laugh at the local priest, certainly, with his wife and children, but they look up to their bishop, and they revere their archbishop. What's more, they expect him to play a part in the government of his country. Why should he not? Why should I not govern as well as bless?"

"Why not indeed, Your Beatitude?"

"But if the communists take over, where will the Church be then? That is my question for you, Dr. Forrester. I want you to think it over."

"I will, Your Beatitude," said Forrester. "I certainly will." And the audience was complete.

"What a charming old man," whispered Sophie as

they made way for the next guests to pay their respects. Forrester grinned and gazed around the room where, lit by the flickering firelight, was gathered the whole panoply of the Greek political establishment. Red-faced Michaelis, peering at the assembly through his monocle like a benevolent London clubman; Constantine Papas, so theatrically political he looked as if he had been playing the part of a politician on some provincial stage; Admiral Plaxos, a garden gnome in naval uniform, and an assortment of individuals who represented most of the Greek political dynasties, the Venezelos, the Dragoumis, the Tsaldaris. Political power in Greece, Forrester knew, tended to be a hereditary business. Above them all towered the distinctive figure of General Aristotle Alexandros, as tall as the Archbishop but whip-thin, his eagle nose projecting over a nutcracker chin, his moustache bristling, his olive-black eyes flashing. As soon as he saw Forrester he abandoned the politicians, strode across the room and embraced him.

"Duncan," he said. "Duncan the digger."

"I never got to dig when I was with you, Ari," said Forrester. "Too many people shooting at us."

"And missing us," said the General. "Because we were too quick for them. Who is this beautiful woman?"

Forrester introduced Sophie, and was amused to see that there was an immediate glint in the General's eye.

"I am at your service, my lady," said Alexandros, and gestured to the assembled company. "Feast your eyes on our film stars."

"Film stars?" said Sophie, surprised, as Alexandros had clearly intended.

"The Greeks think of their politicians as the rest of the world thinks of film stars," he said. "Or the English think of horses."

"From which I infer that Greeks have a serious interest in politics?" said Sophie, smiling.

"Oh, yes," said the General. "Very serious. The poorest cigarette seller has an opinion on who is about to be traded from his team, who is about to be given a starring role in the next production, who is about to be put out to pasture."

"Which generals are going to stage a coup," said Forrester, feeling he ought to say something to repay Lancaster for the ride from the airport.

"Oh, coups," said Alexandros. "They are so old school. Just exchanging one team for another, with a few shots fired at half-time. I think something larger is in the air these days."

"What's that?" said Forrester, but before Alexandros could reply an arm was thrown around his shoulder and gripped him tight.

"What are you doing out in the sunlight, you old mole?" and Forrester turned to see the beaming face of David Venables, last glimpsed boarding an armoured ferry to cross the Channel just after D-Day, following the invading army with a microphone and a BBC Outside Broadcast van. Despite the formality of the occasion he was still carrying over his shoulder the canvas bag in which Forrester knew he kept whichever manuscript he was working on at present, which would be further encased in an odiferous oilskin pouch whose distinctive scent was discernible even here in this maelstrom of hair pomades and perfumes.

Forrester had met Venables under a table in a pub in Soho when they were caught in a raid at the height of the blitz, and been pleasantly carried away on the tide of acerbic wit that flowed out of the man as the floor shuddered with each falling bomb. Venables had begun his working life as a naturalist, and looked at the human race as if they were so many ants milling about an anthill, but he had wisely disguised the cynicism under a coating of cosy wit for his weekly nature broadcasts on the BBC Home Service. "Our Friend the Vole" and "Otters I have Known" were among his most popular broadcasts. When he was in company he felt he could trust, however, he would frequently compare the passions and rituals of the human race to those of the orangutan, the parrotfish and even the amoeba, usually to the disadvantage of *Homo sapiens*.

"I'm digging up Crete," said Forrester, noting out of the corner of his eye that Sophie, with some effort, was in the process of gently disengaging herself from Alexandros. "And you? What poor dumb beasts are you gunning for now?"

"Greeks," said Venables. "Keith and I have come to write our Greek book. Or rather," he added, tapping his canvas bag, "*my* Greek book – Keith will merely draw the pictures."

"Which will be the only reason anybody ever opens it," said the stocky young man beside him. "And once they close the book, my pictures will be all they'll ever remember." He shook hands with Forrester and bowed to Sophie as she joined them.

"Keith Beamish," he said. "Be like Dad – Keep Mum."

Sophie, joining them, looked puzzled.

"Wartime poster," said Venables. "Advising people to keep secrets. Keith did the picture, and it went to his head."

"Always made me laugh," said Forrester. He turned to Sophie. "'Keep Mum' is colloquial English for not saying anything. It's a pun."

"Is it a good one?" said Sophie.

"Not very," said Beamish, "but my picture was terrific. The lady in it, draped over a couch, was very… attractive. Very like you, in fact. What brings you here?"

If Forrester had been the jealous type, he might have resented both Beamish's instant familiarity and the fact that Sophie seemed to reciprocate it.

"I've come to make sandwiches for my archaeologist," she said, smiling, "while he digs up long-lost Minoans."

"Perhaps I'll tag along and draw you," said Beamish. "It'll be a lot more interesting than anything Venables asks me to do."

"What's this I hear about a bloody book?" said a loud voice behind Forrester, and he turned to see the lanky figure of Patrick Leigh Fermor. "Far too many people writing books about Greece, Venables," said Leigh Fermor.

"You have to get in line. You're not writing one too, are you, Forrester?"

"Just a paper," said Forrester. "About the dig. If I find anything."

Leigh Fermor pointed an accusing finger at him. "I've a strong suspicion you were off looking for Minoan ruins when you were supposed to be helping me harass Germans," he said.

"Well, harassing Germans was all very well up to a point," said Forrester. "Looking for ancient Cretans was much more interesting." Leigh Fermor grinned and punched him in the arm.

"Good to see you again, Duncan," he said. "Glad you made it through." There was real affection in his voice, and Forrester remembered again why he had been prepared to follow this man through hell and back during those desperate days in Crete.

"You too, Paddy," he said. "I gather your lectures are bringing down the house all over the Aegean."

Leigh Fermor leant closer. "Let me tell you a secret," he said. "Spinning yarns about the war is considerably more fun than fighting it."

Keith Beamish said something that provoked general laughter, particularly, Forrester noted, from Sophie, and Leigh Fermor used its cover to draw Forrester aside. As he did so he saw David Venables drawing Alexandros in the direction of the kouros.

"Ever heard of a chap called Cornelius Brandt?" said Leigh Fermor. "Dutchman. Medium height. Curly hair. He has a rather bizarre face."

"Doesn't ring any bells," said Forrester. "What do you mean about his face? What's wrong with it?"

"Well, half of it is covered by a tin mask," said Leigh Fermor. "On which he's painted half a mouth and an eye. Not very well, I'm sorry to say."

"And you mention this because…?"

"He's been looking for you."

"What?"

"Hovering around the fringes of some of my lectures. Asking if you were one of the party."

"Did he say why?"

"No. But I got the impression he meant you no good. I was wondering if he had a score to settle."

"I don't recall particularly doing any Dutchmen down during the late hostilities. They were on our side, if I recall rightly."

"What about during one of your escapes?" Forrester knew what Leigh Fermor meant. He had indeed sheltered with several Dutch families when he had been on the run in Holland, and though as far as he knew none of them had been betrayed, the fact was that some of those who had helped British servicemen hide from the Gestapo had subsequently been turned in by their compatriots. Or by the carelessness of those they had aided.

"I don't think so," said Forrester. "I was never recaptured and I never told anybody who'd helped me get out."

"Bit of a puzzle, then, isn't it?" said Leigh Fermor.

"It is," said Forrester. "But thanks for the tip."

"My dear chap," said Leigh Fermor. "I want you to stay in one piece for as long as possible. I can't wait to see what you dig up in our old stamping ground."

"*To chamógeló tou eínai gia mena mia apólafsi kai ta matia tou—*" said a deep voice from across the room. As Sophie turned her head towards the speaker, Forrester whispered in her ear.

"Jason Michaelaides," he said. "The poet." The Greek had displaced Venables and Alexandros from beside the kouros so he could command the room.

"What is he saying?" asked Sophie.

"His smile delights me," said Forrester, "I think he's speaking of the kouros – and his eyes—"

"*—Lámpoun me mia chará pou den tin kséroume apo tote pou oi ánthropoi ítan paichnídia neogennithénton theón.*"

"Shine with a joy we have not known since men were playthings of fresh-minted gods."

As Michaelaides declaimed the last line his hand rested lovingly on the head of the kouros and it seemed for a moment as though the stone figure's lips curled in pleasure.

"Fresh-minted gods," said Sophie, savouring the words. She looked across at the long, mournful face of the poet as Alexandros led the applause that rang around the room. "That's wonderful," said Sophie. "Do you know him too?"

"A little," said Forrester. "Met him in Cairo. Melancholy, as if he's always on the point of saying goodbye to life. I'll introduce you if you like." But as they moved across the room, they were waylaid by a plump man in a dinner jacket decorated with an impressive row of colourful medals. Forrester recognised him as Prince Constantine Atreides, one of the leading Greek royalists. His thick black hair, usually hidden beneath a panama hat, was plastered firmly in place with copious quantities of scented pomade.

"Captain Forrester," he said. "How splendid to see you back in Greece again."

"Your Highness," returned Forrester. "It seems a long time since the Shepheard Hotel."

"To say nothing of the Ritz," replied Atreides. "And their excellent cucumber sandwiches." Atreides had fled Greece with King George when the Germans arrived, and had spent a considerable amount of time in Cairo and London with the government in exile, polishing up his anti-fascist credentials without having to fight any actual fascists. He was lazy, passionate and intensely romantic. Despite himself, Forrester had always liked him. There was something distinctly Ruritanian about him, as if he came out of a novel by Anthony Hope.

"May I introduce the Grevinne Sophie Arnfeldt-Laurvig, Countess of Bjornsfjord?"

Atreides clicked his heels and made a bow that would not have looked out of place in a production of *The Prisoner of Zenda*.

"Enchanted," he said. "I think in fact I met your husband the count once at Gstaad."

"That sounds highly probable," said Sophie lightly, and

there was no hint in her expression of the truth about Ernst Arnfeldt-Laurvig, a drunkard and a vain, foolish gambler who had dabbled in black magic with the notorious occultist Aleister Crowley and nearly brought the estate to ruin in the 1930s. He had been killed when the Germans invaded Norway in 1940.

"I suppose you are here to prepare for the return of your king," said Sophie politely.

Atreides looked comically rueful.

"He cannot come back without a referendum," he said. "Who would have thought the Royal House of Greece would need to subject itself to a referendum before regaining its rightful position?"

"Will you win?" asked Forrester.

"Of course," said the prince. "The Greeks love their monarch. But the communists will try to stop the referendum happening."

"How?"

"I think they will renew the civil war," said Atreides.

"And if they do, do you think they'll win?"

Atreides glanced over towards General Alexandros, still holding court on the far side of the room. "That depends who they have on their side," he said, darkly.

As if sensing the prince's glance, Alexandros turned towards them – and Forrester saw his face grow pale. For a moment he was at a loss: the General's look could not be directed at him, and Constantine Atreides had never made anyone nervous in his life. Then he realised Alexandros was looking beyond them, towards the door, where two beautiful women were entering. The shorter of the two was dark, and exuded an animal energy, her dark eyes gleaming as they flickered around the room.

"Helena Spetsos," whispered Constantine. "She fought alongside Alexandros during the war."

"I've met her," said Forrester. "She's a formidable woman."

Helena was surrendering her evening wrap to a footman as though conferring a blessing.

"And the blonde girl?" said Sophie. Helena's taller, younger companion looked willowy by comparison, her fair hair braided in thick plaits, reminding Forrester of a statue of the goddess Diana.

"Ariadne Patrou," said Atreides. "Helena's muse. You will see Helena's portraits of her in the National Gallery one day. When the king reopens it."

Suddenly a man in a colonel's uniform was embracing the two women, his voice booming through the room.

"The two muses!" he said. "Come down from Olympus to grace us with their presence."

"Giorgios," said Helena Spetsos, firmly trying to disengage herself from the colonel's arms. "Anyone would think you were asking us to dance."

"I am not worthy to dance with two such beauties," said the colonel. "And besides, I prefer to dance alone."

After Forrester had left mainland Greece, Giorgios Stephanides had become Alexandros's top lieutenant, and after the Thebes massacre, his second in command. But long before he had joined the resistance, Stephanides had established himself as one of Greece's leading novelists, most famous for Patros, the elemental peasant who, when troubles threatened to overwhelm him, danced alone on the beach to the sound of the bouzouki.

"Would you like me to show you?" the colonel asked.

"Not yet, Giorgi," said Helena. "Perhaps when I have paid my respects to His Beatitude and spoken to Ari."

"Alas, dear lady," said Colonel Stephanides, "you have just missed the General."

Helena glanced sharply in the direction of Alexandros's admiring circle and Forrester, following her look, realised Alexandros had vanished. Suddenly Helena's eyes flashed with anger and she leant close to Giorgios.

"Doing your master's bidding again, Giorgi?" she hissed, for it was now clear Stephanides's job had been to delay them until Alexandros could leave the room.

"My dear Helena—" said Giorgios, but she cut him short, and Forrester remembered why Helena had been such a formidable member of the resistance.

"Ari has been avoiding me," she said, each word like a hailstone. "But he cannot avoid me forever. Tell him that. Tell him the longer he lets the storm brew, the fiercer it will be when it breaks."

And with the beautiful Ariadne in tow, she thrust Stephanides out of the way and sailed towards His Beatitude the Regent of Greece. The crowd parted before her – and His Beatitude, Forrester could have sworn, gave a nervous swallow as she approached.

He wondered what it was Helena Spetsos needed to speak about so urgently to General Aristotle Alexandros, and why his old friend was so reluctant to confront her.

3

TIN FACE

Forrester and Sophie tried to slip away from the reception, but it proved impossible. Soon after Helena Spetsos's dramatic arrival and General Alexandros's hasty departure, Leigh Fermor had introduced them to his mistress, a charmingly short-sighted photographer called Joan Rayner, who had fallen for Paddy when he came back to Egypt with his captured German general and was now working for Osbert Lancaster at the British Embassy. Then the ambassador himself, Sir Clifford Norton, came to speak to Forrester (with much the same message as his press attaché had already conveyed), and Sir Clifford's clever wife "Peter" arrived to show off her protégés, the painter Lucian Freud and a young British artist called John Craxton, who immediately offered to illustrate Leigh Fermor's travel book, whenever he got round to writing it.

Sophie was yawning discreetly and they were about to get away at last when Maurice Bowra, the acerbic Greek scholar and Warden of Wadham College, turned up with Professor Charles Runcorn, a historian specialising in the Crusades, both now working for the British Council. It was clear, Forrester thought, that however exhausted Britain might be after its epic struggle with Hitler, it was bringing its intellectual firepower to bear on the coming battle for freedom in Greece. Apart from being one of the world's leading authorities on Byzantium, Runcorn was Paddy's boss at the British Council. Without quite knowing how, Forrester and Sophie found themselves being swept out of the Archbishop's reception in the midst of a talkative group that included Paddy, Joan, Venables, Beamish, the painter Niko Ghika, Prince Atreides (once again wearing his panama hat) and Jason Michaelaides, the poet who had declaimed over the kouros.

"Leigh Fermor looked very decorative in the British Council offices," Runcorn was telling Forrester, "but none of us could think how to get any work out of him. He never seemed to do anything except entertain a procession of exuberant Cretans and make the office girls fall in love with him."

"He was always borrowing money from them," said Maurice Bowra, "and rarely paying it back. I disapproved of that."

Forrester liked Maurice Bowra: the don had helped him to get into Oxford when he had come up from Hull for his interview, despite his thick East Yorkshire accent and lack of social standing, and had indeed been the one who had steered him towards the classics. Not many trawlermen's sons from Hull got into Oxford in those days, and Forrester credited Bowra with the fact that he was one of them.

Bowra had served in the trenches in the First World War and had always tried to assist ex-servicemen seeking a university education, famously telling one former soldier who lacked the necessary qualifications that "war service counts as Latin". He had also been at the foreground of the anti-appeasement movement during the 1930s, and the only reason he had not been given a proper job during the last war was that he was homosexual. "However," he was said to have remarked philosophically when taking up a post as an air raid warden, "buggers can't be choosers."

"It was my idea to get Leigh Fermor out of the office and lecturing to the Greeks," Bowra confided with some satisfaction.

"Which has worked rather well," said Runcorn. "Because it keeps him out of everybody's hair."

"Oh, you're just jealous, Charles," said Jason Michaelaides, "because Paddy knows more royals than you do, and therefore more royal gossip."

"Royal gossip is very good," said the historian judiciously, "and political gossip is even better, but according to my friend Steven Runciman, who should know, nothing beats *Vatican* gossip."

They were walking along the street called Leoforos Vasilissis Amalias as he said this, and as they laughed something moved in Forrester's peripheral vision in the gloom of the National Garden. It was a patch of white about the size of a man's face, but not as wide. The half-face vanished almost as soon as it appeared – and then reappeared briefly twenty yards further on, in a clump of trees.

Forrester felt the chill at the base of his neck that was so familiar from his war years – and the almost comforting surge of adrenalin that always followed it. But he was not alone now: Sophie was with him, and his first responsibility was to her. Should they slip away from the crowd that made them so conspicuous, or stay with it to take advantage of numbers? If he had been alone he would have been tempted to walk right into the garden and confront his stalker but he was not alone.

On the other hand, every time the cheerful, chattering party walked under a streetlight, he and Sophie were a perfect target for whatever enemy was lurking out in the bushes. And Forrester knew, in his bones, it *was* an enemy. He found himself counting the steps through the unlit parts of the street until the next light would expose them to a pistol shot. He glanced up at the Acropolis, silhouetted now high above him against the stars: would it be for him, as for Socrates, the last sight he would see?

If so, he thought, there were worse, and he let his mind relax, weighing up all the options. "On his way to Thebes," Jason Michaelaides was saying, "Oedipus encountered the Sphinx, which asked him this riddle: What goes on four feet in the morning, two feet at noon, and three feet in the evening? His answer of course was Man, in his infancy, maturity and senescence. That simple word destroyed the monster. We have many monsters to destroy. Let us think, as we seek to slay them, of the answer given by Oedipus."

"And never forget what happened to Oedipus," said David Venables, and there was a general laugh. "How much better it would have been for him if he had never answered the riddle." They began to cross the street towards the maze of steep alleys leading into the district known as Anafiotika, immediately beneath the Acropolis. Forrester made sure he stayed a pace behind Sophie: if a bullet was to come whistling out of the dark, it would hit him first. And then he thought what a bloody fool he was being: it would probably kill both of them.

No bullet came. They were in Dedalou Street now, climbing steeply upwards, the houses around them simple whitewashed stone, many nestling right into the bedrock, with stone urns on balconies spilling cascades of bougainvillea and old petrol cans on rooftops brimming with geraniums and marigolds. For some reason, Greeks had a real fondness for using brightly painted, slightly rusting old tins in their garden decor, and the fact always gave Forrester an obscure satisfaction, perhaps because it was in such contrast to the prevailing aesthetic of Humberside.

He knew that in classical times no one had lived on these steep slopes below the great temple because the Delphic oracle had said it was sacred ground, but when Athens was expanding in the nineteenth century, stonemasons had been recruited from the island of Anafi to create monstrosities like the Archbishop's residence. These workers had provided accommodation for themselves and a heritage for their children by taking advantage of the Ottoman law that if you could put up a house between sunset and sunrise, it was yours. Which meant their homes, unlike the ones they were building for the rich, had a rugged simplicity and charming eccentricity no architect would have dared essay.

Forrester's eye roamed above, behind and ahead as the noisy, chattering party wound up the cobbled street where ancient vines arched across the street, windows were hidden by peeling shutters and doorways were set deep in crooked walls. He turned sharply as a pair of eyes gleamed from the darkness of an alley – and then realised they belonged to a cat. In fact Forrester was almost certain that there was no one following them along the street up which they were walking but he was vividly aware that on either side of them was a labyrinth of alleys, with outside staircases allowing access to ledges and rooftops from which—

And there he was. It had to be the man Leigh Fermor had warned him about, the Dutchman with the tin face.

Leigh Fermor had not mentioned the one thing about Cornelius Brandt's mask that only a close encounter could reveal: it was a thing of horror. Not just the thought of what tangle of mutilated flesh lay beneath it, but the unnatural stillness of the mask, the unwinking painted eye, the red gash of the crudely painted mouth. Whoever wore such a thing, whoever had painted this caricature of a face, proclaimed himself not just as a wounded man but as one who had set himself apart from the human race.

But Brandt's appearance, so close at hand – the balcony of a Turkish-looking house where he stood on could be no more than thirty feet above them – was the opportunity Forrester had been waiting for. "Stay with the others, I'll find you," he whispered to Sophie, and dropped behind as the chattering crowd flowed on up the street.

As they disappeared, he stayed where he was, looking up at the observer.

It was not so foolhardy as it seemed. Even at this distance Forrester could tell from the man's stance that he wasn't aiming a weapon at him – yet. And if a weapon came out, Forrester had time to step back into the shadows. Instead, the man simply stared at him, his head unmoving, as if drinking him in. And then he vanished.

It was like a disappearing trick: there was no movement, he simply wasn't there any more, as if a dark curtain had been drawn across the balcony. For a moment Forrester felt a stab of superstitious fear, as if Brandt was a spectre, the last lingering embodiment of one of the many men he had had to kill in so many different ways during the war: the reproachful shade of a life he had snuffed out in order to fulfil a mission.

And then he pulled himself together, put such morbid imaginings out of his mind (with almost exactly those words of admonition) and swung himself up onto the wall below the balcony. Balancing on the top he edged along it until he came to a shed that lay beneath another balcony and hauled himself up to the balustrade. Seconds later he was standing on the spot where Brandt had been moments before and realised that the curtain of darkness that had hidden the tin-faced man was not an illusion, but simply a dark blanket hanging on a washing line which the Dutchman must have tugged across to hide himself. And as Forrester smiled, a little ruefully at the realisation of how he had been fooled, he heard the scrape of boots on the tiles above him.

Brandt was on the roof directly over his head.

A beat, as the options raced through his mind. The obvious one was to swing himself up again, over the edge of the roof, but perhaps that was exactly what Brandt wanted him to do. As he came over the edge he would be at the point of maximum vulnerability, and all the Dutchman had to do – if Leigh Fermor was right and the man did indeed have some sort of score to settle – was kick him off the edge and send him flailing down into the street below.

On the other hand, if he stayed where he was, Brandt could vanish into the darkness, and suddenly Forrester felt a visceral need to confront this spectre, to bring him out of the shadows and ask him who he was and why he was stalking him. He glanced across to the house next door and saw that it was separated from this one by a narrow ravine, with a little stream running down it. He calculated the gap as about eight feet, and leapt.

He was out of practice. The months of tutoring undergraduates and dining not wisely but too well at Barnard College's excellent High Table had increased his weight, slackened his muscles and slowed his reactions. He hit the balcony railing awkwardly, pulled himself noisily over it, and knocked over a stool in the process. A dog began to bark in the yard below and a voice called sleepily from inside, "*Poios eínai aftós?*" *Who's that?*

Feeling slightly foolish, Forrester looked back at the roof of the house he had just left. Sure enough, there was Brandt, watching him. Only the tin half of his face was visible, the living part in shadow, but Forrester could have sworn that the painted mouth was smiling.

On the other hand, there was still no sign of a gun. As whoever was inside the house began to unlock the shutters to confront the intruder, Forrester grasped the edge of the guttering of the roof above and swung himself onto it, the tiles smooth and cool beneath his fingers.

As he rose to his feet he saw Brandt turn and walk unhurriedly up to the roof-crest of the house on his side of the ravine, and vanish down the other side. In parallel, Forrester did the same thing on his side – but by the time he reached his roof-crest, Brandt had already made a leisurely jump to the roof of the next building. Forrester did likewise. Still separated by the narrow slot in the hillside, with every yard they covered they were coming nearer to the black cliffs that led up to the Acropolis.

"Mijnheer Brandt, I presume," Forrester called out. The man kept on moving. "My name is Forrester. I gather you've been asking after me." No reply. Forrester kept on moving in parallel. "Is that correct? Do you want to speak to me?"

Still walking, the man glanced across at Forrester, continued for another few yards, and then stopped. Brandt was on a flat roof now, a kind of terrace, flanked by huge amphorae filled with geraniums. The roof Forrester stood on was steeply sloped and covered with semi-cylindrical tiles: a much more awkward place to stand upright. The Dutchman came close to the edge; he was only a yard or two away now.

"What do you want?" asked Forrester. Brandt stared at him, as though drinking him in, and Forrester began to feel a strange sense of unease. It was not fear, exactly, but the sensation of a door opening: a door he wanted to remain closed.

Forrester had left Oxford to join the Special Operations Executive early in the war, and had been on missions in most of occupied Europe and much of the Mediterranean right up to the moment when the Germans had signed the surrender document on Lüneburg Heath. The memories, not just of the dangers he had run, but of the things he had had to do to survive, sometimes rose up to overwhelm him, blotting out the present and plunging him back into a world of terror and violence he wanted only to put behind him. As he looked at the silent, grotesque figure a few yards away on the opposite rooftop, he felt the demons beginning to stir once more. He had to make a conscious effort to keep his voice calm. "Do you want to talk to me about something?"

There was no reply, and without warning Forrester's head began to swim. He tried to breathe deeply; it would be foolish to fall down now, and he knew that, as the memories came flooding back, it could happen all too easily. And then, so fast it was almost impossible to see, the man's hand moved as if he were skimming a stone across a pond, and he flung something at Forrester's head.

Forrester jumped sideways to avoid it and as he did so realised Brandt had not stopped at random: he had waited until his enemy was on the edge of the steepest drop they had yet passed. All he had done was throw a tile – Forrester heard it smash on the roof behind him – but he had timed it perfectly.

In avoiding it, Forrester missed his footing, fell and found himself sliding helplessly backwards down towards the edge of the roof. He was aware of Brandt watching him with almost scientific curiosity as he scrabbled for something to hold on to, failed, and went over the drop.

At the last second his fingers clenched over the sharp edges of the tiles and he hung there, trying to see what lay beneath him. Fifty feet of air, he realised, and a fall that would either kill or cripple him, and then as he looked over he saw the tin face tilt itself into its grim, artificial smile.

In a leisurely way, the Dutchman reached down and picked up another tile. This time there was no way Forrester could avoid it: it was going to hit him full in the face. He felt not fear, but fury at his own foolishness. An unarmed man had outmanoeuvred him – and was about to kill him.

As Brandt's arm went back for the throw, Forrester took a deep breath, and let go of the edge of the roof.

For what seemed like an eternity he fell, and then

he felt an agonising pain as the branch of a cypress tree tore into his calf, and then he was grabbing for more branches and the branches were breaking and he was still going down and there was one of the massive vines that stretched across the alleys and it was breaking under his weight and without warning his shoulder hit the cobbles and the smashed branches were coming down on top of him. There were voices and lights coming on behind the shutters of the whitewashed houses, and as he looked up he saw Brandt, silhouetted against the moon, and he knew that this was not over, and would not be over until one of them was dead.

Not thinking where he was going, and as fast as the pain in his leg would allow him, he limped away from the wreckage, as people began to emerge into the alley, and suddenly he was in Stratonos Street and there were strings of lights suspended from café to café and open windows and music and tables and there was Sophie at a restaurant table in the street, talking with Jason Michaelaides and Constantine Atreides, and Paddy Leigh Fermor kissing Joan Rayner and David Venables arguing with Charles Runcorn about Clement Attlee. He took a deep breath, brushed at his clothes to hide the worst of the damage they and he had sustained, slipped into a spare seat, and ordered a glass of grappa. No one except Sophie seemed to have noticed he'd been gone, and she simply gave him a cheerful grin and continued with her conversation.

"I was just telling the countess," said Michaelaides, "that Odysseus was the ancestor of the Vikings."

Forrester suppressed the pain shooting up his bruised leg. "I think the Vikings relied less on Odyssean cunning and more on large axes," he said, swallowing the grappa, and felt, with relief, its fiery harshness course through him.

"I was thinking of putting Odysseus in my book," said David Venables. "Following him about the Aegean, that kind of thing."

"Perhaps I could draw the countess as Penelope," said Keith Beamish.

"And Leigh Fermor as one of the demanding suitors," said Runcorn. "Being cut down by Odysseus's retributive arrows."

"My dear old chap," said Leigh Fermor, "if I were cut down by an Odyssean arrow, who would win the Greek people over to democracy with his wonderful lectures?"

"There are times, Leigh Fermor," said Maurice Bowra, "when you remind me irresistibly of Mr. Toad, endlessly making up verses in praise of his own magnificence."

"Then you must be Badger, Maurice," said Leigh Fermor affably, "always trying to spoil Toad's fun."

"Only in Toad's own best interests," said Runcorn.

"Well, of course," said Leigh Fermor. "That's a given."

"Who is Mr. Toad?" asked Jason Michaelaides, and as always with any group of English people there was a chorus of voices eager to describe the delights of *The Wind in the Willows*. Keith Beamish even dipped his finger in wine and did a rapid and remarkably vivid sketch of Toad on a napkin, holding it up to Michaelaides, but the poet shook his head.

"I'm sorry, I do not see," he said.

"Well Toad was a tremendous show-off, you see, just like Paddy," said Venables.

"Is not clear," said Michaelaides.

"After defeating the stoats, he came up with a programme for an evening's entertainment, to celebrate his victory," said Joan Rayner.

"The first item was Speech… by Toad," said Maurice Bowra. "Followed by the promise that there would be Other Speeches by Toad During the Evening."

"Then he promised an Address, by Toad," said David Venables.

"A Song, by Toad," said Charles Runcorn.

"And other Compositions, all by Toad," said Beamish, "to be sung by the Composer."

"So you see," said Maurice Bowra, "why Paddy fits the part so perfectly?"

Leigh Fermor shook his head in mock horror at this critique, and Michaelaides opened his mouth to ask another question, but no words emerged. Instead, his eyes widened, his hands came slowly up to his head as if he was performing a charade to which the answer was *pain* – and then he teetered back in his chair like a child at the back of a classroom, lost his balance, and fell into the darkness. There was a sharp crack as his head hit the cobbles.

Seconds later the poet was lying on his back on the roadway and Sophie was kneeling beside him, her hands beneath his head. There was blood running through her fingers.

As Michaelaides looked up at her with surprised, despairing eyes, Forrester knew that Sophie's face was the last thing the poet would ever see. He himself looked up at the roof behind them and there, silhouetted against the stars, stood Cornelius Brandt.

The Dutchman watched silently for a moment, and then vanished into the night.

4

THE SPECULATIONS OF INSPECTOR KOSTOPOULOS

The hours that followed were, for Forrester, a nightmare of conflicting obligations. His first instinct had been to go after Brandt, but there was no way he could leave Sophie at a moment like this, and then the police arrived and then the ambulance and when Jason Michaelaides's body had been taken away they all had to go down to police headquarters to make their statements to a diminutive man in a crumpled white suit, who introduced himself as Inspector Gregory Kostopoulos. Whether they could speak Greek or not, he insisted on addressing the English members of the party in his slightly unreliable version of their own language, and despite Forrester's repeated corrections addressed him throughout as *Forrest*. The title "mister" also received his special attention, and had been abbreviated until it resembled a weather condition.

The last time Forrester had been in Athens police headquarters it had been used by the Gestapo, and he had no desire to spend any more time in it, but Inspector

Kostopoulos was a slow and thorough man, whose interrogative method consisted of repeating whatever had been said to him with a rising inflection, and getting his interlocutor to say it to him again before he signalled his sergeant to write it down, which as the hours passed induced almost as much mental stress as bright lights and rubber truncheons. To Forrester's story of Cornelius Brandt and Leigh Fermor's confirmation of it he listened with polite incredulity, as if this was exactly what he expected imaginative Englishmen to come up with.

"A face entirely of tin," he said thoughtfully. "Is very mythical, Mist Forrest."

"Not *made* of tin," said Forrester. "A tin mask to cover up some sort of disfigurement."

"Like monster," said Kostopoulos. "Greek monster."

"Leigh Fermor saw him and said he was Dutch."

"Ah! Mist Farmer," said the policeman, reclassifying Paddy as a slightly ethereal son of the soil, "everybody loving his stories, me inclusive."

"And I saw the man myself," said Forrester.

"Yes, of course you was," said Kostopoulos. "On roof."

"That's right, on the roof."

"But why Dutchman wanting to kill fine Greek poet? You know that, Mist Forrest? Jason Michaelaides, finest Greek poet of our times."

"I do know that," said Forrester. "And I don't think Brandt was trying to kill him. I think he was trying to kill me, and Michaelaides got in the way."

"In way?"

"Of whatever Brandt was using to try to kill me," said Forrester patiently. "It could have been a gun with a silencer, or he could have thrown a knife. Did you find the weapon?"

"Was no weapon," said Kostopoulos.

"There must have been. Countess Arnfeldt-Laurvig had blood all over her hands when she held his head."

"From cobbles," said Kostopoulos. "From hitting head on cobbles when great poet falling over."

"But something *made* him fall over," said Forrester. "Something happened to him *before* he fell over. I saw it myself. We all did."

"Oh, yes," said the policeman. "Something happening to Michaelaides alright. He was poison."

Forrester gaped. "Poisoned? Brandt couldn't possibly have *poisoned* him – he was too far away."

"You right there, Mist Forrest," said Kostopoulos, "nobody on no roof was killing Jason Michaelaides. Was somebody poisoning his tzatziki."

"Poisoning?"

"How else is he dying?" said Kostopoulos. "With no holes in him? Maybe not tzatziki but something else he's eating."

Forrester said nothing. There was nothing to say.

"Is tragedy," said Kostopoulos. "And somebody going to pay."

Dawn was breaking over Athens when, with Osbert Lancaster's help, they were finally released with the admonition not to leave the city until the case had been cleared up, and all Forrester and Sophie wanted to do was return to their hotel, sluice themselves in the thin trickle of water from the shower, and fall asleep.

When he woke up the next morning, Forrester lay beside Sophie, thinking. Had he been completely wrong? Had Brandt merely been the witness to what had happened, not its instigator? There seemed no reason to doubt Kostopoulos's assertion that Michaelaides had been poisoned – Sophie had confirmed her impression that the blood on the back of the poet's head came from a superficial wound that had happened when he fell – but if Michaelaides had been given a dose of poison, who had done it?

Sophie had been sitting on one side of the poet, Charles Runcorn on the other. Sophie obviously had no reason to do Michaelaides harm, and as far as he was aware neither did Runcorn. He himself had been beside Constantine Atreides and directly opposite, with Maurice Bowra beside him on the right and Paddy Leigh Fermor on Bowra's right. Keith Beamish was on Forrester's left and David Venables next to him. Niko Ghika – who knew him best – was farthest away, at one end of the table, Joan Rayner at the other. As Forrester remembered it, the wine had been poured from a common pitcher, and the tzatziki, hummus, olives, pickled peppers, flatbread and taramasalata had been passed around the table and were being eaten by anyone who felt like it. If any one of these dishes had been poisoned, they would all, or at least several of them, have been affected.

But it had been obvious, as they had waited together at the police station, and when they were released by Osbert Lancaster into the care of the British Consul, that nobody was suffering from anything other than the effects of being kept awake all night.

In short, Forrester reasoned, Kostopoulos was wrong when he said Michaelaides had been poisoned at the restaurant. If he had been poisoned, the poison had to have been administered earlier.

Suddenly Forrester was remembering all the *spanakopita*, *saganaki* and *tiropitas* being handed around the Archbishop's reception, and when Sophie awoke and he told her what he was thinking, she smiled. "I am beginning to realise that life with you will never be dull."

Forrester laughed. "I could do with some dull, and I'm sure you could too."

"If there is to be danger and excitement, though, it is very important it is with people you like," said Sophie solemnly, and put her hand on Forrester's face.

"Thanks," he said.

"Besides," said Sophie, "I liked that poor man too. I liked his poems. I held his poor cold hand in mine as he died. I want whoever killed him to be punished."

"Alright," said Forrester, "let's see what we can do."

Half an hour later Sophie was in a cab to the British Embassy and Forrester was headed back to Skaramangar House. But when he got there, with his list of questions about the reception arrangements carefully prepared, Inspector Kostopoulos was already in occupation, and though he now seemed prepared to agree with Forrester that Michaelaides might have been poisoned before he got to the restaurant, he dismissed the idea of doctored *spanakopita* with a wave of his hand. "You are not seeing trees for wood," he said firmly. "Archbishop already telling me something much more interesting going on here last night. You remembering?"

"There was a lot going on. Half the Greek political establishment was here, to say nothing of most of the diplomatic corps."

"Also to say nothing of *him*!" and the inspector pointed dramatically at the kouros.

"You're not saying the kouros did it?" said Forrester, incredulously.

"With his accomplice," said Kostopoulos, "the name of which will be discovered." He snapped his fingers and a policeman stepped forward and began painstakingly swabbing the statue's head.

"Archbishop telling me of ancient ritual, and Michaelaides reciting beautiful poem with hand on kouros's head. Immediately Kostopoulos realising this is giving murderer perfect opportunity. Place poison on head of kouros just before Michaelaides recite poem, and hey prosto, deadly dose is administered to unsuspecting victim." The policeman was now dropping the swabs into a brown paper bag.

"Surely that would be very tricky," said Forrester.

"You'd have to have a poison that was absorbed through the pores of the skin, you'd have to put it on just before your victim placed his hand on the statue's head, and you'd have to put just the right amount so that the next person in line didn't get poisoned."

"All true," said Kostopoulos triumphantly, "which is pointing to extremely skilled operator."

"I would have thought that poisoning one of the hors d'oeuvres would have been much simpler," said Forrester.

"Not knowing which *saganaki* victim will pick? Impossible."

"Unless," said Forrester, "you simply slipped a poisoned *saganaki* or *tiropitas* onto his plate while he wasn't looking."

Kostopoulos looked disconcerted for a moment, and then waved his hands. "Not enough interesting," he said firmly. "Agatha Christine curling the lip at it. No, Mist Forrest, this going down in annals as Kostopoulos famous kouros murder, of which headlines I am already seeing. Now, you will help me making diagrams of positions of all peoples in room at time. It will be your contribution."

And two more policemen entered the room, carrying an immense blackboard.

Sophie was as surprised as Forrester when they met later that morning to compare notes at a café in Syntagma Square, but she was less inclined than Forrester to be sceptical. "He *is* a policeman," she said. "And it *is* a very ingenious idea."

"Far too ingenious," said Forrester. "And with far too many practical objections. But I have a question for you: were you speaking literally, when you said Michaelaides's hand was cold?"

Sophie looked puzzled. "Was it a metaphor," said Forrester, "or did you mean his hand was actually cold?"

"Actually cold," replied Sophie. "Cold and dry."

"Well you should let the inspector know that, because it may help identify what poison was used, and steer him away from the kouros idea."

Sophie pulled a face: she clearly was not entirely ready to reject the kouros idea yet. "If we're talking about symptoms," she said, "what about blurred vision and blind spots?"

"What about them? Did Michaelaides demonstrate either one?"

"I think he might have done," said Sophie. "Remember when Keith Beamish showed him the drawing of Mr. Toad?"

"Yes."

"Michaelaides said 'I can't see'. And 'It's not clear'."

"Surely as in 'I don't understand'. After all, Keith had done the drawing with his finger, in wine, on a napkin."

"I think he really meant he couldn't see," said Sophie, "and I think somebody ought to be looking for a poison that does that to people."

"Well, it's one of the symptoms of digitalis poisoning," said Forrester. "But Michaelaides might have been taking it for a heart condition and we should pass that thought on to the good inspector too. But whether it was the kouros or a *tiropitas*, whoever did it must have been close to Michaelaides at the reception. Can you remember who you saw around him?"

"Well, David Venables, certainly, and of course General Alexandros," said Sophie. "He had his arm around Michaelaides's shoulder. And he had a motive."

"What?"

"Ah, of course, you don't know. That's what I found out from Mr. Lancaster at the British Embassy. He was very helpful."

Forrester frowned. "Tell me more," he said.

"Helena Spetsos," said Sophie.

"What about Helena Spetsos?"

"She'd been having an affair with Jason Michaelaides since 1945."

"Why would Alexandros care about that?"

"Because Helena Spetsos was General Alexandros's lover during the war." She saw Forrester's surprised reaction.

"You didn't know that?"

"I did not," said Forrester. "She joined the resistance after I left for Crete." He considered for a moment, searching his memory. "I do know they fought alongside each other, so it's perfectly possible, of course."

"You seem doubtful. That they were lovers, or that he cared enough to kill Jason Michaelaides?"

"You saw what happened when Helena Spetsos arrived at the reception: Stephanides delayed her so Alexandros could skedaddle, and she was furious. I assumed she wanted to see him and he was trying to avoid her."

"Which he would if he'd just killed her lover."

"Possibly," said Forrester, frowning. "But it still doesn't add up. Helena was eager to see Alexandros, not Michaelaides. So why would Alexandros be jealous of him? Did you see Helena and Michaelaides together after Ari left?"

Sophie thought, and then shook her head. "No, I didn't."

"They might have had an affair," said Forrester, "but Alexandros was the man she wanted to see. Besides, if Ari had wanted to kill Michaelaides, he'd have shot him, not poisoned him."

Sophie laughed. "That's a very good character reference!"

"What I mean is, he's a soldier, a man of action. Poisoning a rival would seem underhanded to a man like him."

"But what if he wanted to make sure no one suspected him?" said Sophie. "In that case poison would be the perfect means."

Forrester stared out at the ramshackle stream of cars, motorcycles and carts flowing endlessly around the square; despite their noise he could still hear church bells ringing in the distance, and cocks crowing in the houses behind the square. The sun was hot and the Acropolis so bright in the midday sun it was hard to look at it.

"I gather General Alexandros was married when he had his fling with Helena Spetsos," said Sophie.

"He was very happily married," said Forrester, "until his wife shot him."

It was Sophie's turn to look surprised. "Because of the affair?"

"No, not at all. She shot him because she objected to him joining the resistance. Did it in public view at a farewell dinner when he was about to leave Hydros, where they had an estate. Missed. Killed a goat. Alexandros left for the mainland that same night. Penelope, her name was. Penelope Alexandros. Story spread around the whole Aegean."

"How extraordinary."

"Greek women can be very passionate. Think of Clytemnestra or the maenads."

"The maenads? Who were they?"

"Women driven mad by Dionysus. They roamed the woods and tore men to pieces."

"All the same, it seems a pity to shoot one's husband when he wants to go off to war. Especially if he's a professional soldier."

"The army had surrendered by then. He was going to join the irregulars."

"So he's divorced now."

"I'm not sure it was ever formalised. He had other things to think about during the war, as we all did. And Penelope Alexandros is far away on her island. Rules it like a feudal potentate, I'm told."

"How very anachronistic," said Sophie. Forrester grinned. He had forgotten, momentarily, that as Countess of Bjornsfjord, Sophie Arnfeldt-Laurvig was also effectively the ruler of a small and almost medieval domain.

"Touché. But I'm sure you allow your peasants *some* rights."

"They aren't peasants, they're farmers. And they have the same rights as anybody else in Norway. They just look to me for…"

"Leadership?"

"Reassurance. Especially during the last few years."

Forrester, who knew a little about life for civilians in occupied Europe, put his hand over hers. "They were damn lucky to have you," he said. "And I'm damn lucky you're with me now."

And for a moment, amid the glare and noise, they were silent, enclosed in their own world. Then, returning to the present, they reconstructed the scene at the Archbishop's residence, considering in turn Aristotle Alexandros, Charles Runcorn, Keith Beamish, David Venables, Leigh Fermor and the rest.

"The fact is, whether it was the kouros or the hors d'oeuvres, any one of them could have done it," said Forrester.

"But apart from the General, which of them had any motivation to do so?" asked Sophie.

"That," said Forrester, "is what we have to find out."

"Well," said Sophie, "I know who I want to talk to first."

"Who's that?"

"Why, Helena Spetsos, of course. I think she's the key to the whole thing."

"I'm not so sure about that," said Forrester. "But I agree we ought to talk to her, and you'd probably be best for that. Do you know where to find her?"

Sophie smiled. "Mr. Lancaster was most helpful. He

even made me a little drawing of her building and the street it's in." She showed it to Forrester. It was spare, elegant and subtly subversive, as if sending up the pretensions of everyone who lived in that particular location.

"I'd keep that," he said. "It might be quite valuable one day."

5

GOING TO SEE THE GENERAL

Moments after Sophie left in a cab, Forrester spotted Venables and Beamish strolling along the square and beckoned them over. He told them of Inspector Kostopoulos's theories and his own.

"You have been thinking hard," said Venables.

"I'm anxious to get to Crete. I can't leave until this has been cleared up."

"Point taken," said Venables. "The kouros thing points to another Greek, doesn't it? Someone who knew about that particular tradition and planned to take advantage of it."

"It would take some doing, though," said Beamish. "I mean, you'd have to get the poison onto the statue without your victim noticing what you were up to."

"And before anybody else put his hand there."

"And how would you conceal the poison?" asked Venables. "In the palm of your hand?"

"I entirely agree," said Forrester. "I think our man doctored one of the hors d'oeuvres."

"Perhaps you could hide the poison in an Elastoplast or something," said Beamish. "Or, you know, using one of those burn dressings, with liquid inside them."

"Bit far-fetched," said Venables.

"It's not my theory," said Beamish. "I'm just trying to help your friend here find out what happened."

"Friend?" said Venables. "I've always thought of him as just some chap I met under a pub table during the blitz. And then he passed himself off to me, as I recall, as a soldier-scholar, not some sort of Hercule Poirot."

"I've no desire to be Hercule Poirot," said Forrester. "But the sooner we can get this cleared up the sooner I can get off to Crete."

"I'm all for that," said Venables. "Larry Durrell has invited us to come over to Rhodes and we can't go until that bloody policeman gives us the nod. What about that chap Prince Atreides? Bloke with the medals and the brilliantined hair. He was near the kouros and he looked to me as if he'd poison anybody soon as look at them."

"He and Michaelaides were both with the government in exile during the war," said Forrester. "On the same team, so to speak."

"Well it's always chaps on the same team who you want to kill most," said Venables. "During the war I hated my producer at the BBC much more than I hated Hitler."

Keith Beamish nodded sagely. "And I'll probably murder Venables long before we finish writing this book."

"*I'm* writing the book," said Venables. "You're just doing the pictures." He turned to Forrester. "These artists!

So bloody full of themselves, don't you find?"

"Compared to writers," said Forrester judiciously, "I find artists almost saintly."

He found Constantine Atreides finishing a long and leisurely lunch in the Temple of the Golden Dawn, Athens' most elegant restaurant, his panama hat beside him on the table, like a portable shrine. The prince's face lit up as Forrester entered, and he immediately ordered two cognacs in addition to those a neat row of glasses revealed he had already consumed. When the brandy came he raised his glass to Forrester.

"To the late, great poet," he said.

"To Jason Michaelaides," said Forrester, and drank. The cognac, even at two in the afternoon, was very good.

"Did you know him well?"

"We worked together for years during the time of exile," said Atreides. "He was as steady as a banker."

Forrester raised his eyebrows.

"That doesn't sound very poetic," he said.

"I think your T.S. Eliot worked in a bank, didn't he? Jason was like that – a patient diplomat by day, then, at night, in the silence of his own room a wild poet crying out to the heavens."

"Did you get on well with him?"

"I admired him hugely. He saw *me* as part of the furniture. An amusing part of the furniture, certainly, but not to be taken seriously."

"That must have been rather annoying."

"Not annoying enough for me to poison him."

"Connie! I'm not accusing you. Just trying to find out—"

The prince held up a restraining hand, and then leant forward confidentially. "You know Michaelaides had an affair with Helena Spetsos?"

"I did know that, yes."

"And you know why?"

"No."

"Because of Ari Alexandros."

"I don't understand."

"Ari and Helena were lovers during the war. When they were not killing Germans they were making passionate love in caves."

"I'd heard that too. I don't see what it has to do with Michaelaides."

"I will tell you. After the war ended, Ari suddenly became unavailable. Of course he had many excuses – supervising demobilisation, visiting army units on the Yugoslav border, all that sort of thing. But the fact was he dropped Helena like a hot brick. That is your English phrase, isn't it? A hot brick. I like that, which is why I use it."

"And the affair with Michaelaides?"

"Was simply Helena's way of forcing Ari Alexandros to pay attention to her again. After all, Michaelaides is – was – famous. Alexandros couldn't help but notice."

"It doesn't seem to have worked," said Forrester, "if what I saw at His Beatitude's last night is anything to go by. Alexandros clearly wanted nothing to do with her."

For the first time, Atreides looked troubled. "I think the General's mind was on other things," he said, darkly.

Forrester remembered the briefing from Osbert Lancaster. "You mean whether he should stay with the army or join ELAS."

"Alexandros is the most intelligent and efficient general in the country," said Atreides. "If he joins ELAS and civil war breaks out again, ELAS will win and Greece will become communist. It's as simple as that."

"Which makes it all the more puzzling that the army is treating him so badly," said Forrester.

"They are bloody fools," said Atreides bitterly. "They are ashamed that they surrendered to the Germans and Alexandros fought on with the resistance. He is a standing reproach to them. They are determined to freeze him out."

"Even if it means him joining ELAS?"

"He cannot be allowed to join. It would be a catastrophe for Greece."

"What are you doing to stop him?"

"Drinking cognac and talking, as always. You know me, Duncan, a dilettante, a man of straw."

"I don't entirely buy that, Connie. I know King George places a great deal of faith in you to make sure he's invited back."

"I do what I can. But I rely on the wisdom of the Greek people to understand that their best hope for freedom is the return of their rightful king."

"Do you really believe that, or are you just saying it because George is your cousin?"

"I truly believe it," said Atreides, taking another

mouthful of cognac. "Our politicians are self-interested fools. Our army – well, you know our army. All they are good for is staging coups. Greece needs her king back if it is to remain a democracy, it's as simple as that."

"So who do you think killed Jason Michaelaides?"

Atreides looked him in the eyes. "This is between you and me? You swear not to repeat it?" Forrester nodded. "It was Ari. Helena was his woman. Michaelaides had stolen her. He does not like to be beaten, the General. As I think you know. And why else did he leave in such a hurry?"

He signalled the waiter, and Forrester knew he was about to order more cognac.

"Thanks for the brandy, Con," he said, "but I have to go."

"Go? Go where?"

"Well, to see the General, of course. I've got to bring this thing to some sort of conclusion if I ever want to get to Crete."

While Forrester was in the Temple of the Golden Dawn, Sophie was squinting in the sunlight, comparing Osbert Lancaster's drawing of Helena Spetsos's house with the reality, and smiling to herself at the uncanny accuracy with which the press attaché was able to bring out the building's essential features. His descriptive note said: "Turkish Art Nouveau combined with Minoan Revival" and somehow, in its glorious pretentiousness, that was exactly what the house was. Stepping out of the glare of the street with some relief, she opened an elaborately wrought metal gate and found herself in a garden so thickly populated with trees and flowers it was like entering a kind of Eden. It was large too, and it was some time before she found her way through the shade of the lush foliage to the front door. She knocked, waited, called out and received no reply, but convinced there was someone home, walked around the side of the house through ever thicker and more fragrant vegetation, and suddenly she was staring through open French doors into a room at the back of the house, her eyes open in shock.

In the middle of the room a naked woman was bound against a Corinthian pillar, her hands tied above her head, another rope securing her feet, a third around her waist. Her head was slumped sideways on her chest, her blonde hair covering her face. For a moment Sophie stood frozen, immobilised by a combination of astonishment and horror.

And then the bound figure raised its head and smiled at her.

"Darling, I think we have a visitor," said Ariadne Patrou, and Helena Spetsos stepped out from behind an easel.

"Who the hell are you?" she said. "And what the hell are you doing here?"

"I'm terribly sorry," said Sophie. "I knocked and called out at the front door, but nobody came." Taking advantage of the woman's momentary uncertainty, she advanced into the room, her hand outstretched. "My name is Sophie Arnfeldt-Laurvig. We met briefly at the regent's reception last night, but I don't expect you'll remember me."

"I don't," said Helena.

"It's the Norwegian lady," said Ariadne, helpfully. "You're a countess, aren't you? A friend of Captain Forrester.

I'm sorry I can't shake hands. I'm a captured naiad, you see. She's painting the Minotaur separately."

"The countess from Norway? That sounds like something from a film," said Helena Spetsos, wiping the paint from her hands on a rag. "So what does the countess from Norway want in my studio? Have you come to ask to have your portrait painted? Or perhaps you too would like to be a captured naiad?"

As if considering this offer, Sophie came further into the studio, which, just as the garden was over-filled with plants, was jammed to overflowing with all the props of the artist's profession, from plaster casts of famous statues to rich Turkish rugs, dismantled altars and massive weathered pieces of block and tackle. "First of all, of course, I want to offer my condolences," said Sophie. "About poor Jason Michaelaides. I was with him when he died, you see."

A shadow passed briefly across Helena Spetsos's face. "It was very sad," she said. "He was a great man." There was a slight noise from the pillar and as Sophie glanced across at the naked woman, she could have sworn there was a fleeting smile on her face; but almost before it had registered she had turned the smile into a slightly theatrical grimace of discomfort.

"If you're going to talk to our visitor, Helena, could you let me down for a minute?"

"No," said Helena Spetsos shortly. "The countess will not be with us for long."

But Sophie made no move to go. "It must have been a terrible shock. I gather you were very close."

"I have seen a lot of death in the last few years," said Helena. "It has ceased to shock me."

"I wish I had some last words to pass on," said Sophie, determined, for reasons she was not entirely certain of, to break through the woman's reserve. "He actually died in my arms, you know. But sadly he wasn't able to speak."

"They said he was poisoned," said Ariadne, from her pillar. "Is that true?"

"Be quiet, girl," said Helena. "It's none of your business."

"The police say he was poisoned," said Sophie, "but it may not have been at the restaurant, you understand."

"No, I don't understand," said Helena, fixing her with a level stare.

Sophie answered her gaze. "The poison was probably given to him at the Archbishop's reception."

"But we were there too!" said Ariadne. "How terrible!"

"Will you keep quiet?" said Helena with sudden, explosive harshness. "Or do I have to make you?" Then, as if embarrassed by her own outburst, she leant towards Sophie and spoke quietly. "She talks too much. She's a good model but too chatty. Do you find that with girls?"

"I don't know," said Sophie. "I've never tried to paint them." Helena looked at her speculatively. "I think you would be a good model," she said. "I like mature women, I like their shapes. Have you ever posed?" She fixed Sophie with eyes which, from close up, Sophie saw were a deep, dangerous sea-green, and hard to turn away from.

"I haven't," said Sophie at last. "I'm not sure my husband would have approved."

"*Would* have? He is dead, the count?"

"Yes," said Sophie. "For a long time now."

"So you're a free woman."

Sophie smiled. "Not free enough to become an artist's model," she said.

"Good for you," said Ariadne. "It's a dog's life."

Sophie did her best to get the conversation back on track. "I saw General Alexandros with Mr. Michaelaides at the reception just before you arrived. Were they friends?"

From her pillar, Ariadne gave a short, barely suppressed laugh, and Helena's lips compressed in a thin line.

"I don't think so," she said. "Look, it was kind to bring your condolences for my friend's death. Very kind. But now, as you see, I have things to attend to. You can show yourself out through the front door." She turned back to her easel.

As Sophie left the room Ariadne caught her eye and winked, but as she was closing the front door behind her, she heard a high-pitched squeal from the studio, as though Helena had found a way to make her model pay for her impertinence.

She hesitated, decided it was none of her business, and firmly closed the latch. But as she turned a bend in the path towards the front gate, a tall figure appeared before her. It was a moment before she realised it was Professor Charles Runcorn.

He stared at her, just as startled as she was. "Countess!" he said. "What are you doing here?" He seemed flustered and defensive.

"I was talking to Helena and Ariadne about what might have happened last night. To Jason Michaelaides." Sophie spoke reassuringly and she was certain she saw a look of relief on the professor's face.

"Ah, yes, of course. That poor fellow. How lucky we all were!"

"Lucky? That he died?"

"No, of course not, dear lady. Of course not! But we were all at the same table in that dreadful taverna. If we had eaten whatever Jason ate or drank what he drank, we might have been poisoned too."

Sophie considered this, realising that not everybody in the party knew yet that Michaelaides had probably been given the fatal dose while they were all at the Archbishop's. On the other hand, if Runcorn himself had administered the poison, he'd want to stick as long as possible with the idea that the crime had been committed later. She decided to leave the issue unresolved.

"Who do you think might have done it, Professor?" she asked. "You've been in Athens longer than I have. Do you know of anybody who might have wanted to see Jason Michaelaides dead?"

Runcorn considered. "My focus has been entirely on the activities of the British Council and what little spare time I've had, of course, has gone into the Third Crusade."

"Is that why you've come to see Miss Spetsos?" said Sophie and was gratified to see the play of emotions across Runcorn's face as he considered grasping at the lifeline she had offered – and then realised it had a hook at the end of it.

"Oh, no," he said. "By no means. I fear Miss Spetsos has very little knowledge of the Crusades and less interest. I came to see her on British Council business. About her paintings."

"An exhibition?" said Sophie. "That would be interesting." Runcorn nodded gratefully, and Sophie went on. "I've just seen the painting she's doing with poor Ariadne tied to a pillar. I think she's a captive nymph. It should be very exciting."

"It sounds rather risqué for the British Council," said Runcorn carefully. "But I suppose it's a classical theme."

"Very classical," said Sophie. "Well, I mustn't keep you any longer, but if you do have any ideas about who might have been behind last night's events, please do let me know."

This time Runcorn's smile was a little more confident. "Of course, dear lady," he said. "Though I suppose it might be my duty to let the police know first." And with that he strode off down the path with the air of a man who believes he has scored a neat point against an opponent. Sophie noted that she did not hear his steps at the front door or the sound of the bell being rung; apparently he was sufficiently familiar a visitor to be able automatically to navigate his way to the study where Helena was creating her art.

What, she wondered as she stepped back into the brightness of the street, were the three of them getting up to now she was gone? If she was certain of anything, it was that the British Council's cultural programmes had very little to do with it.

General Alexandros was in the stables of the 6th Cavalry Regiment when Forrester finally found him. Forrester had started his search at army headquarters, round the corner from the palace, and had been struck by how unhelpful every senior officer had been when he asked where the General was. Only the lower ranks and junior officers seemed to have any affection for their old commander, and even they were reluctant to show it. It was late afternoon by the time Forrester found himself among the dim, pungent horse boxes, watching Alexandros gently stroking the nose of a big bay that must have been at least seventeen hands high. The General grinned as he saw Forrester approaching.

"My men prefer tanks, these days," he said. "They must be mad."

Forrester looked appreciatively at man and animal: both magnificent specimens, and both, as Forrester knew, bred for battle.

"How did you track me down?" asked Alexandros.

"Couple of helpful NCOs," said Forrester. "The top brass seem determined not to acknowledge your existence."

Alexandros laughed. "I embarrass them," he said. "Don't mean to, but there it is. They surrendered, I didn't. Can't blame them, really, but they *are* quite determined to keep me out in the cold."

"I'm trying to find out what happened to Michaelaides," said Forrester. "I was there when he died and the police say I have to stay here in Athens until it's all sorted out. Have you any idea who did it?"

"None at all," said Alexandros. "He was a damn good poet."

"Somebody told me he pinched Helena Spetsos off you."

Alexandros walked away from Forrester to the next stall. "How are you, my girl?" he said to the gleaming black mare as he held out a piece of carrot. "Any old friends accusing *you* of murder these days?"

"Good God, Ari, I'm not accusing you of anything," said Forrester, joining him. "I'm just trying to find out what happened. Michaelaides died in front of me and it looks as though it was because he was poisoned at the reception. The police think it might have been something smeared on the head of the kouros."

Alexandros said nothing, and went on stroking the horse's nose.

"I saw you near the kouros with Michaelaides," said Forrester. "Not you alone, of course – Venables was there, Connie Atreides, any number of people. But you were in an excellent position to see if anything untoward happened and that's what I'm asking."

"I saw nothing," said Alexandros. "That is, I saw a room full of people eating, drinking, conspiring, politicking, showing off, including those you mention. I saw plenty of people patting the kouros on the head. But I saw nothing that would suggest anyone had put poison there, or was trying to get someone else to put his hand on the damn thing against his will. Michaelaides had to push several people aside, including me, to take up his pose and start declaiming. Pompous ass."

"Alright," said Forrester. "But, would you mind telling me why you left the Archbishop's reception in such a hurry last night?"

Alexandros looked hard at him. "I think you already know the answer to that question," he said.

"Helena Spetsos?"

"You saw her arrive?"

"I did. I saw your pal Giorgi Stephanides delaying her. By the time she'd disentangled herself you'd gone."

"You have sharp eyes."

"I was puzzled. It's not like you to be afraid of a woman."

"On the contrary, I think all men should be afraid of women. It's our only chance of keeping our souls intact."

Forrester remembered the hours in the cave during which Alexandros had expounded his many philosophies on the relations between the sexes. "Someone said that she expected to marry you now the war is over."

"She did. She does."

"But you're not going to?"

Alexandros said nothing.

"If that's even a possibility, the police have to put you on the list of suspects of the Michaelaides murder. You do see that, don't you?"

"Which they will, Duncan, if you go spreading gossip about what Helena Spetsos and I did during the war."

"Ari, you're the last person I'd imagine poisoning anybody. Charging at them with a cavalry sword, yes, but poisoning: not your style."

"Thank you. Let us hope Inspector Kostopoulos takes the same view."

He led them both out of the stables; the sun was beginning its descent, but it was still strong enough to make him shade his eyes as they entered the stable yard.

"Helena Spetsos is a remarkable woman," said Alexandros. "She gave me back my youth. But I would not kill for her."

"I'm happy to accept your word on that," said Forrester.

"Good," said Alexandros. "So our business is complete."

"Sadly," said Forrester, "mine isn't until this thing is cleared up and the police let me go on my way to Crete, which is where I'm really supposed to be."

"Of course you are," said Alexandros, putting his arm around Forrester's shoulder in the gesture he remembered from the night before. "We will have to see what we can do about that."

"What do you mean?"

Alexandros smiled. "Who knows?" he said. "This is Greece."

6

ON THE WATERFRONT

The next morning, as Forrester woke beside a still-sleeping Sophie in the hard, narrow bed in their hotel, he made a conscious effort not to think about what they had learned in their investigations the day before. It was much better, he knew from long experience, to let his unconscious mind filter the knowledge he had gained before he tried to put it into any kind of order, and in the woman beside him he had the perfect distraction.

Her right breast was uncovered by the sheet, and he contemplated the pleasure, which for the moment he denied himself, of feeling its weight in his hand. Then he looked at the shape of her forehead, the way her hair lay across the pillow, the way the sunlight coming in through the blinds lit her eyelashes. "Noble" was the word that came to mind. It meant nothing to him that she *was* literally noble, that she came from a long line of Norwegian aristocrats; what mattered was that she was noble in her soul, that her very presence, in the smallest, least glamorous hotel room in

Athens (which is what he suspected this was) conferred upon it a kind of golden aura – a validation. Anywhere Sophie graced with her being, Forrester felt, had its own validity. And by the same token he felt too that simply being with her justified his own existence.

For a moment he did not think of Cornelius Brandt, or Jason Michaelaides, or Inspector Kostopoulos, or the fact that he was stuck in Athens when all he wanted to do was to get to Crete. Instead, he leant over and gently kissed Sophie's ear. A moment later, her eyes opened.

"Somebody just kissed my ear," she said.

"Yes," said Forrester. "It was me."

"How very forward of you."

"You have very kissable ears."

"I know," she said, "and they've heard a lot in the last twenty-four hours."

Forrester kissed her eyelids. "And these have seen a lot too," he said. Sophie smiled at the butterfly touch of his lips.

"Yes, they have. Though I have to confess nothing quite as startling as Ariadne Patrou tied naked to a pillar in Helena Spetsos's studio."

"Ah, yes, that," said Forrester. "I can imagine."

"All too well, clearly," said Sophie, after a moment. "Don't go getting any ideas about tying me to a pillar."

"I wouldn't dream of it," said Forrester. "Not even any interesting variation on that scenario." He paused for a moment. "Though I have been wondering how Professor Runcorn fits into all these goings on."

"You don't believe he was simply planning an

exhibition for the British Council?"

"He may indeed have been planning an exhibition, my darling, but not, I suspect, for the British Council."

Sophie looked at him thoughtfully. "Me neither. But was it just a coincidence that he turned up then?"

"Well, let's put it this way," said Forrester. "If I was Helena Spetsos and wanted to draw somebody useful into my web, setting up a scene like that might not be a bad way of going about it."

"If Professor Runcorn has a taste for that kind of thing," said Sophie, "Helena Spetsos will be able to wrap him around her little finger."

"To the extent of getting him to poison Jason Michaelaides for her?" said Forrester. "Because nobody would suspect him?"

"How very devious," said Sophie.

"How devious do we think Helena Spetsos is?" asked Forrester.

"Very," said Sophie.

"The problem is," said Forrester, "we haven't established any reason why Helena Spetsos would *want* to have Michaelaides poisoned. Even assuming she was just using him to get Ari Alexandros's attention and didn't need him any more, there was no need to bump him off, was there?"

"Unless they'd had a lover's quarrel," said Sophie. "You can't discount that."

"With someone like Helena Spetsos," said Forrester, sighing, "I suspect one can't discount anything."

Sophie got out of bed, then, put on a dressing gown and

left the room. The bathroom was down the corridor – it was that sort of hotel.

When she came back she handed Forrester an envelope with the address of police headquarters in the top left corner. "The manager brought it up himself. I suspect he was hoping to catch me in my nightgown."

"Well, he will have to just solace himself with his exciting glimpse of your bathrobe then," said Forrester, "which is not a bad consolation prize." He tore open the envelope. It contained a message on police notepaper.

Dear Mist Forrest,

All is good. Investigations tickety boo. Not to leave Greece, but Crete is O.K. Coming seeing me when getting back to Athens.

Signed,
Kostopoulos, G. Inspector

He looked at Sophie, frankly surprised. "What do you make of that?"

"It means you can get on with your expedition," said Sophie.

"Yes, but why is he allowing it? Somebody's pulled some strings."

"Good for them. I'll start packing."

"But listen, does it mean that we were getting too close to the truth? Somebody doesn't want us digging any more?"

"Quite possibly," said Sophie, "but as you were only digging so we could get out of here, does it matter?"

"I suppose not," said Forrester. "I just hope…"

"Hope what?" said Sophie.

"That it wasn't Ari."

"Who pulled the strings? Or did the murder?"

"Either," said Forrester. "Or both. It just seems very odd."

"Let it," said Sophie. "I've had enough of Athens, haven't you? What do you have to do before we can go?"

"Very little," said Forrester. "Apart from a visit to the Athens branch of the Empire Council for Archaeology."

"Then you should go and see the Empire Council for Archaeology," said Sophie, "and then let's get out of Dodge."

"Did your governess teach you that?"

"No, but she had a lover in Oslo, and when we went there, she let us go to see westerns in the cinema so she could spend the afternoons with him. That's where I fell in love with Tom Mix."

"Tom Mix," said Forrester. "I love the idea of you eating sticky toffees and falling in love with Tom Mix." And he kissed her.

The Empire Council was housed in a charming two-storey building complete with balconies, tall, shuttered windows, and a roof topped with statues of gently smiling Greek goddesses in flowing robes, some of them with lyres. Inside it was blessedly cool and dim, with black and white tiled floors and panelled walls rising to the shadowy recesses of the ceilings.

Council Secretary Iris Bulstrode regarded Forrester sternly through steel-rimmed spectacles when he was ushered into her office.

"You are a very fortunate young man to have been given this opportunity," she said.

"I'm aware of that, and very grateful to the council, Miss Bulstrode," said Forrester.

"And you must be very persuasive. The Empire Council's resources are extremely limited. How you convinced London to allocate funds for your expedition is frankly a mystery to me."

Forrester knew there were times when the only path of resistance is not to resist. "And to me too," he said. "I only hope I can justify their faith."

He met her steely gaze with a smile, and after a moment her head tilted and he knew he had momentarily prevailed: even Miss Bulstrode found it hard to trample on unreserved humility. One of the reasons Forrester was so diplomatic, of course, was the fact that he knew the council's arm had been twisted to approve his expedition. He had done a favour to the British government, one that could not be publicly acknowledged, and this was its way of repaying the debt.

Or perhaps of keeping him quiet.

Miss Bulstrode had no way of knowing this, but she sensed it.

"Yes, I can see how you pulled it off," she said. "Let's hope your archaeological skills are equal to your diplomatic ones. Now, let's get down to business. You know there's no question of your taking this stone away, don't you? If you find it again."

"Of course. Basically this is a preliminary expedition, to confirm its location, take photographs, and arrange for it to be protected until there can be a proper dig."

"Good."

"My memory from the brief time I spent in the cave is that at least half the thing is buried in the mud of the cave floor. My plan is to remove some of the earth around it to establish its full size, and then take photographs."

"Which you'll send to us."

"Of course. If you agree with me about its significance, I'll work with you to convince the Greek authorities to give it a proper designation as an ancient monument before transferring it to a museum for further study."

"Do you have all the equipment you need?"

"I plan to get spades and sieves and that kind of thing when I reach Crete. I have a pre-war camera, a tripod, some film and some flash bulbs, but only a limited supply. If you have any more, or any suggestions as to where I could get more, I'd be very grateful."

Miss Bulstrode smiled. "Oddly enough, I can help you there. As you know, the Germans have always been very active in Greek archaeology, ever since Herr Schliemann claimed to have found Troy. Members of the Wehrmacht with an interest in Classical Greece wangled themselves postings here whenever they could, and some of them indeed took over this very building, leaving a certain amount of equipment behind when they retreated. We may be able to find you some things among that material."

Forrester grinned. "Nothing would give me greater

satisfaction," he said, "than to use some of the loot Jerry left behind," and together, like children exploring a forbidden attic, he and Miss Bulstrode went down into the cellars beneath the building to begin their search.

When he left the offices of the Empire Council for Archaeology, Forrester was the proud possessor, among other useful items, of a pre-war Hasselblad, a German flashgun and twenty flashbulbs to go with it. He picked Sophie up from the hotel and piled their luggage in a taxi to Piraeus, where, just before they boarded the ferry for Crete, he telephoned Osbert Lancaster at the British Embassy, letting him know he had permission to leave.

"Delighted to hear it, old man. Best of luck. Have you heard the news, by the way?"

"What news?"

"Your pal Ari Alexandros has disappeared."

"What?"

"Didn't turn up at army HQ this morning, isn't at his house, vanished without leaving a return address."

"What do the police make of that?"

"Well, there's an obvious conclusion, isn't there? And knowing Inspector Kostopoulos, I'm sure he's jumped to it. Whether he'll do anything about it is another matter. Sleeping dogs, you know. But it's not your problem any more, dear chap. Go and dig up your relic. Tell us what King Minos had for breakfast. That's what we're all waiting for – with bated breath."

And the line went dead.

* * *

Later that day, after a smooth, uneventful voyage through the turquoise waters of the Aegean, the ferry was nosing its way gently through a fleet of picturesque caïque into the old Cretan port of Chania, against its absurdly flamboyant theatrical backdrop of the massive snow-capped peaks of the White Mountains. Chania was Forrester's favourite city on the island: he loved it because of the deep sense of continuity it gave him. There had been people living here, beside this sea-strand and on the gentle hill above it, since the Stone Age. Chania had been one of the jewels in the crown of King Minos, revered in the golden age of Greece, a governor's headquarters during the Roman Empire, a prized possession of the Byzantine Empire, a refuge for Christian monks when Islam came storming out of Arabia, and the headquarters of the Pasha of Crete under the Ottomans. Massive Venetian seawalls enclosed the harbour.

"Venetians?" said Sophie. "I hadn't realised the Venetians were here as well."

"Absolutely. They bought Crete from a French knight for a hundred pieces of silver in the year 1204."

"You are teasing me."

"I wouldn't dream of it," said Forrester. "He was called Bonifacio and he came from Montferrat. He'd been given it as part of the loot when the Crusaders destroyed Byzantium."

"But wasn't Byzantium Christian?"

"Yes, but it was also immensely rich, which made it fair game as far as the Crusaders were concerned, so they robbed it blind. After the Fourth Crusade Bonifacio got Crete, among other things, and promptly sold it to Venice. Hence these delightful harbour walls, put there to make sure anybody else who wanted Chania had to pay a much higher price than a hundred pieces of silver."

Sophie shook her head. "The study of history does not do much for one's faith in human nature."

"But it does wonders for one's sense of irony," said Forrester. "Besides, though human beings do terrible things, they also do wonderful things. For example – creating a city like this."

"I love the way your face lights up when you talk about the past," said Sophie.

"I love the way you keep me in the present," said Forrester, "which is much the best place to be." He took her hand, and she leant her head against his shoulder.

The boat landed and they gathered up the ex-army backpacks that now held their luggage and Forrester's equipment, divided at Sophie's insistence, equally between them. They walked together along the cobbled quayside to the *pensione* Forrester had booked, in one of the tall, narrow-windowed Venetian buildings on the waterfront, with a tiny balcony looking down on the immense dome of the Mosque of the Janissaries.

"That's not Venetian," said Sophie, looking at it out of the window of their spare, whitewashed room.

"Well spotted," said Forrester, standing beside her and pushing the shutters fully open. He put his arm around her, breathed in her scent, felt the curve of her hip against him.

"Well?" said Sophie. "I'm expecting an explanation."

"I'm sorry, I was distracted," said Forrester. "The Ottomans besieged the city in the mid seventeenth century."

"And I assume they took it," said Sophie.

"They did. They had a vast slave army known as the Janissaries, and the Janissaries prevailed. Hence the size of their mosque."

"It's huge," she said.

"I imagine they were very excited to be here."

"They're not the only ones, are they?" said Sophie. She pulled the shutters closed again, plunging the room into an inviting shade. "Have you checked out the bed?"

"Not yet."

"I think we should check out the bed," said Sophie.

The bed was comfortable, but with every movement of its occupants it creaked and emitted an absurdly loud metallic squealing noise. "We *are* just above the restaurant," whispered Forrester.

"Then the diners will have some distraction," said Sophie, "while they eat their kebabs."

Afterwards, as they lay beside one another, Forrester felt the tension inside himself beginning to ease. It sometimes seemed to him as if a giant key had been turned in his soul in September 1939, winding his nerves as tight as a watch spring, and every time the spring had uncoiled, as in those weeks with Barbara Lytton before he went back behind enemy lines, something had happened to wind it up again.

Such as returning home to find that she had volunteered to join the SOE and gone to France because she thought he was dead.

Such as learning that within six weeks she had been caught and shot by the Gestapo.

Such as returning to Oxford to resume his academic career and realising his first task was to save his best friend from being hung for a murder he did not commit.

But as it was that quest which had led him to Sophie Arnfeldt-Laurvig, he knew he should be grateful. Knew he *was* grateful. Because if there was one thing that five years of danger and fear had brought him, it was the ability to snatch joy from the moment, however fleeting, and savour it.

As Forrester slept, Sophie lay watching the glory die away over the Aegean, enjoying the weight of his head on her body, running her hand idly over the scars on his arms and chest, wondering, and not wanting to know, how he had come by them. As the dusk deepened she listened to the clatter of pans and dishes from the restaurant kitchen, the cocks crowing in the gardens on Kastelli Hill and the shouts of the children running along the waterside. She thought of the silent pine forests above the water at Bjornsfjord, before her mind drifted to her lost husband and his foolishness and how she had once loved him and how he had vanished into the maelstrom of the war like so much else. And then she too began to doze.

Later that evening they sat at an outdoor table by the waterside eating the fish soup called *kakavia* and watching the people pass to and fro. The last time Forrester had been here he had been watching a group of German officers wolfing down *horta* while he and Leigh Fermor had studied the movements of the sentries along the harbour, wondering if it would be practicable to sabotage some of the shipping that lay there. It would have involved swimming for half a mile carrying a limpet mine, and Paddy had been eager to make the attempt, but the Cretans were wary of sabotage, knowing how ferocious the German reprisals would be, and in the end they had decided against it.

Instead they had come up with the plot to kidnap a German general.

"What was it like here, during the war?" Sophie asked.

"Exciting," said Forrester. Sophie raised an eyebrow.

"Nervous-making," Forrester amended. "But the truth is there *was* something of a boys' own adventure about it. Blame Paddy Leigh Fermor for that. You've met him, you can imagine what he was like given the chance to dress up like a Cretan bandit or disguise himself as a German officer."

"How did the Cretans feel about that? After all, they must have suffered most when the Germans made reprisals."

"True," said Forrester, "though we did our best to make sure the Germans knew the stunts were by us rather than locals. We even left letters explaining."

"That didn't stop them wiping out whole villages, though, did it?"

"It didn't, though that mainly happened after their own guerrillas got overenthusiastic. The fact is that Cretans are a warlike people. There was one old priest, whose youngest son was shot by the Germans, who shook my hand afterwards and said he had two more he was also ready to sacrifice."

"I wonder what his wife thought about it?"

"She was probably as fierce as he was."

"Was it worth it?"

Forrester considered. "Well, the information we gathered about aircraft movements and shipping movements helped Cairo work out what Jerry was up to all over the Mediterranean. By Cairo I mean Allied intelligence."

"And the resistance? What about that?"

"It was war," Forrester said at last. "In war, you fight. You don't know what the outcome will be, but if you stop to consider, you're beaten. The important thing was to keep on fighting."

"That was *all* that mattered, boss," said a voice beside them that sounded like pebbles clattering down a dry mountain streambed, and suddenly Forrester found himself in an embrace that lifted him right off his feet. Yanni Patrakis had found him.

Yanni Patrakis had been Forrester's closest companion among the band of shepherds, millers, shopkeepers, olive-oil makers and bandits who had come together to form the core of the Cretan resistance movement. A giant of a man with huge black handlebar moustaches and hands the size of hams, Yanni was a fisherman with his own caïque, who had once killed two German sentries by banging their heads together before throwing them off a cliff. He was also a philosopher. Forrester introduced him to Sophie, and the Cretan looked her up and down with unfeigned admiration.

"Thou wilt be good for this one," he said, jerking his thumb at Forrester. "He lives too much inside his head."

Sophie smiled. "Where do you live, Mr. Patrakis?"

"Patrakis lives in the earth," said Yanni without missing a beat. "He is also in the olive trees they planted here when Jesus was a boy. He is in the stones they used to build the walls of the harbour." He gestured up towards where the White Mountains lay in the darkness. "He is in the bones of the mountains. Duncan knows this is true, for he has been in the mountains with me, hast thou not, boss? Thou knowest Patrakis *is* Crete."

No one else, thought Forrester, could have brought off such braggadocio, but you only had to look at Yanni to know with him it was entirely authentic. His high-collared white shirt, his heavily embroidered blue jacket, his breeches ballooning like exuberant jodhpurs and tucked into white knee-boots, all proclaimed him Cretan to the core. But whereas most of the guerrillas alongside whom he had fought had offered little conversation during those long weeks in the caves beyond what was the best brand of pistol or whether leather-soled boots were better than rubber-soled ones, Yanni had been full of ideas from the moment Forrester had parachuted down onto the Agostina Plateau. "Like Icarus," Yanni had said then as they hid the parachute, "thou fallest from the sky. But where is Daedalus?"

"Flying back to Cairo," said Forrester. "And keeping well away from the sun." Yanni had laughed and clapped him on the back and Forrester knew he had a friend for life.

Now Yanni joined them at their table and without for a

moment excluding Sophie from the conversation brought Forrester up to date with the adventures of all the *andartes* in their band – Manolis, the shepherd boy, now back with his flocks, Agios the windmill-builder, dead in the massacre at Krousonas, Antonios Grigorakis, the oldest of them all, who had fought the Turks in the uprising of 1897 and used the same musket to shoot at the Germans in 1942.

"A man full of dignity," said Yanni to Sophie. "With a white beard, cut so neatly you would think he had a barber with him in the caves."

"His beard came to a beautiful point," said Forrester. "So he looked like an unusually respectable Elizabethan pirate."

"But very fierce and hard," said Yanni. "He once shot off his own finger for rolling a bad number in a game of dice."

"He sounds quite mad," said Sophie. "But I'm sure he's very charming."

"Oh, he would give Duncan a run for his money with thee, my lady."

"What is he doing now?" asked Forrester.

"Trading in olive oil, boss," said Yanni. "But, as always, with great dignity."

"And you," asked Forrester at last, as the second bottle of wine arrived. "Do you thrive?"

"Patrakis thrives, boss," said Yanni. "There is his wife, bobbing in the water." They looked across the waterfront at Yanni's caïque, with the black and white eyes painted on either side of the prow. "The fish leap into my net, the fishmongers throw themselves at my feet to buy my catch, the sun rises on me in the morning and sets on me in the evening. And now my best friend in the world has come back."

There was silence for a moment, a companionable silence, for Yanni – in addition to his other gifts – knew when there was no need for further speech. But finally Sophie said, "Yanni, Duncan probably won't mention this, but I will, in case you have seen anything. An old enemy has been following him."

Yanni looked at Forrester, puzzled.

"We've probably left him behind in Athens," said Forrester.

"Who is this enemy? Tell me his name, boss, that I might smite him for thee."

So Forrester, half annoyed with Sophie for bringing it up, and half relieved to be able to share the story of Cornelius Brandt with his friend, told him about the man with the tin mask covering his face, and what had happened in Athens.

"He wishes to make thee uneasy," said Yanni.

"He *has* made me uneasy," admitted Forrester. "The problem is I can't think why he's been after me. I mean, the Dutch were on our side."

"What if he is a German, pretending to be Dutch?" asked Yanni, shrewdly.

Forrester paused. "That would make sense," he said. "If I were a German I don't think I'd announce the fact in Greece just now."

"Well, thou and I caused much trouble for the Germans in the war."

"True."

"Perhaps some of them are angry with thee."

"That is quite possible."

"Perhaps it is because of something thou and I did to the Germans here in Greece."

"That could be so," said Forrester.

"I will spread the word," said Yanni. "If he sets foot on my island, boss, thou wilt know."

"Thank you," said Forrester.

Yanni smiled and turned to Sophie. "Did Duncan ever tell thee, my lady," he asked, "about the time we walked into a Christmas party for German officers, and I passed him off as my idiot brother from Agios Nikolaos?"

And he proceeded to relate the story, so vividly that by the time he had finished half the diners at the tables around them were listening too, and the orange moon hung huge in the velvet sky.

7

INTO THE WHITE MOUNTAINS

The bus that would take them to the village closest to the Gorge of Acharius left from Eleftherios Venizelos Square in the middle of the old town. Eleftherios Venizelos had been born near Chania and had led the 1896 uprising against the Turks in which Antonios Grigorakis had fought. As the bus pulled out of the square the driver pointed to a large, shady tree. "That is where the Turks hanged the Bishop of Kissamos for supporting the uprising," he said.

"They never forget, do they?" Sophie whispered to Forrester.

"A little bit," said Forrester quietly. "The bishop was actually hung in 1836."

"You are such a pedant!"

"No, just a historian." An old woman across the aisle was holding two live chickens, their legs tied together with twine; she caught Sophie's eye and smiled, revealing a mouth with just three teeth in it. Sophie smiled back, pointed to the chickens and mimed eating. The old woman grinned more broadly, and indicated the strings of tomatoes and onions she had in her basket. Sophie peered in and breathed in appreciatively as the scent wafted from bundles of herbs.

"That's rosemary," she said.

"*Dendrolivano*," said the old woman.

"And this we call oregano," said Sophie.

"*Rigani*," said the woman, and with a twinkle in her eye held up a velvety plant neither Forrester nor Sophie recognised. Its round green leaves were covered in soft, woolly white-grey hair and its tiny flowers were rose-pink and purple.

"*Thelete na to peíte Díktamo*," said their interlocutor, "*alla oi Krhtikoí to léne éronta*."

Forrester grinned. "She says you'd call it 'dittany', but the Cretans call it *érontas*, which of course is related to the word 'eros'."

"As in erotic?"

"Very much so. They believe it's an aphrodisiac, and young lovers climb the mountains to find it for each other every spring."

Sophie smiled. "How romantic."

"Also, if I recall rightly, Aristotle claimed that if goats that had been wounded by arrows ate dittany, the arrows would fly out of their bodies."

"Then Aristotle was more gullible than I had imagined," said Sophie, but to the old woman she gestured to the plant and repeated, to her interlocutor's great delight, "*Erontas*."

As she spoke the roar of yet another unmuffled engine caused Forrester to glance idly down as a noisy motorcycle came alongside the bus and its rider looked up at them.

It was Cornelius Brandt.

For what seemed like eternity the disfigured man steered neatly between the carts and animals meandering along the street, glancing up every now and then through the dirt-smeared window at Forrester, as if taunting him.

Then suddenly his gloved hands twisted the throttle and the bike accelerated, pulled ahead of them, and disappeared down the road.

Forrester glanced across at Sophie. Now in conversation with a little girl who was showing her a peg doll, she had seen nothing. Forrester wondered whether to tell her, and then decided he must. If she continued on the expedition with him she must do it with her eyes open.

"I've just seen Brandt," he said quietly a few moments later. "He passed us on a motorcycle."

Her eyes met his calmly, and the smile did not leave her face but it was clear she was thinking rapidly. "He'll know where we're going, won't he?" said Sophie. "From the sign on the bus."

Forrester realised she was right. "We'll get off at the village before the last stop," he said. "Not the one on the sign. I know how to get to the gorge from there."

"What if he's going to the gorge himself?"

Forrester hesitated. For the first time he began to wonder if there was some connection between this bizarre apparition of a man and the reason he himself was returning to Crete.

"There's no particular reason to think that," he said at

last. "I think he's just following us. But I take your point: it would be better to get there before him." Then another thought occurred to him. "Perhaps it might be better if you stayed in the village instead of coming to the gorge. Or came back to Chania on the bus instead of getting off."

"The hell with that, Dr. Forrester," said Sophie. "If you're going, I'm coming with you."

They were heading eastwards now, along the foothills of the mountains, past little chapels that looked as if they dated from the time of St. Paul, whose red-tiled roofs, despite the years of war and occupation, were well repaired, the walls whitewashed, the porches swept clean, the little gardens that surrounded them neat and well-tended, their fig, almond and lemon trees swelling with fruit. Each of them looked like a little bubble of peace, and Forrester longed to enter one – as he had sometimes during the war – and sit in the cool quiet, breathing in the lingering scent of incense and wishing he still believed.

"Tell me about the Gorge of Acharius," said Sophie after a while. "How exactly did you come to be there?"

"Because of kidnapping General Kreipe," said Forrester.

"Then start by telling me about that," said Sophie. "Why were you kidnapping General Kreipe?"

"The original idea was to abduct another general, a chap called Friedrich-Wilhelm Müller, because he'd just destroyed seven villages, taken eight hundred and fifty people hostage and killed five hundred, including women and children. In short he was a bastard and apart from the propaganda value, we'd have been lifting a scourge from the back of every Cretan.

"But halfway through planning the kidnap Müller was replaced by General Heinrich Kreipe, who'd just been transferred from the Eastern Front, and though we didn't have anything against him personally we decided for propaganda purposes kidnapping one general was as good as kidnapping another."

"One general was as good as another," repeated Sophie, as if testing the phrase. She gave Forrester a sideways look.

"Well, that's what we told ourselves. The first plan was to kidnap him from where he was staying, Arthur Evans's old headquarters, Villa Ariadne near Heraklion, which the Germans had requisitioned, but it was too well guarded. Instead we decided to catch him on his way home from the divisional headquarters at Archanes, which was about five miles away, and there was a point where the road sloped down steeply and his car had to slow down to a crawl. It was a good spot because it was surrounded by rocks and bushes and there were trees to hide in. I know because I spent days in those trees scouting it out."

"I can just imagine you," said Sophie. "Like a boy playing Red Indians."

"Well, there's something in that," said Forrester. "Anyway, the kidnap was going to be at night, so Yanni and I took a lot of trouble to work out how to identify Kreipe's car in the dark. By the time we'd finished we knew the exact sound of the engine and the exact shape of the slits in the black-out coverings over the headlights. We also spent a lot of time studying the German checkpoints in Heraklion, because once Kreipe had been taken we knew we'd have to drive through it."

"Heraklion must have been full of Germans," said Sophie. "How did they not spot you when you were doing your reconnaissances?" Forrester smiled to himself: it was rare and oddly pleasing when Sophie made a tiny error in her delightfully correct use of the language.

"Because by that time I looked like a Cretan shepherd," said Forrester. "And Yanni, of course, looked like Yanni. And then it nearly all went wrong. A German sentry asked for a cigarette and Yanni offered him a packet of Senior Service."

"Senior Service?"

"A brand of English cigarette. I thought we were done for, but Yanni dealt with it beautifully: he said he'd got the cigarettes on the black market after the British were defeated in the Dodecanese, and we all laughed. You should have seen us strolling through that place, swastika flags everywhere, and German voices. We even walked past Gestapo headquarters."

"Were you afraid?"

"To be honest, I was exhilarated. It was like going into the lion's den."

"Men," said Sophie.

"I know," said Forrester. "Fools, all of us."

"And the kidnap itself? How did you do it?"

"Paddy and a chap called Billy Moss, who looked like a film star, dressed up as German corporals. As Kreipe's car slowed down at that bend Paddy waved a red torch and the driver pulled up. Paddy leaned in and asked the General for his papers and the minute Kreipe reached down to get them Paddy grabbed him, hauled him out and shoved a pistol against his chest."

"Did he resist?"

"Oh yes, he struggled like mad before we could get the handcuffs on. Billy coshed the driver and we dragged him out and tied him up at the side of the road. Then Paddy took the General's hat and sat in the passenger seat and Billy Moss took the wheel and the rest of us sat in the back with the General, making sure he didn't say anything or squirm free. We checked the tank was full and turned the car round for Heraklion."

"Why go through Heraklion if it was full of Germans?"

"We had to. It was the only road that would let us get to the mountains. On the way Paddy identified himself as a British major and told Kreipe he was now a prisoner of war and would be taken to Egypt."

"How did he react?"

"He was furious, but I think he was also relieved we weren't going to kill him on the spot. Anyway as we were coming up to the first checkpoint we pushed him down on the floor and Yanni held a knife to his throat so he kept quiet."

"And they let you through?"

"They let us through the minute they saw the General's hat, which as I say was now on Paddy's head. Fortunately Kreipe was known to get shirty with sentries who held him up, so as soon as they saw the gold braid they scrambled to oblige. Also there was a blackout, which made it hard to see anything, and Billy Moss hooted the horn with such Teutonic arrogance the soldiers on the streets started saluting."

Sophie could not help smiling at the absurdity of it. "How many checkpoints were there?"

"Twenty-two," said Forrester.

"My God," said Sophie.

"After the first few we felt absolutely entitled to be waved through, and I think that helped," said Forrester. "But that's not to say we weren't hugely relieved when we were out on the coast road again."

"And did you let the General up off the floor?"

"We did, and he immediately demanded that Paddy explain the object of what he called 'this hussar stunt' and the truth was Paddy found that a bit difficult. But we didn't have much time for explanations; we had to get rid of the car, get Kreipe onto a mule and head up into the mountains."

"Because you were on the north coast and the boat to take him to Egypt was going to land on the south coast."

"Yes. That was where Paddy and I split up: he and Billy Moss and most of the *andartes* went off with Kreipe, and Yanni and I and a few other chaps set off in a westerly direction."

"Why was that?"

"Well, we knew it wouldn't be long before the Germans came after us, and when they found the car they'd know the point at which Paddy and his gang had gone up into the mountains. Our job was to lay a false trail up into the hills by another route, and then lure Jerry into following us."

"Which must have been dangerous."

"Not to put too fine a point on it, it was. All Paddy and Billy had to do was to keep hidden and keep the General moving. Yanni and I had to hang around, get seen, and then get seen again often enough to keep them coming after us. It was a bit like Hare and Hounds."

"Hare and Hounds?"

"A game we used to play as kids. Cross-country running."

"Except in cross-country running I imagine your opponents aren't trying to kill you."

"Well, it's fair to say it was quite intense. By contrast Paddy and the General spent weeks on the other side of the island hanging about waiting for the submarine to pick them up. There was even a point when they were on Mount Ida in the snow and Kreipe started reciting Horace."

"Horace?"

"Latin poet. Wrote odes. Turned out Paddy knew by heart the particular ode that Kreipe was reciting, and he said it made him realise, as he put it, 'we had both drunk at the same fountain'. I'm not sure they became friends, but apparently things were much easier between them after that."

"And you? Did you have anyone to recite Latin poetry with?"

"There wasn't much time for that. Kretzmer was hot on our trail."

"Kretzmer?"

"The chap they sent out after us. Oberleutnant Hans Kretzmer. He didn't introduce himself, of course, but I doubled back once and listened in on them from the top of a gully. I heard them use his rank and name then."

"But he didn't catch you."

"Came damn close, though, several times. And he did me a favour, really."

"A favour? In what way?"

"He forced me to go into the Gorge of Acharius – and that was where I found the cave."

The bus was climbing into the mountains now, and the red earth of the maquis began to vanish under a covering of tamarisks, cypresses and oaks. Then as they approached the village of Meskla an intoxicating scent came in through the open windows, and they could see groves of lemons and oranges growing alongside the ruins of ancient walls.

"*Cyclops*," said the old woman to Sophie, pointing to them. Sophie looked at Forrester for explanation.

"She's saying the walls are Cyclopean," said Forrester. "Because they look as if they were built by giants."

"*I Spiliá tou Kýklopa eínai edó kontá*," said the old woman.

"And she also says the Cyclops's cave is near here."

"Wasn't that near the sea?" said Sophie. "I seem to remember the poor creature throwing stones at Odysseus's boat when he realised that he and his men had escaped."

"Quite right. You'll find the Cretans have annexed quite a lot of Greek mythology and shifted it to their own island. Apart from Cyclops they claim not only to have the cave where the immortal Zeus was born but also the cave where he died."

"Which is a little bit contradictory."

"Very much so. If Zeus was immortal, how could he die? But the Cretans love stories for their own sake. How true they are is of less importance. And I suspect these ruins didn't have much to do with the Cyclops either: they're most likely Minoan."

The bus came to a halt in the centre of Meskla, opposite a Byzantine church with two elaborate whitewashed towers and a dome topped with a cross. As they retrieved their backpacks from the luggage compartment Sophie took a deep breath: the scent of citrus blossom was just as exhilarating here as it had been on the bus, and as they inhaled it they looked up at the wooded hills rising up all around the village, red-tiled roofs and white-sailed Cretan windmills glowing in the sunlight among the green canopy of the trees.

"I think I like it here," said Sophie.

"Good," said Forrester. "I'd hoped you would."

A donkey laden with baskets of oranges trotted past them, its hooves clattering sharply on the cobbles, and the big, bald man guiding it called out a cheery good day as they set out. Their course was along a brawling stream, shaded by chestnut trees and bordered by massive lichened rocks over which little falls plunged into deep pools.

Every twist of the stream brought them higher into the mountains, whose silver-grey rock glinted in the sun. Every now and then Sophie would reach into the stream, scoop up handfuls of deliciously cold water and throw it over her head and chest.

Forrester grinned. "I remember doing that the first time I was here," he said. "I never imagined I'd be back with someone like you."

"Not someone *like* me," said Sophie. "*Me.*" And she threw a handful of water over him too.

At last the chestnuts and oaks gave way to pines, and the pines grew shorter and the ground more rocky until instead of trees there was the deep-green, scented maquis: lavender, thyme, verbena and blue sage, where the bees droned lazily between plants heavy with pollen.

The stream they were following was narrow now, flowing swiftly between banks of wildflowers, and as Sophie exclaimed over them, naming them in Norwegian, Forrester glanced upwards and saw the dark slash in the white cliff-face.

"There it is," he said.

"The Gorge of Acharius?" said Sophie. Forrester nodded.

Suddenly they were both aware of the silence. In the distance, very faintly, the tinkling of goat-bells, but somehow the sound served only to emphasise the great noiselessness of this upland world, as if it was holding its breath, waiting for something to happen. Forrester felt his stomach tighten.

"Did the Germans pursue you along this stream?" asked Sophie.

"No," said Forrester. "Yanni and the rest of us had

gone around the outskirts of a village called Theriso, which is a few miles east of here. We didn't actually go into any villages because we didn't want to put them at risk. Kretzmer and his men were about a mile behind us at that point, but getting closer. I decided the time had come for us to split up. Some of the *andartes* headed back to their own hideouts. Yanni and three other men carried on westwards on the north side of the mountains."

"And you went into the Gorge of Acharius."

"I went into the gorge."

They were walking up towards the cliff now, the ground becoming steeper with every step, the vegetation more sparse, as an eagle wheeled. They looked through the slot in the cliff-face that led into the gorge, but accustomed to the brightness on the mountainside, their eyes could make out little in the dimness. By their feet the stream, just inches deep here, slid silently over a lip of rock on its journey down to the sea.

"Ready?" asked Forrester.

"Ready," said Sophie, and they squeezed through the gap.

The first thing that struck them both was how cool it was between the towering walls after the heat of the exposed mountainside. Sophie glanced behind her: through the entrance she could see a dazzling world of silvery rock and, in the distance, the green hills surrounding Meskla. But in here the sun's ferocity was tamed and the light was thin, and diffused. The sky was a ribbon of bright blue, high above.

The stream, a mere trickle now, slid along beside them

and there were ferns growing in niches in the rock; a few steps in Sophie had to turn aside to avoid treading on a purple orchid. There was a strong scent of damp, ancient rock.

"You were very lucky to find this place," said Sophie.

"Oh, Crete's riddled with them," said Forrester. "The mountains are made of limestone and the acid in rain dissolves it. When the water gets down to the bottom of a gorge, it makes pools, and the pools eat into even more rock, and that's how you get so many caves."

"Including your cave."

"Including my cave."

Now the walls of the gorge were no more than a dozen feet apart, the rock face alternating bands of green and purple rock. Twisted pines thrust their way out of cracks in the limestone, like prisoners pushing their arms through the bars of their cells, and round a corner they came upon a grove of cypress trees clustered together like mourners at a funeral.

"Cypress trees grow very old in Crete," said Forrester. "These might have been planted while Byzantium still ruled the island."

"The last days of the Roman Empire," said Sophie.

"Absolutely," said Forrester. "The Eastern Empire, anyway." He did not see the secret smile on Sophie's face as he made his automatic scholarly correction.

"How close behind were the Germans when you were here?"

"To be honest, I don't know. I'm sure they didn't see me come into the gorge, or they would have been much more thorough. At the time I hoped they didn't know I was here at all, which was why I took the chance of hiding in the cave."

"Is it much further?"

Forrester smiled. "As they say in the pantomimes, *it's behind you.*"

Sophie turned, and found herself looking at a gnarled and ancient pine tree, not much taller than she was. Its deeply indented bark looked like the skin of a crocodile. It was only when she ducked beneath its outstretched arms that she saw the crack in the rock.

"Discreet, isn't it?" said Forrester. "You can see why I chose it."

Sophie eyed the black hole doubtfully.

"Don't worry," said Forrester. "It gets wider once you're inside."

"I'm not worried about how wide it is," said Sophie. "I'm worried about whether your Dutchman or German or whatever is already there, waiting for us."

"Highly unlikely," said Forrester. "I'm sure we've shaken him off by getting off early. But let's have a look," and he swung the pack off his back and knelt on the rocky floor of the gorge. Sophie watched as he examined the ground and the fragments of moss, twigs and pinecones that had fallen from the tree. Without getting up, he said, "It might be better if you didn't come in."

"You think he *is* in there?"

"I'm not sure, but someone has been here in the past few hours."

"If he's in there, you shouldn't be," said Sophie.

Forrester stood up. "I don't think I've got much option," he said.

"You've got the option of walking away," said Sophie. "This man already tried to kill you once; he's now got the perfect place to finish the job."

"Well, forewarned is forearmed."

"That's ridiculous. If he's waiting for you in there, what chance do you have?"

"I suppose I'll find out when I meet him."

Suddenly Sophie was overcome by anger. "That's ridiculous!" she said. "For a rock?"

"Yes," said Forrester. "For a rock."

"Listen—"

"No, listen to me, Sophie. Please. The Minoans wrote. They wrote a lot. We have the tablets, we have the inscriptions. But we don't know what any of them mean. The stone in this cave could be what allows us to read all of that."

"I don't care about what the Minoans wrote, or a damn piece of rock they wrote it on, Duncan," said Sophie. "I care about you."

Forrester took her hands in his. "What's in there is part of who I am," he said. "You tease me about living in the past; it's true, I do, part of the time. It's part of me. I'm a link in a chain going back a hundred thousand years, probably more. And if I have a purpose in life it's to understand that past, to see how it shaped us, so we can look ahead and see where we're going.

"You're right about the war: most of it was just pointless

killing and suffering. But the gods were good to me here: they gave me something that made it all worthwhile, for me anyway. I'm not going to throw that away because some crazed foreigner has a grudge."

"I lost my husband to the war, Duncan," said Sophie. "I don't want to lose another."

"You're not going to lose me," said Forrester. "Find a patch of shade, sit down and wait for me to come out. I promise you I'll be back."

And he turned sideways and slipped through the entrance to the cave.

8

MINOTAUR

There are an estimated four thousand caves in the four great limestone massifs that constitute the bony spine of Crete, which is one of the reasons the island has proved so productive of bandits, pirates, guerrillas and outlaws of all kinds: they have places to hide.

Forrester had reason to be grateful to these caves, and he remembered how often they had given him a sense of security during the long, tense months of his Cretan mission – but he had never liked them. He did not like the darkness, the narrowness, the sheer senselessness of their architecture. Man used them, but they had not been made by man. The erratic, irrational processes of the physical world had shaped them, and man had to adapt to them, not the other way around.

And before man, other creatures had made these places their home, and were sometimes still there. Blind snakes, slow-moving, endlessly scavenging insects, swarms of devil-faced bats.

Still, none of these thoughts had passed through his head as he had slid backwards into its darkness that first time, with Oberleutnant Kretzmer in hot pursuit. Then it had seemed like a sanctuary indeed: exactly what he needed. He had been tucked away in what he believed was the back of the cave about twenty feet from the entrance when he heard the rattle of their boots on the stones out in the gorge and the metallic clink of their equipment.

Kretzmer's confident, authoritative voice echoed between the limestone walls of the gorge. "*Schnell, schnell. Bauer, nehmen Sie Ihre Zug und die linke Seite der Schlucht ausfindig zu machen; Mullhaus, die rechte Seite.*"

Forrester had crouched there in the darkness, waiting for the sound to die away down the gorge. It did not. He stayed there, not breathing, waiting for them to pass the pine tree that hid the entrance.

They did not pass it. Forrester heard the excited shout as the man called to his comrades.

But by the time the first German helmet appeared in the slot, he had already discovered that the cave did not end where he thought it did; that there was a narrow cleft behind him, hidden in the darkness. As the soldier entered, Forrester was already forcing himself backwards into the cleft, fighting the terror of being trapped there, and suddenly the cleft had become a sloping tunnel and he was sliding silently backwards into—

He had no idea. He still had no idea when he landed. He had no idea where he was even as he listened to the sound of jackboots crunching around the floor of the main cave above him. He sensed the space was spherical, or dome-shaped; he could feel a steeply curved wall against his back.

He knew there was something in front of him too, something about two or three feet high. He sensed it was in the centre of the chamber.

He knew too, in his bones, that this was a sacred place, that it had been a place of awe and terror for thousands of years, that men had come here to communicate with the divine – and they had left something behind them.

Something that stood in the centre of the chamber.

But he suspected he would never discover its nature: above his head, the soldiers searching the cave were coming closer, and soon, he knew, they would find the entrance to the shaft by which he had entered. And the grenade would be tossed down it, and if he was lucky he would be dead.

Then he heard again Kretzmer's harsh voice outside in the gorge, shouting something urgently to the searchers.

He did not find out until much later that it had been Yanni who had saved him by deliberately showing his head above the top of the gorge, a hundred feet vertically above the searching Germans. Yanni had decided not to go westwards with the other *andartes*, but had doubled back on the slopes above them. He had known he could do this safely because it would take at least thirty minutes for Kretzmer's men to get out of the gorge and scramble up to the skyline where he had shown himself.

But nothing had obliged him to do it. It had not been part of the plan. It was just Yanni. It was who he was.

In the distance there was the rattle of machine-gun fire, and more shouts from Kretzmer as Forrester heard the sound of the searchers' boots retreating from the cave. But he was scarcely thinking about it, because by that time his fingers had felt their way over the object in the centre of the chamber, and he was beginning to understand what he had found.

It was a long time before he had dared strike a match to examine the rock, and by that time all sounds of activity outside had long ceased. By that time too his fingers were confidently tracing the shape of the incisions – and he knew exactly what they were.

There was the circle with four straight lines in the middle. The bird's beak shape. The wheatsheaf. The heart split in two.

Linear B – it was all Linear B. The lost language of Minoan civilisation.

But that was on one side of the stone. As he traced the outlines on the other side his mouth went dry. When he finally struck the second match and saw it, he literally felt his heart leap within his chest.

Hieroglyphs.

He had found his Rosetta Stone.

The original Rosetta Stone had been discovered at Rashid in Egypt in 1799 by a soldier in Napoleon's invading army. It had been carved two hundred years before the birth of Christ to proclaim a decree by Pharaoh Ptolemy V – and Ptolemy had ordered the decree written not just in Egyptian hieroglyphs, which had remained a mystery since the end of the Egyptian empire, but also in ancient Greek. Once the ancient Greek text had been translated, hieroglyphs could finally be deciphered – and after two thousand years of mystification archaeologists finally had the key to Egyptian civilisation.

And now Forrester had found a stone that had not only the undecipherable writings of the Linear B script of the ancient Minoans – but texts in hieroglyphs, possibly even Egyptian hieroglyphs. If these texts were the same as what was written in Linear B, Forrester knew he had found the route to the heart of the labyrinth.

But there had been no time, of course, to find out whether that was the case. He couldn't stay here and he couldn't take the stone with him. And any time now the Germans would give up their wild goose chase after Yanni and come back.

He had made the greatest discovery of his life and he had no option but to leave it, to inch his way back up the tunnel, crawl to the entrance, make sure the gorge was still free of his pursuers, and continue his escape.

With a heavy heart he did all these things, made his way safely, a week later, to the rendezvous with his fellow SOE operatives, and got out of Crete in the same launch that took Leigh Fermor, Billy Moss and General Kreipe to Alexandria.

But almost every night since then he had dreamt of the stone; he had moved heaven and earth in London to get the funds and permissions needed to come back to confirm its existence, and now he was here again, in the same cave.

All he had to do was reach it.

Provided a crazed Dutchman did not kill him first.

Pressing himself into the cleft at the back of the cave wasn't hard; wriggling himself into the tunnel that led down to the chamber was easy enough. But forcing himself to let gravity take hold and slide down into the blackness where anything might be awaiting him took all his mental strength.

The second his feet hit the floor he rolled and then slammed himself against the back wall, ranging the barrel of the Luger across the chamber.

Yanni had left the gun at the hotel reception desk the night after their reunion, wrapped up in a brown paper parcel tied with string; the parcel also contained a small cardboard box with a dozen bullets inside. Forrester remembered when they had taken them from the ammunition pouch of the German sentries before Yanni threw them over the cliff.

But he was not thinking of that now – nor of any danger to himself. He was staring down the beam of his flashlight at the centre of the cave, where the stone had been.

All that remained was a hole in the cave floor where it had been embedded.

"You bastard!" he said. "You goddamn ignorant bloody *Hun*." He felt sick with grief and anger.

"*Hun?*" said a voice. "That is very old-fashioned."

Forrester looked around him. The voice seemed to be coming from everywhere and nowhere.

"Brandt, is that you?"

"There is no 'Brandt'," said the voice. Despite the echo created by the chamber, it had a creaky, almost metallic quality. "My name is Oberleutnant Hans Kretzmer."

Forrester felt his stomach contract.

"The poor German fool you outwitted here in this very gorge."

Forrester heard the words with a sickening sense of inevitability. Of course it was Kretzmer. At some subconscious level, he felt, he had known it all along.

"The poor German fool who is about to have his revenge."

"You tried to catch me, Kretzmer. I escaped. Such things happen in war."

"You shamed me. You prevented me from rescuing General Kreipe. And you ruined my life."

Forrester decided to ignore the accusation. "So why have you moved the stone, Kretzmer?"

"You will understand in good time."

"Where have you taken it?"

"Not far away. It's perfectly safe. In fact, if you wish to see it again, there's nothing to stop you doing so."

Forrester's eyes narrowed. And then he saw, low down in the chamber wall, the entrance to another chamber.

"You can see it, can't you?" It was as if the German was watching him.

"Yes."

"Would you like to come down and examine your beloved carving?"

Forrester knew there was no point in prevaricating.

"Yes," he said. He aimed the torch down the drop: it was no more than six feet to the chamber below, and he could see one edge of the stone, leaning against one wall.

"I assume you are armed," said the voice. "You must throw down your gun before you come. You have my word I will not shoot you if you do that."

A beat, and then there was the distinctive sound of a gun rattling down the shaft and hitting the floor of the cave below. Forrester slid after it immediately, before Kretzmer could reach for it, and there was the man, staring straight at him.

For a moment, Forrester stopped breathing: the painted tin mask had been removed.

The face it had hidden truly was a thing of horror. It looked as if a great purple birthmark had been smeared across the flesh of one side – and then the face itself gouged out. The cheek was missing, and the shattered remains of jaw and teeth clearly visible through it. One eye was gone, and the red eye socket stared steadily at Forrester over the barrel of a pistol.

"Raise your hands, please, Captain. And don't think of reaching down to retrieve your weapon. I promised I would not shoot you and I will not. Instead, you may examine the prize you have lost." And he shone his torch across the cave.

The stone was propped up against the east wall of the cave about ten feet from Kretzmer, who was leaning casually against an outcrop of rock on the far side, giving him a commanding position. Something deep in

Forrester's mind told him there was another significance to this arrangement, but all that mattered to him at this moment was the stone.

It appeared to be intact. He moved towards it, consumed with the need to run his hands over it – and then, prompted by some instinct he did not understand, stopped, just feet away, in the centre of the cave.

"You understand how valuable this is, Kretzmer?" he said. "Not in monetary terms, but for scholarship."

"I am perfectly familiar with the challenges of deciphering Linear B, Captain Forrester, and can clearly see how important this object could be to achieving that."

Forrester looked over at the smashed face in surprise.

"Before the war, you see," said Kretzmer, "I was not a mere soldier. I was a distinguished student at the University of Berlin. In the Department of Ancient History, no less. I worked hard to engineer my transfer to Crete and you can imagine my happiness when I first gazed on the throne room of Knossos, the pillared colonnades, the Hall of the Double Axes. I felt as if I was coming home. During my free time I explored the mountains, searching for just such objects as this. When I came back to the gorge after your escape, I found it."

"Why didn't you take it then?"

"I intended to. As soon as I had returned to Heraklion and gathered the necessary equipment. It would, as you can imagine, have made my name, assured me of a career after the war. But you smashed that dream, didn't you?"

"Me? Don't be ridiculous. I must have already been in

Egypt by the time you came back."

"But you had sealed my fate long before that. You had sealed it between checkpoints sixteen and twenty on the road to Chania."

"What are you talking about?"

"I was the officer in charge of the sector between those checkpoints."

Suddenly, Forrester's mouth was dry.

"Because of you I was blamed for my part in the disaster of General Kreipe's kidnapping. My only chance of redeeming myself was to rescue the General. But you ensured that would not happen, did you not? You led me on a wild goose chase that ended here in the Acharius Gorge. So I think it is only fitting that the penalty should be imposed here, don't you?"

"Penalty for what?"

"The penalty for having me transferred to the Eastern Front."

Forrester said nothing. It was becoming clear at last.

"The Eastern Front was the price I paid for your amusing stunt with the General," said Kretzmer. "Three weeks after you and your friends escaped with him, I was in Belarus."

"Hardly my fault," said Forrester. "What you should ask yourself is why the hell you invaded Russia in the first place."

Kretzmer's eye flashed with rage. "Because you cowards wouldn't fight them!"

Forrester blinked. "What?"

"You still don't realise! Bolshevism is the enemy,"

spat Kretzmer. "The Führer knew that. You fools did not. Now they will destroy you, as they destroyed us. As they destroyed me."

"Listen—" said Forrester.

"No, you listen, English," said Kretzmer. "I want you to know about the place where you sent me. I want you to smell the stench of rotting bodies. I want you to hear the noise of the tanks as they crushed our men beneath their tracks and left them to die. You think we ever rested? No – there was a sniper on every rooftop. You think we could sleep at night after we had fought them all day? No – because it was night they liked the best. Their favourite weapon was a sharpened spade. You know the noise a spade makes when it bites into a man's skull? I want you to imagine it, English. So we lay awake waiting. Night after night, week after week, month after month, never sleeping. Gradually going mad.

"You know where they got me in the end? In the ruins of the university. In the wreckage of a lecture room. Appropriate, no? They came at us with grenades. I was hit, and I was captured. You see the result before you. I hope you are proud of it."

"Listen—"

But Kretzmer did not let Forrester finish. "There were two thousand wounded prisoners packed into the cellars. No light, no sanitation, just screams for help. Prayers, sometimes. Never answered. No bandages, no medicine, no clean water. I should have died, Forrester. I should have died as they operated on me, without anaesthetic of course, because there was none, but one thing kept me alive. It was the thought that one day I would find you, that I would take the stone, and I would have my revenge."

"Revenge for your sufferings?" said Forrester. "*Your* sufferings? You're alive, man. Sixty million people are dead. Count your blessings."

But it was as if Kretzmer could not hear him. "It is ironic I would not have been able to track you down if it had not been for the help of your famous Empire Council for Archaeology. Once they had decided to fund your expedition, they announced it, and my path was set."

"I'm very sorry about what happened to you," said Forrester, "but holding me responsible is insane."

"But you *are* responsible," said Kretzmer. "And now you will pay."

"The whole world will pay if you destroy these inscriptions," said Forrester, looking down at the stone.

"I have no intention of destroying them," said Kretzmer. "I intend to take the stone with me. But you, Captain, will remain here, in this cave, as mute witness to my success."

"I thought you gave me your word not to shoot me."

"I did, and I will not shoot you, but you will die here anyway, that I promise you. But you may take one last look at your prize if you wish."

Forrester hesitated.

"Go on, feel free: I do not break my word."

"For God's sake, Duncan. He's going to kill you." Forrester's heart sank as Sophie slid down the shaft that led into the chamber. But Kretzmer's ravaged face seemed to smile.

"Ah, Grevinne Arnfeldt-Laurvig. How convenient of you to join us."

For a moment Sophie said nothing, silenced by her first sight of the man, and then she said, "What use is revenge, Herr Kretzmer? What good does it do? Anybody?"

"It will soothe my soul," said Kretzmer, and Forrester knew the end was about to come.

"You have no soul, Kretzmer," said Forrester, "it's all gone," and as Sophie fired the flashbulb on the Hasselblad Miss Bulstrode had lent him, momentarily blinding Kretzmer, the gun slid from Forrester's sleeve into his hand. The torch still lay on the ground where he had rolled it down the shaft to convince the German he was unarmed.

Both weapons fired simultaneously – but Kretzmer's was aimed not at either of his human opponents, but at the roof of the cave. As the bullet struck the keystone and dislodged it, half a ton of rocks crashed to the floor and Forrester knew that if he had accepted Kretzmer's invitation to look at the inscriptions, he would been crushed like an insect beneath them. Of course the German could not afford to have a body, even a skeleton, with a bullet wound in the cave where he had made his find. But a dead Englishman crushed in a rockfall – that need have nothing to do with him at all.

Or a dead Norwegian woman, for that matter. Jesus!

The cave was full of dust now, blinding, choking dust.

"Sophie! Sophie! Are you alright?" and he saw that

though the main rockfall had not hit her, one of the rocks had knocked her to the ground, and she lay still with blood on her face. Mouthing incoherent prayers he lifted her out of the rubble, fear coursing through his body like freezing water.

When she opened her eyes and stared at him groggily he felt as if it were he who had come to life again. He looked up: Kretzmer had vanished. The cave was unrecognisable – it seemed almost the entire roof had come down.

"Jesus, I'm so sorry, I'm so sorry."

Sophie smiled.

"I came of my own free will, Duncan. And I think it was a good thing I did. Now, start looking for your stone." A beat, and then he laid her down and began pulling aside the rocks that lay between them and the cave wall where he had last seen it, but long before he reached the wall he knew what he would find.

The stone had gone along with Kretzmer.

Sophie looked at the shaft that had brought them in here. "He couldn't have gone that way," she said. "He could not have got past us without us seeing him."

"I know," said Forrester, and began burrowing through the debris until he was on the side of the cave where Kretzmer had been when he fired.

And there was the third shaft, vanishing up into the mountainside.

"Don't go up there," said Sophie. "He'll kill you if you do."

Forrester shook his head. "Don't worry. I've been a

bloody fool today, and nearly lost you. I'm not going to take that risk again."

"I'm glad."

"But I'm not giving up," said Forrester. "I'm just not going to make it easy for him. Come on, let's get out of here."

9

THE HUNTER AND THE HUNTED

Because the tunnel through which Kretzmer had escaped had led upwards, Forrester guessed it came out on the mountainside above the gorge; the walls of the gorge, as Kretzmer no doubt knew, were too steep to scale without mountaineering equipment, and that meant that when they emerged from the cave they had to trek back to the entrance before they could head up the mountain to the point where he might have emerged.

By the time they finally scrambled out of the gorge and onto the upper slopes the sun was beginning to descend towards the west, but its glare still reflected off the rocks and they had to squeeze their eyes half closed to see. It took twenty more frustrating minutes before they found where Kretzmer had come out of the tunnel leading up from the cave, but the marks, where he'd dragged the stone out into the light, were unmistakable.

More significantly, as Forrester knelt down and examined them, he smelt engine oil, and a few yards further on found the indentations left by Kretzmer's motorcycle. Despite himself, Forrester had to acknowledge Kretzmer's ingenuity: not only had the motorcycle allowed him to get to the gorge well ahead of them – it had also allowed him to get away with the stone, doubtless stuffed into a pannier bag, so fast they had no hope of overtaking him.

"No hope at all?" said Sophie.

"Not while he's on the bike," said Forrester. "But at some point he has to get off."

"How do you mean?"

"Well, we're on an island. If he's going to smuggle that thing out of Crete he's got to do it by boat."

"From Chania?"

Forrester examined the motorcycle tracks in the fading light; they weren't tracks really, just marks in the fragrant, low-growing scrub covering the mountainside, but there were just enough of them to make out the direction.

"He's headed north and west, which is the way to the Chania road. You're right, it is the obvious jumping-off point, because it's where most of the caïques are."

"Too obvious?"

"Possibly. But he may have made an arrangement at some little fishing village nearby. That would have been the smart thing to do."

"And he's smart."

"Yes," said Forrester ruefully. "He's smart."

"What should we do?"

"We need to get to a telephone as soon as possible."

But reaching a telephone proved, as Forrester had

suspected, no easy matter. As dusk fell, the journey back down the course of the stream to Meskla became more and more treacherous, and their pace slowed dramatically. The gurgling of the stream beside them and the cold depths of its pools were no longer an attraction, but a constant source of danger. Even turning an ankle on one of the slippery rocks could have wrecked their plans. By the time they reached Meskla it was dark, they were exhausted, and the last bus was long gone. Also, it turned out there was no telephone in the village.

Responding to Forrester's urgency, the local doctor agreed to take them down in his horse and cart to the police post on the main Chania road, and Forrester telephoned from there. Finally, after going through many operators, he roused Osbert Lancaster in Athens and explained what had happened.

"Well, from what you say your chap shouldn't be too difficult to spot," said Lancaster, "if he comes through Athens."

"I don't think he will," said Forrester. "If I were him I'd hire a caïque and get them to drop him somewhere well outside Greek territory: Sicily perhaps, or Albania, and not at one of the big ports either – some cove or other."

"So effectively he'll probably make a clean getaway," said Lancaster.

"Partly depends on how well he does in hiring his boat. If you could get onto the British Consul in Chania he might be able to help. I'll be speaking to the Chania police myself."

"Consider it done," said Lancaster.

Forrester spent another half hour getting a call through to Miss Bulstrode at the Empire Council for Archaeology in Athens. When he finally got through, that redoubtable lady, without wasting a moment in unnecessary comment or questions, promised to enlist the assistance of the director of the Chania Archaeological Museum, whom she knew well.

It was not until the next day that Sophie and Forrester themselves reached the port on the Chania bus, having spent an uncomfortable night dozing in the police post, and Sophie went straight back to their hotel to clean up while Forrester went first to the consul and then to the archaeology museum to enlist the aid of its director, a silver-haired man called Evangelous Apostopolous.

A bitter look came into Professor Apostopolous's eyes when he heard what had happened: his brother had been one of the hostages machine-gunned by General Müller's men at Kedros.

"The harbourmaster will tell you about caïques from Chania," he said. "I will call him to make sure he does everything he can. I myself have many relatives in the fishing villages to the west of here. I will send messages to them in case the German left from there." He looked hard into Forrester's eyes. "Don't worry, my friend, we will track this monster down."

Forrester nodded, and shook Apostopolous's hand, but there was little confidence in his answering smile. Kretzmer was a too formidable opponent for that.

The urgent requests from Miss Bulstrode and Osbert Lancaster had ensured that the local police were also doing their best to help, and it turned out the harbourmaster was Evangelous's brother-in-law. But he shrugged his shoulders expressively when Forrester asked if any of the Chania caïques was missing, pointing out that as usual a third of them were out on fishing expeditions, a third were delivering cargo along the coast, and most of the others were taking cargo to and from nearby islands. Yanni Patrakis himself was out at sea somewhere. The one useful thing Forrester was able to establish, when the harbourmaster brought the leader of the dockers' union into his office, was that no one remembered seeing a man fitting Kretzmer's description in the last twenty-four hours. Forrester guessed that if the German had ridden his noisy motorcycle down the dock, and anybody had seen that grotesque mask, or indeed the face beneath it, they would have remembered.

Which meant that if he had taken a caïque, he must have taken it from somewhere else.

At this point Forrester himself returned to the hotel, cleaned himself up, changed his clothes, and ate a late breakfast with Sophie: a meal in cheerless contrast to their dinner two days previously, when Forrester had felt so near his goal.

"Have you asked Yanni?" she said.

"Out fishing," said Forrester. "Nobody's sure when he'll be back."

"Well," said Sophie, "I've got something that may be useful," and to Forrester's surprise she brought out a map. Examining it, Forrester realised that it was a German wartime map of coastal defences.

"Where on earth did you get this?"

"From a second-hand stall in the marketplace," said Sophie. "I think they were quite surprised anyone wanted to buy it."

The map was creased and beer-stained, and depicted only an odd mushroom-shaped peninsula to the east and north of Chania; it was an entirely random acquisition, but Forrester decided to take it as a sign.

"The director of the museum is enquiring in the villages west of here," he said. "But this map covers the east. I think we should take advantage of it and check out the peninsula ourselves."

"There seem to be a lot of places there where he could have got a boat," said Sophie, tracing her finger across the map. "Agios Onoufrios, for example. Or the coves around Kalathas. I suppose we'd better go round each one."

Forrester considered. "We may run up against a certain reluctance to say anything that might get a local man into trouble for smuggling antiquities."

"Then perhaps we'd better not mention that," said Sophie. "We could say Herr Brandt – I imagine he'll still be calling himself Brandt and pretending to be Dutch – is a great friend of ours who's accidentally left his wallet behind in Chania."

Forrester looked at her and grinned. "I hope you're never on my trail," he said.

"As long as you never go anywhere without telling me," replied Sophie levelly, "you have nothing to worry about."

* * *

They hired a local taxi and began a long, hot, weary afternoon spinning their story to suspicious fishermen and their families at the little villages around the Katafigio peninsula – and getting nowhere. Dozing dogs eyed them narrowly as they trekked through whitewashed alleys heavy with the trapped heat of the day's sun. As they stood waiting for people to answer their knocks the endless chirp of the cicadas seemed to mock the futility of their quest. And no one seemed to know anything about a man with a strange-looking face on a motorcycle asking to hire a boat. Halfway round the peninsula, after visiting four fishing settlements, the cab broke down and the driver announced there would be a half-hour wait while he made running repairs.

It was stiflingly hot by now, and the chorus of cicadas was louder and more mocking than ever. Seeking shade, Sophie suggested they walk down to the beach to bathe their feet in the water. A little way along the beach was a ruined chapel, and without giving the matter much thought, they strolled along to visit it. It was a relief, however brief, to get out of the sun into the cool dimness of the church and put their quest behind them for a moment. To Forrester's surprise, despite its ruinous appearance, much of the interior was intact, and there was even, beneath a surviving section of roof, a faded Byzantine fresco.

"It's beautiful," said Sophie. "It looks like a ship in a storm."

"I think that's exactly what it is," said Forrester. "And look – one of the people on board has a halo, so he's a saint. St. Paul, I'd guess. He was always getting caught in storms while he was crossing the Mediterranean."

"Spreading Christianity."

"Absolutely. Nothing was going to stop him: not the weather, not shipwrecks, not the Romans, nothing until he'd got his new religion off the ground."

At which point Sophie put her finger to her lips and pointed. A young girl was kneeling at the far end of the chapel, praying.

"*Kai as érthei písosto chróno gia ta genéthlia tis mitéras tou.*"

Sophie looked at Forrester for a translation.

"She's praying that somebody comes back in time for her mother's birthday," whispered Forrester, and Sophie's eyes softened.

"*Makári o Agios Christóforos na tou chamogelásei kai to téras den tha ton vlápsei,*" prayed the girl.

"May Saint Christopher smile on him and the monster not hurt him," said Forrester. His eyes met Sophie's, and as the little girl ended her prayer, they backed out of the church so she would not find them standing over her when she opened her eyes.

Instead, when she emerged, they were sitting on the sand, looking out to sea.

"*Kali sas méra,*" said the girl, gravely. Good day.

"*Kalispéra sas,*" Forrester replied politely. The girl looked at them, curious and uncertain, but reassured by the fact that they were sitting down and she was standing up and able to run away if she chose to do so.

"*Eínai o patéras sou psarás?*" asked Forrester – Is your

father a fisherman? – and when the girl replied, hesitantly at first and then more volubly, Forrester followed up for a moment or two with a series of apparently casual questions. Then the girl said her goodbyes and headed for home.

"Well?" said Sophie when she was out of earshot.

"Her name is Calliope Laskaris and she says a man with a bad face gave her father money to take him somewhere in his boat," said Forrester.

"*På målet!*" said Sophie.

"*På målet?*"

"It means on target in Norwegian. Bang on target. Any more?"

"Her father left with this man last night. She's worried that he hasn't come back."

"It has to be Kretzmer."

"Yes," said Forrester. "She also mentioned he came on a motorcycle."

"What should we do? Get the police?"

"No," said Forrester, getting up. "It's too late for that and I don't want to get the family into trouble. But I think we should have a chat with Calliope's mother."

They followed the girl at a discreet distance until she reached a cluster of whitewashed houses clustered around a small cove and disappeared inside one of them. They waited, giving her chance to talk to her mother, and then went up to the house themselves. Slightly modifying their story about being friends of Brandt to account for the family's obvious unease about him, but reassuring the woman – whose name was Anna – there would be no trouble with the authorities if she told them where her husband had gone, they gradually got the story out of her.

The husband – Spiros Laskaris – had met the Dutchman at a bar in Chania two nights ago, and had agreed to take him out to one of the islands. No, her husband had not told her which island – the Dutchman had sworn him to secrecy – but the little girl interjected to say she had seen the man studying a map on which the island of Antikythera featured. The Dutchman had put it away quickly when she saw him looking, and she could not be certain Antikythera was the island to which her father was going, but that was what she had seen.

She also added that she did not like the Dutchman. She did not like his strange face and she did not like the way he ordered her father around. Her father, who owned the best caïque on the peninsula!

Forrester thanked the woman and her daughter with great politeness, and asked them whenever their man returned to send a message telling his friend Evangelous Apostopolous at the Chania Archaeological Museum. At this point the taxi, now repaired, came cruising along the coast road looking for them, and when they were back aboard Forrester told the driver to take them straight back to Chania.

"Do you think the little girl was right about Antikythera?" said Sophie.

"I don't know," said Forrester. "There would be no point in taking the stone there, because it's still in Greece, but if you were heading for Sicily or somewhere on the Adriatic, Antikythera is in the right direction."

"And he probably wouldn't have told Laskaris that he wanted to leave the country."

"I'm sure he wouldn't. He'd wait till the man was committed."

"So what do we do?" asked Sophie.

"Well, first of all we give this information to Evangelous, and contact the authorities on Antikythera. I think it's governed from Piraeus, but there should be some local official. And then we head there ourselves."

"By ferry?"

"Ferries in this part of the world are a bit unreliable. I think we might need our own personal transport."

"Yanni?"

"If he's come back, Yanni would be ideal."

To Forrester's great relief, when they returned to Chania, they found Yanni on his boat beside the dock, fish spilling through his hands like silver, extolling the virtues of his catch to the merchants. As he listened Forrester knew what it must have been like to have been in the presence of Homer as he recited the *Odyssey*. Yanni saw him, but did not pause in either his spiel or the frenzied haggling that followed it, in which he acted in rapid succession the parts of an insulted lover, exhausted sailor and lordly, generous sea-god, until the deals had been done to everyone's satisfaction and the fish taken off by its new owners in large wheelbarrows.

Only when the last merchant had gone did Yanni step towards them, arms widespread, though to Sophie's relief, in view of the generous layer of fish scales that now clung to him, he did not actually embrace them.

"Thou art both in mourning," he said shrewdly. "And yet full of strange energy. What has happened? No! Do not tell me now. Tell me at the Sign of Aphrodite, for I have a thirst that cannot be denied."

And over plate after plate of stuffed vines and hummus, washed down with retsina, they told Yanni their story. By the time the bill had been paid, Yanni was already making arrangements for his caïque to be refuelled and provisioned so they could set out at first light the next morning.

"Never fear, my friend," he said to Forrester. "We will get the stone back for thee, and for the people of Crete."

10

CYCLOPS

They motored out of Chania harbour into a still, white morning. As Forrester cast off, the sun came up, lighting up the milky haze that covered the sea. At the wheel, Yanni's pose reminded Sophie of the statue of the sea god Poseidon at Cape Sounion, and Forrester suspected that Yanni had adopted the stance to produce exactly this effect. As Crete slipped below the horizon behind them he could still smell the island's herb-filled scent on the breeze.

Despite what he knew to be the diminishingly small chances of overtaking Kretzmer before he left Greek waters, Forrester felt his spirits lift as the caïque slid away across the glassy Aegean. For a while there was nothing ahead but its vast calmness, and then, gradually, distant islands appeared ahead, their peaks floating above the morning haze like immense airships.

As the mist burned off, these islands became clearer, some dark, mysterious humps, some forbidding, waterless rock fortresses, others green and tree-clad, inviting them to bring their boat to shore and enter their locust-eater domains. It was easy to imagine the temptations that had led Odysseus astray as he struggled home to Ithaca. On one headland they could see the dazzling crystal whiteness of a ruined Doric temple; the next was crowned with the ramparts of a massive castle once used by the Knights of St. John. Even the tiniest islet with its deserted coves seemed like the haunt of some god from the dawn of time.

But by lunchtime the breeze had died, the sun was beating down on them, forcing them into the shelter of the canvas awning, and the sea had turned to the colour of golden honey. Somnolent with heat, Forrester took a spell at the wheel while Yanni and Sophie served the octopus stew that had been simmering all morning in onions, tomatoes, garlic and its own juices.

"I can see why you like being out here instead of on shore, Yanni," said Sophie. "It feels like freedom."

"Greeks invented freedom," said Yanni, "because they live by the sea. Look at all these islands – every one a world unto itself." He pointed to a distant speck. "From that isle came a pirate fleet that spread fear throughout the Aegean." He glanced to starboard. "There they built the ships that destroyed the navy of Xerxes the Great. And yonder the lord of the island sank wells, and dug ditches, and brought water to the parched earth. Even today his orchards grow the best lemons in the world. Breathe in – you can smell their scent from here."

"The *lord* of the island?" said Forrester. "So were his peasants free too? The ones who sank the wells and dug the ditches?"

"Who knows?" said Yanni. "Some would have been free however much they were told to do, others were slaves no matter how little they laboured. A man's freedom is inside his own head, or nowhere at all. This, I think thou knowest, Duncan, truly."

Forrester grinned. He knew there was no besting Yanni in an argument.

Not long after their course brought them alongside a lateen-rigged boat, perilously low in the water, its passengers squeezed in among crates of chickens, tins of cooking oil, tethered goats and huge pottery jars. Old women gossiped with one another, children played, and the crew dodged in and out among them, hauling on ropes and shifting sails to catch the cat's-paws of breeze. Yanni hailed the captain, whom he knew, and Forrester translated their conversation for Sophie.

"He's asking him if he's seen Laskaris's caïque," he said, "or a man with some kind of mask on his face. Not very likely but…" then Forrester stopped talking and listened hard. Moments later the other boat was past and Yanni was clenching his fists in satisfaction.

"They saw Laskaris's boat yesterday. He had engine trouble – big black clouds of smoke coming from the exhaust. Instead of heading for Antikythera he changed course to Koros, because there is a repair yard there."

"How far is Koros from here?"

"Two or three hours," said Yanni. "We should be there by this evening."

"He might have finished his repairs today and already

have left," said Sophie, but Yanni shook his head.

"This is Greece, my lady," he said. "Nothing happens that fast." He thought for a moment. "Except death."

They reached Koros that evening. It was one of the more fertile islands, and the brightly coloured houses of the port seemed to explode up the hill like fireworks from the waterfront, their windows catching the light of the sinking sun as the lamps came on in the cafés and tavernas below. A gleaming white gin palace of a boat, pompously named *Notre Futur*, sat directly in front of the squat lighthouse that also housed the harbourmaster's office, and Yanni spat contemptuously into the water when he saw it.

High above the town was the massive bulk of the Monastery of Saint John, turning rose-pink in the last light of the evening. Forrester knew that the evangelist had written some of Revelations in a clifftop eyrie here before retiring to a presumably more attractive cave on Patmos. He could imagine him, wild haired, wild eyed, his mind quite possibly disordered by some hallucinogenic plant, looking out over the wine-dark sea and seeing the Beast with Seven Heads and the Whore of Babylon rising from the waves.

Yanni took a berth as far from the main part of the waterfront as he could, to at least slow news of their arrival reaching Kretzmer. And because Kretzmer knew Forrester and Sophie by sight but not Yanni, it was Yanni who went to see the harbourmaster and make discreet enquiries as to the whereabouts of Laskaris's caïque.

Forrester used the time to scan the harbour with the binoculars, and by the time Yanni returned, he was fairly certain that Laskaris's boat was one of three berthed beside a wharf on the other side of the harbour. The wharf seemed to be piled with significant quantities of discarded maritime equipment, some of it housed under a corrugated tin roof covering.

From what Yanni had learned it seemed he was right: the local boat builder had been at the taverna, and it was he who was repairing Laskaris's caïque. But Yanni had better news still: Kretzmer was staying at the monastery on the top of the cliff until the repairs were completed, which would not be at least until noon tomorrow. Forrester glanced up at the brooding bulk, and knew that in all probability Kretzmer, rather than take the stone all the way up there, might have left it hidden on Laskaris's boat.

"We should at least look," he said, and the others agreed. Yanni would keep watch at the taverna so he could warn them if Kretzmer returned to the waterfront, and helped them work out a route through the winding alleys of the town that would allow Forrester and Sophie to make their way around to the repair dock without being seen.

As darkness fell, they set off.

What had seemed like the simplest part of the operation, detouring behind the waterfront along the back streets, turned out to be much more difficult than they had imagined: the narrow cobbled streets twisted around each other like so many snakes, and from the lamp-lit interiors curious eyes glanced out at them through open doors. As they found themselves at the end of yet another blind alley or treading gingerly down a set of worn, unlit steps, Forrester was increasingly certain that at any moment Kretzmer would step out from the shadows to confront them.

But finally they were back by the water, the lights and noise of the tavernas to their left now, the cluttered darkness of the boat repairers ahead. The owner had clearly taken advantage of the vast number of wartime wrecks of British, Greek and Italian craft that were now scattered around the islands, and had been bringing engines, propeller shafts, pumps, navigation equipment and anything else he could lay his hands on to his quayside lair, where they lay in glorious profusion waiting for a new berth. Forrester and Sophie made their way carefully through the tangled mass, but the first caïque they came to was obviously not Laskaris's: it looked as if its repairs had been started shortly before the Italian invasion and postponed on a weekly basis ever since. The second boat had no engine, which removed it from the equation. The third exactly fitted the description Laskaris's wife had given them.

It was in a considerable state of disrepair. The decking had been pulled up to reveal the engine, and the damaged exhaust stripped out. An array of potential replacements for the damaged parts had been laid out on the worn planks of the wharf beside it. Forrester contemplated the tangle, and then glanced along the quay to the taverna where Yanni was keeping lookout. They had arranged that if Kretzmer appeared and seemed to be coming in their direction, Yanni would step out into the light of the sodium lamp by the harbourmaster's office. But there was no sign of him, so Sophie stayed on the wharf to watch out for that signal while

Forrester climbed down onto the caïque and made his way along the cluttered deck until he reached the boat's cabin.

It was dark and stuffy in there, but Forrester had a flashlight, and being careful to keep it from being visible beyond the boat, began a methodical search. He started with the obvious places like lockers and under bunks, then went on to the ceiling panels to see if any of them were movable, and finally got down on his hands and knees to find out if any of the floor planking had been shifted. As far as he could tell, none of it had. Then he left the cabin and crawled into the exposed engine compartment to examine every possible place that might be big enough to take the stone.

It was while he was jammed between the engine block and the side of the caïque that he heard a scuffle of footsteps.

And then silence.

By the time he had extricated himself from the engine housing and risen to his feet, Kretzmer was on the wharf, one arm around Sophie's shoulder, the other holding a Luger to her temple. Forrester felt the weight of the gun in his own pocket, and knew there was no possibility of using it.

As Forrester rose, Kretzmer tilted his head, producing the effect of the smile without a smile. "The monastery of *der heilige Johann*," he said, "is not just a refuge: it is a lookout. Did you not think of that? Did you not imagine that I would examine every vessel that came into harbour while I am here, and every movement of their passengers? Did you not imagine I would have anticipated exactly what you are trying to do now?"

"Touché," said Forrester. Inside, he felt sick: Kretzmer

was right – he should have thought ahead. But he had been too eager to find the stone. So eager his mistake might cost Sophie her life.

"Touché indeed," said Kretzmer. "And how pleasant it is to be in such intimate contact with your Norwegian friend." He turned to Sophie. "I like your perfume, Countess. Balenciaga, I believe?"

Sophie glanced at him for a moment before she spoke. "If you think knowing about women's perfumes makes you a civilised man, Herr Kretzmer, you are mistaken."

"Really? We will discuss that in more detail later," said Kretzmer, "when I have more leisure." He turned back to Forrester. "But it is in fact useful you are here, English. Reach beneath the engine."

Forrester stared at him and did nothing.

"When I give a command, I expect it to be obeyed immediately," said Kretzmer, and Forrester heard Sophie's grunt of pain as he jammed the gun harder into her temple. "Kneel down again and reach beneath the engine."

A beat, and Forrester did as he was told. As he searched, he was aware, out of the corner of his eye, that Kretzmer was kicking at one of the bollards on the wharf, and then another, but he was too low down to see exactly what he was doing, and too preoccupied with the task before him to figure out why. Suddenly, as his fingers felt through a mass of oil and metal shavings, he felt the outline of something hard beneath a thick layer of sacking.

"Well done," said Kretzmer, "you have found it. Now pull it out."

Forrester did as he was told, and felt an involuntary surge of excitement run through him: there was no doubt it was the stone. "Now, bring it over to the wharf, reach up and put it down on the planks."

A dozen scenarios ran through Forrester's mind as he heaved the stone up and took careful steps across the dismembered decking, but none of them ended with Sophie still alive. He looked up at her frightened eyes and knew that, vast though the stone's value was to him, it was nothing compared to her. Reaching up, he slid the bundle of oil-soaked sacking onto the wharf.

"Very good," said Kretzmer. Then, to Sophie, "Pick it up."

"I'm not sure I'm strong enough," said Sophie.

"You will be strong enough," said Kretzmer, "if you want to live."

Sophie drew in a long breath, and then bent down to retrieve the filthy object, her breath growing shallower with the effort. As Kretzmer watched her Forrester slid his own gun from his pocket and thumbed the safety off, knowing perfectly well as he did so that there was no way he could use the gun while Kretzmer's weapon was so close to Sophie. He heard her grunt of effort as she stood upright, cradling the stone in both hands.

"Stay where you are, Captain Forrester," said Kretzmer, "and I promise she will come to no harm. If you make any move against me, she will die. You know enough of me now not to doubt my will, I think."

"I don't doubt your will, Kretzmer, but face facts. We've caught up with you. The authorities all over Greece know what you've done. They're going to catch up with you too. If you give this thing up now we can come to some arrangement. If you carry on you're an outlaw."

"I've been an outlaw for a long time," said Kretzmer. "You made me one."

Then he kicked at the bollards again and Forrester understood what the man had been doing while he was extracting the stone. The loosened ropes slid free and the caïque slid away from the wharf into the dark water.

"Bon voyage," said Kretzmer, and then, to Sophie, "Come." And together, they disappeared into the darkness of the wharf.

As the caïque drifted away into the dark waters of the harbour, Forrester sought desperately for a way to bring it back to the shore. What Kretzmer had done was crude but efficient: he had effectively prevented Forrester from following him. The crippled caïque was gliding further from the wharf with every second; soon the only way back to shore would be by swimming. Desperately, he flashed the torch around the debris of the dismantled engine – and found, half buried in the mess, the boat hook. He hauled it out, saw the rusted engine block of a German E-boat on the wharf, and lunged.

The rusted metal began to disintegrate almost as soon as the hook caught in the block, but the hold was just enough to check the forward momentum of Laskaris's boat, and with just five feet between the two vessels, Forrester leapt, crashed onto the rotting deck of the first caïque.

Then he was back on his feet and racing along the deck

to make the leap back to the wharf. Gun in hand, he peered into the darkness towards the sodium lamp by the lighthouse, half expecting to see Yanni silhouetted in its glare – and then realised what lay between him and the taverna.

Notre Futur.

Notre Futur, with two figures aboard it.

As he sprinted he saw Kretzmer behind Sophie, forcing her to climb from the deck of the motor yacht up to the bridge, and he knew the German had already cast off the ropes. Then *Futur*'s engines roared throatily into life and Forrester jammed the gun back in his waistband and made his third leap of the night.

He made it, just. As his fingers closed over the stern rail, the boat bucked under him like an angry horse and began to accelerate towards the harbour mouth. Behind him, on the waterfront, he could hear the shouts of surprise and dismay – doubtless from the boat's owner as he saw it being stolen from under his nose.

Fighting gravity and the boat's acceleration, Forrester hauled himself over the rail, hit the deck and began to run at a crouch towards the companionway leading up to the bridge. But before he had reached it Sophie suddenly burst out of the wheelhouse door, grasped the stairway rail and swung herself over it.

Kretzmer, still at the wheel, fired blindly after her, assuming she had gone down the steps. Then he glanced to one side, saw her hand still clinging to the stair rail and aimed right at her – as Forrester opened fire and the wheelhouse windows exploded into fragments. He had no idea whether he had hit Kretzmer, but it didn't matter: the diversion had given Sophie time to drop down to the deck. Seconds later he was by her side and as the bridge door swung open and as Kretzmer leaned out with the gun, Forrester grasped her hand and pulled her with him to the rail.

"Jump," he said, and as Kretzmer's bullets split the air around them, they leapt into the darkness and fell into the churning water of the *Futur*'s wake.

Treading water, they watched the boat racing towards the harbour entrance as, on the quayside, they heard Yanni commandeering a dinghy, no doubt to come and get them.

"I thought I'd lost you," Forrester said, and Sophie looked at him, and shook her head.

"Not so easy," she said.

11

POSEIDON

Within half an hour of being fished out of the water they were pursuing *Notre Futur* in Yanni's caïque. The harbourmaster had alerted the authorities on every neighbouring island to the theft, and the furious owner, a Swiss, was berating the *Futur*'s captain for failing to leave any of the crew aboard while he "ate and drank like a pig" at his, the Swiss's expense. But Forrester knew that officialdom would have no effect on Kretzmer's escape. The German now had exactly what he needed to get out of Greek territorial waters.

In truth, Forrester was well aware there was little chance of Yanni catching up with *Notre Futur*. The caïque could do little more than five knots; Yanni had already established from the owner that *Futur* was capable of ten.

Down in the cabin, as Yanni steered and Forrester peered through the binoculars into the night, Sophie made soup. After forty minutes the moon rose and disclosed the *Futur* two or three miles ahead, heading northwest. Yanni altered course, but there was no jubilation in his face.

"What's the matter, old friend?" said Forrester.

"Hold tight," said Yanni, and as Forrester steadied himself against a bulkhead, the first oily swell hit the boat. It rocked, as if it had gone over a little hill.

"There'll be another one in a minute," said Yanni. "But that's just the beginning." He directed Forrester's attention to the sky, where the moon's brightness was now reflecting off towering cumulonimbus clouds.

"Go all round the boat," he said, "and fasten down anything that's loose. Oh, and find the hand pumps. We may need them."

As he spoke the next swell hit them, and for a moment the caïque wallowed in the force of it. Then came the first crack of lightning and seconds later the first roll of thunder, as if the gods were announcing the beginning of a play.

They were sailing into the middle of an Aegean storm.

For the first quarter of an hour Forrester and Sophie took little notice of the deteriorating weather; they could hear the wind getting up, and feel the buffeting of the waves on the elderly planks of the boat, but they were concentrating on their tasks, largely ignoring what was going on in the sea around them.

When they rejoined Yanni in the wheelhouse, Sophie pulled out a bundle of woollen jerseys and oilskin coats and insisted that they put them on. By now the wind was moaning steadily, flattening the wave-tops. There was a sleety rain driving at them from the north and forks of lightning splitting the sky at regular intervals.

"Can you still see him?" Sophie asked.

"Just," said Yanni. "He's further into the storm than we are, and it's slowing him down."

"Will he be able to cope?" asked Sophie.

"It's a much more powerful boat," said Forrester.

"Yes," said Sophie. "But he has to sail it on his own."

She was right, but her guess about the difficulties Kretzmer might be facing brought no satisfaction to Forrester. If *Notre Futur* went down, so did the stone. He wanted to catch the German; he had no desire to preside over his destruction.

But there was nothing he could do about that now; the rain was sheeting down vertically, so torrentially heavy it seemed to draw a curtain between them and the rest of the world. The swells had become waves, and with every passing minute the waves were steeper and higher. Time after time the caïque laboured uphill to reach the summit of a wave, teetered there for a moment and then plunged sickeningly down into the trough on the other side. Yanni's face was set and grim as he strained to retain control of the wheel, for there was no respite. As soon as they were at the lowest point of the valley between the waves, he had to force her head up again to make it to the top of the next. Beneath the banshee howling of the wind Forrester could hear the planks creaking and straining.

"Time to start pumping?" shouted Forrester above the noise.

"Time to start pumping," said Yanni.

Then began an endless time of bent backs and aching

arms as he and Sophie strove to get the water out of the engine bay with the ancient hand pumps. Beside them, wreathed in the smell of hot oil, the elderly engine strained and groaned and through a miasma of diesel fumes Forrester willed it to keep going, because he knew that once it gave up the ghost they were lost.

It felt like being on a diabolical funfair ride. Looking up, he saw the wheelhouse silhouetted against the lightning as the caïque climbed yet another wave, and then the stern, foaming with phosphorescence, high above them as the ship careered down the other side. Sometimes they could see the propeller itself, high out of the water, churning fruitlessly, and he prayed that the packing that kept the water out of the propeller shaft would hold firm.

And then the waves became so steep and so close together that as the caïque reached the bottom of each trough its bows began hitting the wall of the next wave instead of climbing it, and the shuddering crash of each collision made it seem as if the ship was being shaken to pieces. Forrester began to wonder how long Yanni would have the strength to hold on to the wheel, but there was no chance to go and relieve him, because he knew all too well that if either he or Sophie stopped pumping, the engine would die, and with it the ship.

He looked at Sophie, her eyes red with salt water, her face sagging with weariness, her hair a tangled mess as she worked on without complaint – and knew that whatever other uncertainty there was in life, he loved this woman and always would.

It seemed then that the wind ceased to be a predictable force of nature and became a wild, mad thing, blowing not from one direction but from all directions, one after another, backing from north east to north west to south west to south east, shrieking in crazed glee, bent, it seemed, on nothing but their destruction. It was as if someone with a vast hammer had smashed the symmetry of the sea, the very pattern of waves and troughs, so that all around them was broken water, and the old boat was no longer climbing and descending the waves but swinging wildly from one side to another. Forrester was certain then that the caïque would simply fly apart, the wheelhouse spinning off into the sea, each plank separating from its fellow so that the water rushed in and swallowed them all. He could see, in his mind's eye, the engine falling away into the liquid darkness and spiralling down to rest beside the ancient wreckage of some Greek trireme. He reached out and took Sophie's hand and it was as cold as ice.

"I'm so sorry," he said, but his words were torn away as they left his mouth.

Sophie made no attempt to speak: she simply met his eyes, and smiled. It was a forgiving smile, but it was more than forgiveness. It was love. If that was the last sight Forrester saw, he was content with that.

And then the wind died.

The waves returned. Not the steep waves of fifteen minutes before, and not calm waves either, but suddenly there was a pattern in the waters instead of madness and incoherence. Forrester looked up and there, to starboard, reared a headland, and he knew that Yanni had steered them out of the full force of the storm into the lee of some island, and there was now a chance at least that they would survive.

"Keep pumping, boss," yelled Yanni. "We're not home yet."

But gradually the boat's wallowing slowed and steadied, and suddenly, when neither of them was expecting it, Yanni cut the engine.

Forrester stuck his head up to see, to his astonishment, they were gliding silently up to a jetty.

"Tie her off!" shouted Yanni, and Sophie and Forrester stumbled back to the deck and fumbled with frozen hands for the ropes.

They were in a deep inlet, and though the wind and waves were quieter, when Forrester turned his gaze out to the sea from which they had come, out beyond the headland, he could see the storm still raging as fiercely as ever, the sky still repeatedly split by lightning.

"You should be at the bottom of the sea, all of you," roared a voice from the darkness. A dark figure was coming down a set of steep steps from somewhere above. "How in the name of Poseidon did you manage to get through that?" Forrester's salt-caked eyes opened wide as he heard the voice.

Because the figure coming down the steps was General Aristotle Alexandros.

12

PENELOPE'S ISLAND

For a long moment Forrester and the General stared at each other, and then Alexandros threw his arms wide.

"Duncan!" he cried. "And his countess! Welcome to Hydros."

"This is Yanni Patrakis," said Forrester. "He's the only reason we're not at the bottom of the Aegean."

"Then I owe you a lot, Mr. Patrakis," said the General. "For these are good friends of mine. Here, wrap yourselves in these." And he swung a rucksack off his back, pulled out a bundle of blankets and handed them out. "Come, let us get you up to the *kastello*. You have arrived on night of great significance."

"What's so special about tonight, Ari?" asked Forrester as they plodded up the steep main street of the village that lay below the *kastello*.

"I will tell you when we are out of the storm and you are warm and dry," said Alexandros, because the wind was still howling around them. Then began a long climb up steep switchback steps until they turned a corner and there, above them was the great bulk of the fortress, soft yellow light from its windows spilling out into the night; the smell of woodsmoke perfuming the wind. Despite his weariness, Forrester was conscious of something strangely familiar about the shape of the building, spread as it was along a long crest in the hillside, just one storey high for most of its length, buttressed by sturdy pillars. At first he was unable to make the connection, then, with a start, he realised the shape was subtly reminiscent of Minoan palaces, and as they were about to make the final ascent to the massive front door, he remembered something else.

"You didn't see a motor yacht," he asked Alexandros, "coming from the same direction we did?"

"I did not," said the General. "I only saw you because I was looking out for Giorgios Stephanides, who has been on the other side of the island. He was supposed to be back hours ago."

At which point the front door swung open, the light flooded out into the wild night, and a woman stepped out of the mythical past into their present.

"Allow me to present my wife," said General Alexandros as the door, mercifully shutting off the noise of the wind, slammed firmly behind them.

The first thing Forrester noted about Penelope Alexandros was that she was tall and beautiful, her dark hair still rich and thick, her large dark eyes alight with life. The second thing was that she seemed quite capable of killing anyone who got in her way.

"Welcome to Kastello Drakonaris," said Penelope Alexandros. "The servants will find dry clothes for you." Then, to her husband, "Did you find Giorgios?"

"No. He must have taken shelter at Limani Sangri."

Penelope nodded and burst into a volley of orders in Greek, summoning servants variously introducing themselves as Agathe, Adonis, Theodosius and Socrates, and almost before they knew it Sophie, Forrester and Yanni had been swept off to large, stone-floored bathrooms, stripped of their sodden clothes, sluiced with hot water, dried with large, rough towels and provided with approximately appropriate garments. So efficient was the operation that it was less than fifteen minutes before they emerged in their borrowed clothes in the main room before a blazing fire, opposite which the windows looked out at the dark sea beyond the bay.

Almost before they were through the door, glasses of brandy were being pressed into their hands and they were basking in the warmth of the resin-scented logs in a huge stone fireplace. The walls of the room were covered in ochre-coloured plaster and hung with ancient rugs, their faded colours glowing in the firelight. Kelims were draped over most of the chairs and sofas, and provided a covering for a huge ottoman in front of the fire. The light that did not come from the fire radiated softly from oil lamps dotted about the room. There were bookshelves against one wall filled with leather-bound volumes, and another wall was covered in ancestral oil paintings and what looked to Forrester like a seventeenth-century map of the archipelago. When he came closer he saw it was full of tiny holes.

"Where my ancestor took his prizes," said Alexandros.

"Prizes?" said Sophie, clearly imagining some sort of awards ceremony.

"Taking prizes is a polite way of saying capturing ships," said Forrester.

"Of course!" said General Alexandros. "Lambros Leonides was a pirate – one of the most successful in the Aegean. You are standing in the fortress he took from the Venetians."

"*Our* fortress," said Penelope Alexandros, handing round a tray of mezes, which caused Yanni to give a moan of pleasure.

"Thou must introduce me to thy cook, my lady," he said. "I will marry her."

"Then I certainly will not," said Penelope. "Because I intend to keep her for ourselves." But she did not look displeased by the compliment, or with Yanni's presence, and Forrester was not surprised: he could see at once that she and Yanni and Ari were all cut from the same heroic cloth. She turned graciously to Forrester and Sophie.

"I say this is *our* fortress," she said, "because I too am descended from a pirate clan, the Drakonari. The Drakonari defeated Ari's ancestor and took the *kastello* from him."

"But fortunately," said Alexandros, smiling, "my pirate forbear had a beautiful daughter, and a marriage was arranged between the two clans."

"Or, to put it another way," said Penelope sweetly, "the Drakonari took not only Leonides's fortress, but also his daughter."

"Who thereafter ruled him with a rod of iron," said Alexandros, "which, perhaps, was divine judgment. But enough of ancient history. Tell me how you came to give us the pleasure of your company tonight."

"We were in pursuit of someone who has stolen the stone I told you about in Athens."

"*Germanós*," said Yanni.

"A German?" said Alexandros. "Where is this swine? I will make him wish he had never been born."

"He stole a motor yacht in Koros," said Forrester. "That was how we sailed into the storm."

"Where did you last see him?" demanded the General, jabbing a finger at the map. "Show me!"

Yanni looked at the map for a long moment and then pointed. "Four miles east of this cape."

"Had the storm begun? Was his vessel in trouble?"

"The storm had begun," said Yanni. "And we were the ones in trouble. But though his was a much larger ship than mine he was sailing it alone."

"Give me details," said the General, and examined the map closely. "You have probably lost him," he said at last. "His boat should have been able to ride out the storm, and in that case he will be well on his way out of Greek waters by now. But if his engine failed, or he met with any other accident, the Peloponnesian current will have brought him here."

"The Peloponnesian current?"

"Why do you think our ancestors chose this spot for their headquarters?" said Penelope. "That current rules this part of the Aegean. They knew that sooner or later every ship that had lost its battle with wind and waves would be swept here – and into their clutches."

They stared at one another – but Penelope was no longer looking at them: she was staring out of the window, over the sea.

Where a red distress flare had risen high into the sky and was now curving slowly down back into the storm.

"Perhaps the gods are with you," said Penelope, "and the man you pursue is here already."

It was as well Forrester and Yanni had eaten, drunk and put on dry clothes, because the rest of the night was a blur of action. At Penelope's insistence Sophie stayed behind in the house, but Forrester and Yanni joined the rescue party organised by Alexandros, and soon, draped in oilskins, they were among a dozen villagers rounded up by their host, streaming down to the waterfront.

Within fifteen minutes Alexandros's boat was motoring out into the bay, with Yanni and Forrester peering ahead through binoculars for their first glimpse of *Notre Futur*. But it never came. As the stricken vessel limped around the headland it was clear this was no luxury yacht, but a converted minesweeper. And far from being piloted by a lone fugitive, its decks were crowded with people.

And as the minesweeper came close enough, Forrester's mouth fell open, because he recognised nearly all of them.

"I say," said David Venables, "you couldn't throw us a line, could you?"

13

THE THUMB OF ST. PETER

"I was beginning to wonder what we had done to annoy Poseidon," said David Venables as he settled into one of the armchairs in front of the fire. The rest of the party, unrecognisable in the darkness and shrouded in blankets, had been hurried into the house by the servants and were busy drying themselves off. Venables looked around the room. "But now I'm wondering if he was actually doing us a favour."

"He may have been doing *us* a favour," said a slight, fair-haired man coming into the room as he pulled a jersey over his head. "But what has poor Mrs. Alexandros done to deserve an invasion like this?" The man, who always put Forrester in mind of a small blond firework, bowed towards Penelope. "Lawrence Durrell, of the *Aegean Times*."

Penelope smiled. "Endangered travellers have been offered hospitality in this place for many centuries, Mr. Durrell," she replied. "It is my privilege to be able to help you."

"And mine," said Alexandros, shaking hands. "But what were you doing out on a night like this, when you were supposed to be safely in Rhodes, editing your newspaper?"

"Tour of inspection," said Durrell. "The paper's a British Army rag, as you probably know, and I'm supposed to visit our correspondents in the islands from time to time."

"But how come everyone else is with you?" asked Forrester. "You seem to have brought half of Athens."

There was a brief, awkward pause before Venables spoke. "Don't you remember, old chap? I told you Beamish and I were planning to visit Durrell for our book. And various friends insisted on coming with us."

Forrester turned to the editor. "I'm surprised you have a correspondent on Hydros, Larry," he said mildly. "It seems a very far-flung outpost even for the *Aegean Times*."

Durrell smiled. "Well spotted," he said. "In fact we were simply in the vicinity and there was a collective enthusiasm for paying Hydros a visit. The storm simply made our arrival a little more dramatic. By the way, I don't expect you to put us all up, General. Now the boat's tied up we can go back down and bunk there till the storm clears."

"Not to be thought of," said Alexandros. "We have plenty of room here, have we not, Penelope? And we can find space in the village for those we can't accommodate. How many are you?"

"The tally will rise, I'm afraid," said Charles Runcorn, coming in. "I feel like one of my Crusaders, perhaps Count Bohemond, with his stolen relics, struggling home from the Holy Land. But hopefully, more grateful for your hospitality than they ever were."

"Stolen relics?" said Forrester. "What relics?"

"Perhaps the most mysterious objects ever mentioned in the Bible," said Runcorn. "Too long a story for tonight, but I plan to lead an expedition to the ruins of his castle on the far side of the island, if you're interested."

"Speaking of relics, here I am," said Constantine Atreides, doffing his panama hat with all the elegance of the born courtier. Somehow, in the space of half an hour, he had transformed himself from a bedraggled survivor to someone who could have been presented without embarrassment to his master King George.

"Prince Atreides!" said Alexandros, gesturing for the newcomer to approach the fire. "You turn up everywhere."

"Wherever Greece needs me," said Atreides.

"You are most welcome, Your Highness," said Penelope, smiling graciously as Atreides bowed, but Forrester noted that the smile did not reach her eyes.

"And as for me, I only beg to be here long enough to draw you, Mrs. Alexandros," said Keith Beamish, who was just behind Atreides. "And hereby call on the muses to give me the talent to do you justice."

"He can only do pictures," said David Venables. "It will be my privilege, if you permit it, dear lady, to immortalise you in prose," and he tapped his ever present canvas bag. It was for adventures such as this, thought Forrester, that the oilskin pouch had been designed.

"I can vouch for Mr. Beamish's skill as an artist," said a young woman from the doorway. "He has drawn me at least five times since we set out. Indeed, he never seems to stop."

Forrester glanced towards the woman and drew in his

breath. It was Ariadne Patrou. As he looked at Alexandros, he saw the colour drain from the General's face, followed by the expression he recognised from the Archbishop's reception. Because if Ariadne had been on the minesweeper, she would not have been alone. Indeed, as the girl finished her sentence, she stepped aside from the doorway to let the last arrival make her entrance.

"General Alexandros, Mrs. Alexandros: it is so kind of you to offer us your hospitality," said Helena Spetsos. Her glance took in the earthy opulence of the room. "And such a joy to me to enter your enchanted castle. Thank you. Thank you both." And she came forward and clasped Penelope's hands with both of hers. Alexandros stared at her as if he had been hit with an axe.

When he thought about the evening afterwards, Forrester returned again and again to the poise shown by Penelope Alexandros at the arrival of the woman who had been her husband's lover, wondering whether it was because she then knew nothing of the affair, or that she had decided to *pretend* she did not. Almost before she had a chance to reply, however, Lawrence Durrell shifted the direction of the conversation. "I've been wanting to visit Hydros for a long time, you know, because of the Maia legend."

"Maia of Hydros?" said Keith Beamish. "Wasn't she one of the lesser Greek goddesses?"

"Hardly lesser," said Durrell. "She was the product of a sacred union between Atlas and Demeter, the goddess of growth."

"I stand corrected," said Beamish. "She sounds quite formidable. So this is the island where she lived."

"She fled here," said Penelope. "When Zeus fell for her."

"Ah," said Runcorn, "the old, old story. Don't tell me Zeus followed her disguised as a bull?"

"Not exactly," said Penelope. "She made her escape from Olympus so efficiently that no one could find her. Zeus sent several of his sons to search her out and finally Ares tracked her down to Hydros."

"Ares the god of war?" said Keith Beamish.

"Ares, the god of war," said Penelope. "When the women of the island refused to say where Maia was hiding, Ares destroyed all the trees and crops."

"Typical," said Helena.

"Didn't Maia call on her brother Dionysus for help?" asked Constantine Atreides. "I seem to remember that as part of his story."

"She did," said Durrell, "and Dionysus apparently so inflamed the women of the island with drink that they turned into maenads and tore the poor god of war to pieces."

"As he deserved," said Helena Spetsos.

"His blood replenished the fields and orchards," said Penelope, quietly, "which is why Hydros is so fertile. You must remember that story, Ari."

Alexandros smiled, but to Forrester the smile looked forced. "A version of it," he said. "There are a dozen versions of all these legends."

"How did yours differ?" asked Durrell, but before Alexandros was obliged to answer there was a violent knocking on the front door, and when it was repeated, Alexandros hit himself violently on the forehead with the flat of his hand.

"Oh my God," he said. "I had completely forgotten."

Penelope raised an eyebrow. "Yes," she said, "I thought you had." Then her hostess smile returned to her face as the living-room door opened and Archbishop Damaskinos's twin brother walked in.

Everyone rose, and as he did so Forrester realised his initial impression had been wrong – the man, with his huge beard, massive Frankenstein boots and dramatic clerical garb, merely resembled the Archbishop. And whereas the Archbishop had spoken softly, Abbot Vasilios Spyridon had a voice that could shake mountains. "What a gathering! What a noble gathering for a noble occasion," he boomed, lifting his arms in a hieratic gesture. "It gladdens my heart to see so many gathered together to re-consecrate a union sundered by war."

"These are unexpected guests, Vasilios," said Alexandros, "rescued from the storm. It may be best to postpone—" But the Abbot shook his head decisively.

"Not to be thought of, my General. Penelope has waited long enough. And besides, Chrystomatos has gathered up every holy icon in the monastery and brought them all to bless the occasion." He gestured to a rabbit-faced youth, also in clerical garb, who was carrying a tray, and with a dramatic gesture whipped off the covering cloth to reveal an extraordinary collection of painted images, tiny wooden chests and elaborate silver caskets.

Forrester noted that the servants had slipped into the room behind the Abbot and his acolyte, and were staring in awe at the treasures.

"The Thumb of St. Peter," Chrystomatos said excitedly, pointing to one of them, "also the Tears of the Blessed Virgin, and St. John's—" He stopped, leant over to the Abbot and whispered loudly, "I've forgotten what it is of St. John's, Father Abbot."

"Never mind, dear boy," said the Abbot grandly. "All that matters is that we have all the right sacred objects to go with tonight's ceremony, and we will perform it as promised."

"I hope you don't mind me asking," said Lawrence Durrell, "but I'm not quite up with the play here. What is this fascinating-sounding ritual we're about to witness?"

"That is very simple," said Penelope Alexandros. "When Greece fell and my husband decided to join the resistance, he knew the Germans would come to this island and take their anger out on me. It was essential that in their eyes my husband and I were on opposite sides. Ari therefore arranged a theatrical event, attended by many of the leading citizens of the archipelago, including the Abbot here, during which I urged him not to join the resistance and, when he refused, appeared to try to kill him. He then fled for the mainland, where he resumed his fight to save our country. Needless to say, the murder attempt was a subterfuge, and the only casualty was a goat, which was later eaten. The story, of course, spread rapidly through the islands, and as a result people believed we were divorced. In consequence, despite Ari's activities on the mainland, the Germans did not persecute me during the war, and the island was spared many atrocities. Now the war is over, Ari and I wish to make a public proclamation that our love for each other never faltered."

"My dear lady," said Charles Runcorn. "I feel profoundly privileged to be a witness, however unexpected, to so romantic and historic a ceremony."

"Charles speaks for us all," said Lawrence Durrell. "And I'm sure if there were any of his beloved Crusaders present they too would cheer you on." As Forrester seconded his words the room burst into applause. Well, not the entire room.

Even as he applauded, Forrester was unable to prevent himself looking over at Helena Spetsos. For her, this must be the worst possible news. She had clearly moved heaven and earth to get here and reclaim her wartime lover, and had nearly been drowned in the process – and it had all been in vain. Indeed, worse than that, she was about to become an involuntary witness to the reconfirmation of the marriage that would rob her of Ari Alexandros forever. Ferocious and elemental though she was, Forrester felt a twinge of sympathy for her. But there was nothing, he thought, the poor woman could do except bear mute witness.

He was wrong.

Even as the clapping died away, Helena Spetsos closed her eyes and fell, unconscious, onto the tray containing the sacred objects.

For a moment everyone stared in unabashed horror as painted *ikons*, silver caskets and wooden chests crashed into the fireplace, sending coloured liquids and shrivelled saintly body parts rolling into the ashes. Then there was a mad scramble to rescue them and replace them on the tray, while Chrystomatos emitted a high-pitched wail, the servants crossed themselves in superstitious terror and the Abbot growled deep in his chest like a bear.

Helena, still unconscious, lay ignored until Lawrence Durrell and Charles Runcorn lifted her to her feet and hurried her out of the room.

When everything had been picked up and put back, everyone stared at the tray, which now looked like the contents of a rubbish tip. Forrester could see the effort the Abbot was making to say something that would rescue the disaster – and finding himself utterly unable to do so. Indeed, as the man's massive chest heaved, Forrester began to fear he was going to have a heart attack, but after a long moment he regained control of himself and met the eyes of his temporary congregation.

"It seems the saints do not regard tonight as an auspicious time for the ceremony, General," he said at last. "Perhaps you will have your servants accompany us back to the monastery. We will revisit this matter when order has been restored."

And with great dignity the Abbot gestured to Chrystomatos to follow him, and left the room.

"Well," said Durrell confidentially to Forrester, "that was what we in the armed forces refer to as a major balls-up." Forrester nodded but secretly he took his hat off to Helena Spetsos.

He could see now why she had been such an effective guerrilla fighter.

14

THE BAY OF LIMANI SANGRI

When Forrester woke early the next morning and opened the shutters, the storm was over and the sun was shining from a sky washed clean by the rain. Indeed, as he looked down at the village below the fortress, it felt as if the whole world had been renewed by the tempest.

The bay itself gleamed turquoise in the morning light. The crescent of white sand around it looked as if it had been laundered. Even the caïques and minesweeper tied up at the jetty shone under their veneer of dew. But what delighted Forrester most was the village of Drakonaris itself, whose whitewashed houses, their tiled roofs glowing red in the sunshine, tumbled down towards the water below the fortress as if they had been spilt out of a box of children's building blocks. Orange trees glowed like lamps in tiny green gardens, and swallows ducked and dived above hidden squares built around wells where villagers were already filling jugs and buckets for the day's needs. Slender, arrow-straight wisps of aromatic smoke rose from the chimneys into the still air.

"Do you have a sentence in English that means balancing on a bomb?" said a voice from the bed. Forrester turned to look at Sophie and thought for a moment.

"The English phrase is 'sitting on a powder keg'," he said. "A keg is a small barrel and the powder in question is gunpowder."

Sophie smiled. "Then we are sitting on a powder keg," she said.

Forrester gestured out of the window. "A very beautiful powder keg," he said. Then he came over to the bed. "And speaking of beautiful powder kegs…"

"No," said Sophie, taking his hand away. "We have to think what we can do to help these good people."

"I'm not sure there's anything we can do. Helena Spetsos believes she has a claim on Ari. She's come here to make trouble. As you saw last night she has some expertise in that department. But I think Penelope Alexandros can more than hold her own."

"Without someone being murdered?"

"I'm sure it won't come to that."

"How can you be sure of that, after what happened in Athens?"

"We still don't really know what happened in Athens," Forrester said. "All we can be certain of is that somebody at the Archbishop's reception arranged for Jason Michaelaides to be poisoned."

"And that General Alexandros might have had a motive because Michaelaides was having an affair with Helena Spetsos."

"Well—"

"And as soon as you told Alexandros about your investigations, somebody pulled some strings and we were allowed to leave Athens and continue on to Crete."

"That could be just coincidence—"

"Oh, Duncan, stop pretending. I know he's your friend, I know all about you fighting together against the Germans, but face facts. Is there a better suspect for Jason Michaelaides's death than General Alexandros?"

"I don't know. But surely that's something we can leave to the police? You're not seriously suggesting there's going to be another murder, are you?" Sophie did not reply, but lay back again in the bed, staring up at the ceiling.

"Maybe not, but if I were Penelope Alexandros, I'd be very tempted to set the maenads on Helena Spetsos as soon as the opportunity arose."

Forrester grinned. "I'd better make sure I never get you mad at me, then."

Sophie looked at him. "Yes," she said. "You better had," and she reached up and pulled him down towards her.

They were awoken from their doze by a loud impatient knocking at the front door somewhere below them. "Socrates will get it," said Sophie sleepily. "Or maybe Theodosius." But Forrester swung his feet out of bed, convinced, for some reason, that the knocking was for him.

He was right, but not in the way he expected, because the early morning arrival was Colonel Giorgios Stephanides.

Alexandros's wartime second in command, the man who had interposed himself between Helena Spetsos and the General at the Archbishop's reception, was in the main room when Forrester finally found his way there along the innumerable corridors and staircases, talking in low tones to his old commander. Both men looked up with an oddly guilty air as Forrester came in, and then, with an effort, Alexandros beamed at him.

"I have good news for you, Duncan," he said. "You asked last night about a big motor yacht. Giorgios may have found it for you."

"Ari tells me you were chasing one of those fucking Nazis in a stolen boat," said Stephanides.

"White, wide bridge, twin engine," said Forrester. "*Notre Futur* painted bow and stern."

Giorgios nodded. "I was over at Limani Sangri last night," he said. "Far side of the island. There was a motor yacht in difficulty and I started to round up some of the villagers. Before we could even get the first boat out it had gone on the rocks."

"Did anyone get ashore?"

"Don't know. By the time we got there the thing was smashing itself to pieces. There was definitely nobody aboard then, and the chances of anybody getting ashore before we got there are pretty much nil. I'm guessing the body will have been washed up on Sangri beach by now."

"Duncan says the German had a stolen artefact, the stone he was looking for in Crete," said Alexandros. "Any sign of that?"

Giorgios shook his head. "Not that I saw," he said. "But

then, I wasn't looking for a stone. It was all I could do to keep upright in the wind."

"Do you think the wreck will still be there this morning?" asked Forrester.

"Probably not," said Giorgios. "I suspect it's so much matchwood by now."

"Well, we'll see," said Forrester. "What's the quickest way to get to Limani Sangri?"

It turned out that the quickest way to Limani Sangri was to hike there across the middle of the island, so, leaving Yanni to sleep, Forrester and Sophie set off alone, secretly relieved to be away from the emotional cauldron of the *kastello* before all its guests had emerged.

For a quarter of an hour they climbed steadily uphill until both the fortress and the village of Drakonaris were far below them. Then a great bell began to toll and they turned to see, to their right, the sprawling whitewashed complex of the Monastery of St. Thomas where, doubtless, the hapless Chrystomatos was even now trying to put the right relics back in the right reliquaries.

Then the path levelled out and they were in the forest, the scent of the warming pine needles rising like incense in the heat of the morning sun; above them, through the dark green of the trees, the sky was a deep, perfect blue. Soon, as the carpet of fallen needles swallowed their footfalls, it was as if they were walking out of the ordinary realms of existence into a separate, timeless world. Sophie put her hand on Forrester's arm and they stopped for a moment and listened to the silence. Even the tolling of the monastery bell had disappeared.

"It's very easy to imagine meeting Dionysus in a place like this," Sophie said softly. "You might just glance through the trees and see him standing there."

"All too easy to imagine," said Forrester, thinking of the maenads. Then he put a finger to his lips and pointed ahead through the trees. Something white moved in the shadows of a glade ahead of them, about waist height. A tiny movement, left to right, and then the white thing was still. They looked at each other. "Most likely somebody herding goats," Forrester said. But as they followed the path towards the shape, he placed himself ahead of her, just in case.

"Good morning," said Keith Beamish, when they reached the glade. He was seated on a three-legged canvas stool, sketching. The movement Forrester had seen was his white-shirted arm as it moved across the paper. "Peaceful spot, isn't it?"

"Sacred, I would say," replied Forrester, looking across the glade at four marble columns supporting a pediment. "Perhaps to our friend Maia."

"There's rather a nice statue in there," said Beamish, "which might be her. There's a stone amphora by her feet with a spring flowing from it. But be careful if you go inside – it doesn't look entirely stable."

Sophie and Forrester walked over to the little ruin, and cautiously mounted the shallow steps to the marble platform where the columns, their fluted stone deliciously cool to the touch, leant gently towards one another. The effigy of a woman, much smoothed away by time, stood at the back of the shrine, a carving of a stone jar at her feet. A tiny trickle of water emerged from the jar and slid away over the edge of the plinth into the forest.

"She has a lovely face," said Sophie, and her fingers stroked the woman's cheeks. "You could almost believe she was alive."

"No hint of Dionysian fury," said Forrester.

"No," said Sophie. "She looks very serene."

"Do you think I've got her?" asked Beamish. He came up after them, showing them his notebook. Sophie studied it.

"You draw beautifully. You'd think she was still with us."

"Thank you, Countess," said Beamish.

"By the way, Keith," asked Forrester, "did you talk to anyone down at the *kastello* before you came up here?"

"I did not," said Beamish. "I was determined to get away from that emotionally tense venue before anybody woke up." He looked through the trees in the direction of the house, as if expecting its inhabitants to appear, en masse, to disturb his peace.

"What did you make of last night's shenanigans?" asked Forrester.

Beamish raised an eyebrow. "It made me realise why Helena Spetsos was so determined to get here," he said.

"So she was the one who got Larry to add Hydros to his itinerary?"

"She and Charlie Runcorn, though I think it was chiefly her. She's quite a force of nature, isn't she?"

"You know about her affair with Alexandros during the war?" said Forrester.

"From her own lips," said the artist. "And according to her it wasn't just an affair, it was a cosmic event, two great souls coming together to change the future of Greece."

"So she must have been quite shocked to discover Alexandros was going back to his wife," said Sophie.

"Incandescent with rage, I'd have said. But that was a pretty neat trick, fainting on the relics. Stopped everything in its tracks pretty effectively, I thought."

"Mind you," said Forrester, "Penelope Alexandros is a force to be reckoned with too. She's not going to let that woman steal her husband after she's waited for him all these years."

Beamish looked at them uncertainly for a moment, and then said, "I don't like to be crude, and I know it seems odd in view of her passion for Alexandros, but do you think she's a lesbian? Helena, I mean."

Sophie grinned. "You're thinking about her relationship with Ariadne?"

"I am, to be honest," said Beamish.

"And you want to know because…?"

"Well, because I'm rather keen on Ariadne myself, and I've begun to wonder if I've been barking up the wrong tree."

"By barking up the wrong tree he means—" Forrester began, but Sophie held up a hand.

"Mum's the word," she said. "I know what he means." Then to Beamish: "I think Helena Spetsos makes love to whoever she wants, whatever their sex. I'm sure Ariadne is under her spell at the moment, but spells like that can wear off."

"Particularly if Helena's preoccupied with trying to get Ari back," said Forrester.

"I'm glad to hear you say that," said Beamish, "because Ariadne and I began to get to know each other on the trip here, and I got the impression Helena didn't like it."

"She wouldn't," said Sophie. "But I wouldn't let that put you off. In fact, I think it would be a good thing for Ariadne to be rescued from her captor. She deserves gentler treatment than Helena has been meting out to her."

"Thanks," said Beamish. "I'll take your advice to heart. And now I'm going to do a close-up of this amphora." And he squatted down beside it, the pencil already moving across a fresh sheet of paper.

"Show us the result when we get back," said Forrester. "We're off to Limani Sangri."

"Have fun," said the artist, already absorbed in his work, and Sophie and Forrester set off again through the wood.

When they finally emerged from the pine trees they were on an undulating upland plateau; there were windmills on the hilltops and flocks of sheep grazing on the short, sage-scented grass. Half an hour later as they reached the centre of the plateau, they came upon a small lake, where they lay down on the springy turf and Sophie rested her head on his chest.

"Will Penelope prevail, now her Odysseus has returned?" she asked. "Or will the wicked suitress claim her prize?"

"Perhaps the gods will intervene and decide the matter for themselves."

"All the way from Olympus," said Sophie, closing her eyes.

"'As flies to wanton boys are we to the gods'," said Forrester as Lear's lines came unbidden into his mind. "'They kill us for their sport'."

"Do you really think so?" said Sophie. "That sounds rather fatalistic for you."

"You're right," said Forrester. "I'm not sure why I thought of it. I like to think of the gods as kinder than that."

For several minutes they lay there in companionable silence, watching tiny clouds drift across the blue bowl of the sky.

"The gods help those that help themselves," said Sophie at last, rising to her feet. "Come on, let's go and look for your lost treasure before Oberleutnant Kretzmer spirits it away again. If he's still in the land of the living and hasn't been turned into a tree."

"Or a merman," said Forrester, and more of Shakespeare's lines came unbidden to his mind. He sometimes found that when one piece of poetry came into his mind, others followed, almost as if he had opened the lid of a chest that lay there, waiting to be rediscovered. "'Full fathom five thy father lies. Of his bones are coral made. Those are pearls that were his eyes. Nothing of him that doth fade. But doth suffer a sea-change—'"

"'Into something rich and strange'," finished Sophie. "My governess taught me that."

"I first read it in Palgrave's *Golden Treasury*, sheltering from the rain under the canopy on Hull Pier," said Forrester. He remembered looking up from the book and gazing out through the rain across the wide mud-brown waters of the Humber, wondering if that was the only river he would ever know. Well, he had moved beyond that. Far beyond.

He looked up at Sophie, marvelling at her beauty, and smiled as she said, "In fact I think it would be a mercy for that poor creature to be turned into something rich and strange, as long as he leaves your stone behind."

And then she was striding ahead of him along the edge of the lake and the memories came flooding back once more and he called after her. "'Then went Sir Bedivere the second time, across the ridge and paced beside the mere, counting the dewy pebbles, fixed in thought…'"

Moments later they were walking together, side by side, her hand in his. "You are feeling poetic today. What was that about?"

"It's Hydros," said Forrester. "It's definitely a magic island. And the poetry was from Tennyson's 'Morte d'Arthur'. Sir Bedivere has promised to throw the enchanted sword Excalibur in the lake, but he can't bring himself to do it, and when he returns to Arthur and lies about what he's done, the king sends him back to finish the job. For a moment as you walked along the shore, you reminded me of Bedivere."

* * *

The inlet of Limani Sangri had a very different aspect from the bay below Drakonaris. It was surrounded not by wooded hills but by open country covered in windswept shrubs. The littoral was composed of grey pebbles interspersed with jagged rocks, instead of white sand, and the village itself was a secretive huddle of houses that seemed to turn their backs on the outside world. Altogether, despite the bright sunshine, there was an air of foreboding about the place. The path leading down to it from the plateau was steep and narrow. A few hundred yards above the village they paused at a turn in the path and scanned the shore from left to right. At first it seemed as though the storm must have destroyed whatever trace remained of *Notre Futur*, but then, a quarter-mile to the east of the village, Sophie spotted something. As they stared the image resolved itself, and finally it became clear that it had to be the remains of a vessel, smashed into so many pieces it looked as if it had been crushed in a giant fist.

"If our German friend survived that, he's superhuman," said Forrester.

A black dog came out onto the path and barked fiercely at them as they neared the village. Forrester walked straight towards it, his eyes never leaving the animal's, and as soon as he was above it reached down to the back of its neck and gently ruffled its fur. Instantly the barks died away and were replaced by increasingly satisfied growls.

"How on earth did you do that?" asked Sophie.

"I was trained to, actually. In case I ever had to deal with a Doberman Pinscher behind enemy lines."

"And did you ever have to?"

"Couple of times."

"Like that?"

"Not exactly," said Forrester. "The dogs I came across didn't seem particularly susceptible, so I shot them. But I did use a silencer. Nice to know the trick can work, though."

Apart from the dog, the village seemed to be deserted as they made their way carefully down its steep streets to the narrow waterfront. Beside the water sat an old man mending a net with fingers that looked as if they had been carved out of arthritic oak, and he did not look up when they greeted him. They turned right, walked to the end of the quay and scrambled down onto the jagged rocks that lined the inlet.

It took them twenty minutes to reach the wreck, and by the time they got there they were scratched, bruised from several falls, and beginning to feel tired. The remains of *Notre Futur*, spread among the rocks half in and half out of the water, were so tangled that searching them seemed pointless, but they began, methodically, to turn over every piece of wreckage they could reach.

After forty minutes, they had found nothing.

"Alright," said Forrester. "Now for the hard part."

"How do you mean?" said Sophie.

"The rest is underwater, so I'd better go down and have a look." He saw the expression on Sophie's face, reached into the pack and pulled out the Luger. "You know how to use this, don't you?"

Sophie nodded, and took it. "Do you really think he's still alive?"

"No," said Forrester. He looked round at the silent

village, the grey, forbidding cliffs at the entrance to the bay. "But after Koros I'm not taking any chances."

He stripped down to his shorts and removed a facemask and snorkel from the pack.

"Be careful," said Sophie.

"Of course," said Forrester, and slipped into the water.

He swam a little way out first, because the waves were banging hard against the shore and he wanted to avoid being thrown against the rocks. Besides, he wanted to know how widely the wreckage of the boat was scattered before deciding his plan of attack. Finally, twenty feet out, he pushed his head down and kicked his way towards the bottom.

As the sea closed over him he felt instantly at home, with the brightly coloured fish darting to and fro over the sea floor: entering the water felt akin to entering the past. And then he saw the first piece of wreckage – an ugly, broken leatherette seat from the *Futur*'s cabin – and knew where he had to begin. He surfaced again, checked that Sophie was still where he had left her, waved, and dived once more.

For the next thirty minutes, diving and surfacing at regular intervals, Forrester turned over every piece of debris he could reach, without success. Then, when he felt he knew the rhythms of the water well enough, he risked going right up to the rocks against which the *Futur* had foundered, feeling into the crevices between them in case the force of the storm had jammed the stone into one of them. And suddenly, without warning, his fingertips were tracing tiny incisions that could only be the shapes of Linear B, on a stone that felt exactly like the one from the Gorge of Acharius. With his heart thumping wildly in his chest Forrester began to haul it out.

Or tried to, but within seconds it was clear it was too strongly wedged. He shot up to the surface, took a deep breath, waved to Sophie to reassure her and dived once more, thrusting both arms into the crevice until he could close two hands around the rock. Bracing his feet against the rocks, he began to pull – as a long, lazy tentacle snaked out of the crevice and wrapped itself around his forearm, clamping its suckers on his skin.

Jesus! How could he have forgotten the bloody octopi? A second tentacle slowly followed the first, enclosing his upper arm in its clammy grip. Ignore it. Pull. Pull the damn stone until it's free. Don't think about the head emerging from its lair, the beak snapping. Think about the stone. No – don't think, bend your knees, keep your grip, brace your feet – and heave.

He heaved. The stone came out as if it had been fired from a gun. Forrester shot backwards in the water as if *he* had been fired from a gun. The octopus, ripped from its hiding place, its tentacles still wrapped around his arm, came out with him. Suddenly he was desperate for air, shooting up towards the surface, and as he exploded from the water there was Sophie, up on the rocks with the gun in her hand and without thinking he called out and threw the stone towards her.

As it left his arms he knew he was a fool, that it would fall short and smash to pieces on the rocks that had destroyed *Futur*. But to his amazement in one swift, sure movement she dropped the gun, opened her arms and caught the stone as delicately as if it had all been rehearsed.

Before the octopus could disentangle itself Forrester was smashing it against the rocks, until the water went black with the creature's ink. The dead tentacles still gripped him as he scrambled out of the water, until he scraped them off against a piece of wreckage, leaving ugly cuts up and down his arm before he clambered over to Sophie to look down at his prize.

Which was a lozenge of mudstone in which ancient sea snails had carved loops and whorls of mindless creativity. It was not the inscription stone: it was a mocking parody.

"I'm so sorry," said Sophie.

"It's alright," said Forrester. He nodded towards the dead octopus. "At least we can bring something for dinner tonight."

15

THE PEDIMENT

From the wreck they made their way back along the edge of the inlet to Limani Sangri where the old fisherman was still mending his nets. They climbed down beside him and questioned him in slow, patient Greek about what he had seen the night before when the *Futur* foundered, and whether anyone had come ashore. The old man's reaction was odd. He listened carefully, met their eyes with a shrewd, humorous gaze, and said absolutely nothing, returning to the process of mending his nets as if they had never been there. He was apparently neither deaf nor mentally deficient, nor hostile: he just seemed determined not to answer. It was an altogether curious and baffling encounter, which concluded with them thanking him politely and returning to the streets of the village, which were as deserted as ever.

The trek back across the island was as long and wearying as the trek out that morning had been full of promise, and halfway there Forrester began to regret bringing the octopus, whose ink was still leaking steadily into his shirt.

And then, as they reached the glade where they had seen Keith Beamish that morning, he forgot the octopus, his discomfort and even the missing stone, because the peace and silence that had permeated the glade when they first saw it had utterly vanished.

The first thing that struck them as they entered was that there was something horribly wrong with the shrine where they had examined the statue. Two of the pillars now lay flat on the ground, pointing away from the rest of the shrine like skeletal fingers. The pediment they had supported had fallen too – and beneath it lay the broken body of Giorgios Stephanides with General Aristotle Alexandros kneeling beside him. Alexandros turned to look at Forrester.

"I need help, Duncan," he said. Forrester grabbed the largest pine branch he could find, thrust it under the pediment and began to lever the massive marble block up, allowing Alexandros and Sophie to pull Stephanides free. The General examined his friend with the swift efficiency born of years on the battlefield.

"His head is injured, but I think the skull is not crushed," said Alexandros after a moment. He felt Stephanides's arm. "His shoulder is broken, but a moment ago he could move his feet, so I think not the spine. But we need to get him to the monastery as soon as possible."

"I'll rig up a stretcher."

Alexandros nodded, and began to take off his jacket; Forrester went in search of more branches. Sophie knelt down in his place.

"How did it happen?" she said.

"Giorgios found me here while I was waiting for you and Duncan," said Alexandros briefly. "There was an explosion and the shrine collapsed."

Forrester began to slide the branches through the arms of the jacket and shirt to create the stretcher.

"Waiting for us? Why?"

"Because of your message," said Alexandros.

"There was no message from me," said Forrester as he worked. "We were on the other side of the island, searching for the stone at Limani Sangri."

"A shepherd boy brought it. He said you sent him."

Together, they slid the unconscious man onto the improvised stretcher.

"Then somebody wanted to lure me here," said Alexandros.

"Well, it wasn't us," said Forrester. "Ready to lift?"

Giorgios groaned as the two men raised the stretcher. Then, with Alexandros at Stephanides's head, Forrester at his feet, Sophie following behind carrying everything the two men had had to put down, they set off for all the world like some ancient funeral procession.

Behind them, silence returned to the clearing, the goddess looked out from the remains of her ruined temple, Stephanides's blood began to soak into the pine needles, and the evening midges came out to hover in the glade.

The previous night the Abbot and Chrystomatos had seemed somewhat comic figures to Forrester, but as he and Alexandros carried Stephanides in through the massive wooden gates of the monastery, they were all calm efficiency. The Abbot gave the orders, half a dozen monks came running, and within minutes Stephanides was lying on a wooden table in the monastery's hospital, his bloodied clothes being gently cut away by a surprisingly calm, unhurried Chrystomatos as Brother Thersites, the monastery's resident doctor, examined the wounded man's injuries and instructed other monks to bring his surgical instruments, to heat water, and to begin preparing certain herbs.

The Abbot beckoned them away and gestured for them to follow him through a labyrinth of vaulted corridors until they reached his spartan, whitewashed study, its window looking out over a bay now being steadily gilded by the setting sun.

"Sit," he said, and began pouring four glasses of liqueur from a stone bottle. Without further words, he handed the glasses round and raised his solemnly towards them, as though conferring a blessing.

"To your comrade's survival," he said to Alexandros. "He is in good hands."

"I know, Vasilios," said Alexandros.

"What happened, Ari?" asked the Abbot, and as they spoke Forrester began to realise they knew each other much better than either of their formal positions would suggest.

"I received a message asking me to meet Captain Forrester and his lady at the shrine," said Alexandros. "While I was waiting Giorgios found me there and began a conversation. Then there was a small explosion and the shrine collapsed. I ducked out of the way but Giorgios was closer – the pediment struck him as it fell."

"We sent no message," said Forrester. "Somebody else wanted Ari there."

"To bring Maia's shrine down on top of you?"

"So it would seem, my friend," said Alexandros.

"So the question is," said the Abbot, looking hard at Alexandros, "who would do such a thing?"

There was a pause.

"Who indeed?" said the General.

An hour later, when Brother Thersites had finished his operation and Stephanides was asleep in the infirmary, Alexandros, Forrester and Sophie left the monastery and began to walk along the path that skirted the edge of the woods back towards the *kastello*.

"Do you think this is to do with ELAS?" said Forrester.

Alexandros shot him a dark look. "It had better not be," he said.

"Elas?" said Sophie. "I've forgotten, who is Elas?"

"ELAS is the army the communists are putting together," said Alexandros. "They want me to lead it. Needless to say there are those who would go to any lengths to prevent me."

"Have you decided?" said Forrester.

"Greece has seen far too much bloodshed. I have no desire to plunge it into another civil war," said Alexandros.

"Then why might anyone think you would?" asked Sophie.

Alexandros gave a short, mirthless laugh. "Because they know I have been frustrated and isolated since I returned to my official position," he said. "My fellow officers hate me because when they surrendered I fought on against the Nazis. They fear me because many of the brave men with whom I campaigned against the Germans are the same men who are putting ELAS together today. And because they know I despise most of the politicians who are now sinking their talons into Greece. These are the reasons why people might think I would accept the offers ELAS has been making."

"But you're not going to?" said Forrester.

Alexandros turned and fixed him with a hard stare. "If whoever destroyed that beautiful shrine did so in order to prevent me from joining my old comrades in their struggle, they are making a very bad mistake. They might achieve exactly the opposite of what they want. Or the Americans want. Or the British."

Forrester met his eyes. "Ari, let's be clear about one thing: whatever has happened, it has nothing to do with me. Whoever lured you to that clearing simply used my name to deceive you, that's all."

"But the British are desperate to prevent Greece falling into communist hands – and you work for the British government, do you not?"

"No," said Forrester. "I'm here on an archaeological expedition, as I told you."

"Paid for by the British government."

"Funded by the Empire Council for Archaeology, which is not the same thing."

"But you have been working with Major Archibald MacLean since the war ended."

Forrester hesitated: he hadn't realised Alexandros would be so well informed. But when he thought about it, it made perfect sense. Of course, Soviet intelligence in London would have passed news of his reconnection with MacLean to the communists in Greece – the very people who had been trying to recruit Alexandros.

"I worked with Archie MacLean to help save a colleague who was wrongly accused of murder. I'm not employed by the War Office or MI6 or any other organisation. Besides, I'm your friend. You don't seriously think I'd try to kill you, do you?"

"No." Alexandros shook his head. "I don't know. Truth is, I don't know who to trust any more, Duncan."

Forrester turned to face him, forcing him to meet his gaze. "Well, you can trust me, Ari. Deep down, you know that. You saved my life at least twice during the war; I probably did the same for you."

"Beyond a doubt you did," said Alexandros.

"What you decide to do about ELAS is not my business, though I won't pretend I've any time for the communists or that I think another civil war would do Greece any good."

"Believe me, neither do I," said Alexandros. "That's what makes this whole thing so crazy. If they'd just leave me alone—"

"They may *be* leaving you alone," said Forrester. "This may have nothing to do with ELAS."

"Constantine Atreides is here," said Alexandros. "Is that a coincidence?"

"Connie?" said Forrester. "Can you see Connie murdering anyone?"

"He wants to bring the king back, and all the fascist swine who lorded it over us in the thirties."

"But seriously, Ari – Connie?"

"I know, I know. But we have a whole boatload of British here – Durrell, Runcorn, Venables, Beamish—"

"To say nothing of some fiery Greeks like Helena Spetsos and her lover."

"Helena would never—"

"Would never try to kill you? Are you kidding, Ari? She practically caused a shipwreck to get here and she smashed half the relics on the island to stop you remarrying Penelope."

"I never divorced Penelope, it was—"

"Yes, we understand. But the point is the woman is capable of anything."

"So what should I do?" asked Alexandros.

"Make sure you stay alive," said Forrester simply.

"Which is hard when I don't know who is trying to kill me." They walked on for a moment in silence, and then Alexandros turned to Forrester. "Would you try to find out who it is, my friend?"

Forrester glanced at Sophie. "Of course," he said. "I'll do anything I can."

"Thank you," said Alexandros. "It is good to know you are on my side. By the way, did you find anything at the wreck?"

"Nothing," said Forrester. "Except a bloody octopus."

"I'm sorry," said the General. "So your stone is lost at sea?"

"So it would seem," said Forrester, but even as he spoke, he began to wonder.

16

BITTER HERBS

There was a lot of explaining to do when they got back to the *kastello*, but Forrester left that to Alexandros and concentrated on watching the reactions. They were gathered in the big lamp-lit room overlooking the bay, almost as they had been when Helena Spetsos's collapse had disrupted the ceremony the night before.

"This is appalling," said Lawrence Durrell. "You think somebody deliberately blew up that lovely shrine in order to kill Colonel Stephanides?"

"Why should anyone even want to kill the colonel?" asked David Venables. "I don't understand."

"No one wanted to kill Giorgios," said Alexandros. "I believe the target was me."

"Colonel Stephanides was just there by chance," said Forrester. "It was Ari who'd been lured up there with a note saying I'd asked him to meet us there."

"Are you sure it didn't just collapse of its own accord?" asked Runcorn.

"I heard the explosion," said Alexandros. "Not a big one, but enough to cause the pillars to fall."

"And Giorgios? What about him?" demanded Penelope.

"He will live," said Alexandros, shortly.

"If I find out who did it, I will kill them myself," said Penelope.

"I was sketching in that grove half the day," said Keith Beamish. "I didn't see anything. Needless to say, to save anyone the trouble of asking, I had nothing to do with it. I'm as horrified as everyone else."

"Who sent you the message to wait in the grove?" asked Helena Spetsos. "Because whoever did that is the one to blame." There was a sudden silence in the room. She stared around defensively. "Why are you all looking at me like that? I had nothing to do with it. Why would I want to kill Giorgios?"

"You probably wouldn't," said Penelope Alexandros. "But you are quite capable of wanting to kill my husband when you found you couldn't have him for yourself."

For a moment no one said anything – and then Helena smiled. "What makes you think I can't have him?" she said. "We have been through much more together than you and he ever have. We faced death together, we survived defeat together, we led men and women into battle and brought victory to our nation. Ari knows it was destiny that brought us together – not just our destiny, but the destiny of Greece. He has grown beyond you, Penelope, and he knows it. Last night's little ceremony would have been no more than a charade. I think you know that."

Hardly had she finished speaking than in one swift

movement Penelope Alexandros swept up the oil lamp from the table and flung it with deadly accuracy across the room. Only the younger woman's reflexes allowed her to duck neatly away as the lamp smashed into the wall – but before she had straightened up Penelope strode across the room and slapped her violently across the face.

"You know nothing about Ari, you whore," she said, "and you know nothing about me. Ari has finished with you. And so have I. Perhaps that's why you tried to kill him, and bungled it."

Alexandros stared at his wife, as though frozen in place by her fury – as Ariadne Patrou stepped in between the two women. "That's enough!" she said, firmly. "She doesn't need your husband, she doesn't need any of you. She has me."

Pulling himself together, Alexandros turned to his wife. "Let's get you upstairs, my love."

Penelope glared at him, her eyes bright with fury. "Are you mad?" she said. "I'm going to the monastery."

"The monastery?"

"To be with Giorgios," said Penelope. "Or had you forgotten about him?"

"Well," remarked Lawrence Durrell, after Penelope and Alexandros had gone, "this will make a splendid story for the *Aegean Times*."

"I hope you're joking, Larry," said Charles Runcorn. "It's a shocking state of affairs, and a private matter as well."

"Of course I'm joking," said Durrell, though Forrester

wasn't at all certain he had been. He suspected that even if the journalist in Durrell could be restrained for a moment, the writer knew a good dramatic situation when he saw one. "I'm as upset as the rest of you by what's happened. But Alexandros is a public figure. It's going to be very hard to keep something like this quiet."

"That rather depends on us, doesn't it?" said Constantine Atreides. "I think this should remain private, and surely it's up to us to do it."

"I have been accused of murder," said Helena Spetsos. "And until that accusation is withdrawn I have no intention of remaining silent."

"Penelope spoke in the heat of the moment," said David Venables. "Nobody took her seriously."

Helena looked at him speculatively. "For that matter, perhaps she tried to kill Ari herself when she realised he was going to come to me instead of her."

"That sounds like wishful thinking," said Keith Beamish.

"There's no wishful thinking about it," Helena snapped back. She turned on Ariadne. "And as for you, I had no need of your protection from Penelope Alexandros or anyone else. I'll thank you to let me fight my own battles in future."

"She wanted to kill you," said Ariadne sullenly. "I wasn't going to let her."

"We'll discuss this in private," said Helena. "But if the rest of you want to go on speculating who might have wanted to kill Aristotle Alexandros, perhaps you should concentrate on Constantine Atreides."

And with that she left the room with Ariadne in her

wake. Atreides looked around with bewildered ignorance.

"How could she accuse me?" he asked, his eyes wide.

"Because you are afraid General Alexandros will join ELAS, old chap," said David Venables, "as a result of which the communists will take over Greece and your precious king will never dare show his face here again."

"That's a lie," said Atreides. "Why would I think Alexandros would ever start a civil war?"

"He might not want to start one," said Venables, "but if one is coming might he not want to make sure the right side wins?"

Runcorn looked at him quizzically, with a curious half-smile on his lips. "What makes you so certain the communists *are* the right side, Venables? Don't tell me you want to see Stalin running Greece as well as the rest of Eastern Europe?"

"I think the communists would be preferable to a bunch of fascists and collaborators," said Venables, "and I don't accept that if the communists took over in Greece Stalin would dominate. Look at Tito in Yugoslavia – he's independent enough."

"My dear fellow," said Durrell, "how long do you think Tito will be able to stand up to the Kremlin? Months, if I'm any judge of it. And the same would apply to Greece if the communists take over."

Venables shrugged, and poured himself a glass of ouzo. "You could be right. It's not my fight. I'm just upset because someone has tried to kill a good man."

"And succeeded in nearly killing another one," said

Keith Beamish. "Was Stephanides badly injured, Forrester?"

"Yes," said Forrester briefly. "He'll recover but it'll be some time. You really didn't see anybody skulking around the temple while you were there?"

"I did not," said Beamish. "I was sketching till about noon and I can assure you that if anybody had been trying to booby-trap that shrine I would have noticed."

"Did you see anyone going in that direction as you came back to the *kastello*?" asked Charles Runcorn.

"I did not," said Beamish, "otherwise I would have said so."

"Naturally," said Runcorn.

At which point Socrates came in and announced that supper was about to be served. It turned out to be Forrester's octopus.

17

THE TRIO

As the party broke up after the meal Forrester spoke quietly to Yanni Patrakis. "Can you meet us down by the waterfront in about a quarter of an hour?" he said. Then, in a lower tone: "And it might be as well if nobody noticed you leaving."

Forrester and Sophie slipped away from the others as soon as they could discreetly do so and made their way down through the village streets towards the water. The scent of jasmine hung heavy in the air and through the open doorways they could see families finishing their evening meals and preparing to retire. It was all profoundly peaceful, and yet Forrester knew, less than a year ago these islands had been at the mercy of German troops quite prepared to torture and kill as it suited them. It was extraordinary how the human need for peace could reassert itself; how the horrors of the past could be forgotten – or at least confined to the vault of memory.

Once down on the cobbled seafront they walked westward away from the moored boats until they came to an old wooden bench by a slipway where they sat, listening to the lapping of the water beneath a sky studded with stars. There were doves cooing gently in a dovecote somewhere behind them.

"Do you think you can really help Alexandros find out who was trying to kill him?" asked Sophie. "Isn't it something the police ought to be doing?"

"Absolutely they should," said Forrester. "But I don't think there is a policeman on the island – and by the time they bring anybody over from Athens the killer might have another go. Besides, from our experience of Inspector Kostopoulos I don't have very much faith in the Athenian constabulary. Do you?"

"What worries me," said Sophie reluctantly, "is that if you don't succeed and General Alexandros *is* killed, you'll blame yourself."

"Well that's a great encouragement for me to get it right, isn't it?" said Forrester, smiling.

"Get what right, boss?" said a soft voice in the darkness. They turned to see Patrakis standing behind them.

"Come and sit down, Yanni," said Forrester, shifting along the bench to make room. "I'm talking about the fact that General Alexandros has asked me to help him work out who might have been behind this afternoon's events. I wondered what you thought might have happened."

"Who might have wanted to kill Colonel Stephanides?" said Yanni.

"He probably wasn't the one they intended to kill," said Forrester.

"Why not, boss?" said Yanni.

"Well because—" began Sophie but Forrester had heard something in Yanni's tone, and stopped her.

"Let's assume for a moment that Giorgios *was* the intended victim. Do you have any thoughts as to who might have wanted to do it, Yanni, and why?"

"Where is the General's wife right now?" asked Yanni.

"You know as well as I do," said Forrester. "She's up at the monastery with—"

"Colonel Stephanides," said Yanni. There was a pause.

"Why shouldn't she be?" said Sophie. "He's her husband's friend and he's been injured. It's only natural."

"Don't forget I spent the day here while thou sought thy stone, boss," said Yanni. "And like always, my ears were open."

"And heard what?" asked Forrester.

"Conversations," said Yanni enigmatically.

"Between whom?"

"Between the lady of the house and her friend the colonel."

"You're not suggesting there's anything between them?" asked Sophie.

"Well, I also talk to people," said Yanni. "People who have been on this island for a long time, and they have a story to tell about those three."

"Let's hear it," said Forrester.

"They say," replied Yanni, clearly relishing the moment, "that Giorgios and Ari and Penelope were all children here together. They say when they were young that Giorgios and Penelope could not be separated, and that if anyone had asked which of them was going to marry the other it would have been those two, not Penelope and Alexandros. Stephanides was a young man of great beauty and they say that she had eyes only for him."

"But she married Ari," said Sophie. "Why?"

"That I cannot answer, my lady," said Yanni. "But they say that the reason Giorgios was in Limani Sangri the night we arrived was that he and Alexandros had quarrelled about what the Abbot was going to do in the evening. With the relics."

Forrester thought back to the strained conversation between Alexandros and the colonel that he had interrupted that morning – and began to see it in a different light.

"You think it's possible that Alexandros was trying to kill Stephanides himself?"

"I don't know, boss," replied Yanni, "I wasn't there. But if I had seen my wife whispering to a man the way I saw Mrs. Alexandros whispering to Giorgios, I might have decided to kill him just to be on the safe side."

"But the false message, the one that brought Ari to the shrine, was just for him. Giorgios was only there by chance," said Sophie.

"And how do we know that?" said Forrester.

"Because Ari… told us," said Sophie, her voice trailing off as she realised the significance of what she was saying.

"Exactly," said Forrester.

"But surely we saw Ari trying to help Giorgios?" said Sophie. "When we came into the glade?"

Forrester stared at her, reconstructing the scene in his mind. "We saw him kneeling beside Giorgios, certainly. I assumed he was trying to lift the stone, but when I think about it I can't be sure. It was only when I got a branch and we used it as a lever that we actually shifted it."

Forrester tried to imagine a version of what he had seen in which Alexandros was leaning over the injured Stephanides, gloating. But it was hard.

"Anyway, weren't the colonel and Ari comrades in arms during the war?" said Sophie. "And doesn't Giorgios still seem to be Alexandros's right-hand man? Remember how he headed Helena Spetsos off at the Archbishop's reception?"

"That doesn't stop there being bad blood between them over the woman," said Yanni. "This thou knowest, boss."

"All the same," said Forrester, "I find it very hard to think of Alexandros trying to kill Stephanides by bringing down the shrine on him. If he wanted to do him harm he'd have attacked him face to face."

"You made a very similar argument in Athens," said Sophie, "when we began to wonder if Alexandros had used poison to kill Jason Michaelaides. You said a man like him wouldn't use something like poison. And now you say a man like him wouldn't blow up a shrine to crush his enemy."

"Fair point," admitted Forrester. "It does sound rather like special pleading. But there is the fact that he himself asked me to try and find out just what happened this afternoon."

"That wasn't quite what he said," Sophie pointed out. "What he actually asked was for you to find out who was trying to kill *him*. Which, if *he* was trying to kill somebody else, would be a very good piece of distraction."

"It would," said Forrester, "but I have to admit I find it

difficult to believe that's what he was doing."

"Well," said Sophie implacably, "perhaps you should try harder."

Sensing the clash between them, Yanni deftly shifted the topic of conversation. "So what was happening at Limani Sangri?" he said.

"We found the wreck but not the stone," said Sophie.

"And no body?"

"No body," said Forrester.

"It looks as if both Kretzmer and the stone were lost at sea," said Sophie.

"That man has nine lives," said Yanni. "I think he still has several to live."

As Forrester opened his mouth to reply he suddenly found himself replaying the conversation with the fisherman at Limani Sangri: the bizarre conversation in which an obviously compos mentis individual had behaved as if he were an imbecile. And suddenly he knew why.

"Kretzmer was in the village all along," he said as the thought formulated itself in his mind. "He was holding somebody hostage. That was why the old man said nothing. He wouldn't lie but he wasn't going to create a situation where we might go blundering into the village and get somebody shot."

"You're just guessing," said Sophie. "Aren't you?"

"Yes," said Forrester. "But I've still got to go back."

"What makes you think, even if you're right, that he's still there?" said Sophie.

"He may not be," said Forrester, "but I think we have

to go back. And even if he's left the village he may not be far away."

"Unless he's taken another boat," said Sophie.

Forrester cast his mind's eye back to the waterfront of Limani Sangri. There had been very few boats there and none of them had been suitable for going long distances across the Aegean Sea. As he thought about boats, he realised something else. "If we go back we should go by sea," he said. "He won't be expecting us that way."

"My boat is ready," said Yanni. "When dost thou wish to leave?"

18

THE GUN EMPLACEMENT

When Forrester woke the next morning it was still dark, but the first hints of light were already appearing in the sky and he knew he had to return to the grove before they left for Limani Sangri, because there were questions there that had not been answered. He got out of bed quietly, dressed, scribbled a note for Sophie promising to be back within the hour, and let himself out of the *kastello*.

As always, those first breaths of morning air energised him and made him feel as if he was alive at the beginning of the world, and it seemed only minutes before he was up among the pines and walking swiftly uphill towards the grove. The stones of the shrine and its fallen pillars glowed white in the semi-darkness, and with her covering gone, the statue of Maia seemed to be looking directly at him from her plinth. He stood for a long moment, taking in the geography of the scene, from the pediment to the stone amphora from which the spring still trickled, unperturbed.

As it had done, of course, long before man and his troubles came to the island.

Then he went over to the shrine, knelt down at the base of the pillar, which he calculated must have fallen first, and sniffed. Yes, there it was: that pungent almond smell he remembered so well. Nobel 808, the standard plastic explosive of the SOE. He remembered the feel of it in his hands, so like the plasticine he had played with as a child, but green, always green. And after four years of warfare in these islands, there was no mystery about how someone had come to get their hands on it: the stuff was everywhere, left by commandos, partisans, bandits and regular troops. On the other hand, not everyone had been trained to use it. He shone his torch on the marble, picking out the black soot left by the explosion and working out exactly where the explosive had been placed. Then, kneeling close to the ground, he moved slowly away from the shrine, looking for something among the pine needles. Within three feet he had found it: the remains of the tiny cylinder that had been ejected when the plastic went off, away from the direction of the explosion. He had used dozens of the things during the last few years – the timers that allowed the operator to get away before the charge went off. He examined it closely: this one, he knew, would have given the killer just ten minutes to get away after he had planted his bomb.

But of course it wasn't a bomb, really. It was a demolition device. An odd way to try and kill someone, Forrester thought. If the idea was to murder either Ari Alexandros or Giorgios Stephanides, surely it would have been simpler to have planted a proper bomb in the grove rather than trying to bring a shrine down on top of them? And if the would-be killer had intended to kill Stephanides alone, or indeed Alexandros alone, how could he be sure that either one of them would be in the path of the falling pediment?

He looked into the blank white eyes of the goddess. "What did you see, Maia? What did you think about the bastard who was setting out to destroy your shrine?" The goddess stared back at him, her lips still curved in the ambiguous smile she had worn for two and a half thousand years. She was impervious to such insults, serenely detached from all the desperate intrigues of mortal men and women.

Pine needles don't echo. They don't ring to the noise of footsteps but rather deaden sound. Nevertheless Forrester heard it: the soft sound of a shoe as someone moved into the trees behind him, and without conscious thought he threw himself to the right as the shot rang out, and rolled swiftly into the shadow of the trees even as he landed.

The Luger was out of his pocket and in his hand before he had come to a halt and he fired back blindly in the direction from which the shot had come. He knew there was almost no hope of hitting anyone, but that didn't matter: as much as anything he wanted to make sure that his attacker's second shot went wide.

But there was no second shot; even as Forrester dived from the position in which he had fired to the shelter of the nearest tree he knew that his assailant had fled. The ground sloped steeply down from where the shot had come and whoever had fired it had clearly gone straight down the hill.

By the time Forrester found himself racing down that same slope there was no sign of anyone ahead of him.

Suddenly he was out of the trees, with the path leading to the Monastery of St. Thomas on his left and the trail to Kastello Drakonaris on his right. Which way had his assailant gone? He stood still for a moment, drew in a deep breath and began to move swiftly along the right-hand path.

The first person he met when he went through the front door was Yanni Patrakis. "I was coming to wake you, boss," he said. "It's time to set off." Forrester was highly tempted to go through the *kastello* to find out if there was anyone awake and smelling of cordite, but decided it was simply not practical, so he went to wake Sophie. Half an hour later all three of them were in the tiny cabin of the caïque as it emerged from the bay and turned east along the coast.

By the time the sun rose they were motoring through a milky sea of mist with Yanni at the wheel, still turning over the previous day's events in his mind.

"What about the English?" he said, as Sophie handed him a mug of coffee. "The English from the boat. Any of them might want to kill the General?"

"Well, we should consider it," said Forrester. He had left a note for Alexandros reminding him to track down the shepherd boy who had delivered the message about the fake rendezvous in the grove, and find out who had given him his instructions, but he had a strong suspicion whoever had done so would have made sure this line of enquiry was a dead end. And of course if Alexandros had engineered the whole thing, the message would have been fictional too. But they had at least forty minutes motoring around the island before they neared the Sangri inlet and going through the available information would be time well spent. "Let's go through the list. As far as I know Durrell has never met either Ari or Giorgios before. He's a poet, really. This newspaper job is just something the army has given him. I met him a couple of times in Alexandria – all we talked about was writing. My instinct is that he has nothing to do with this. Charles Runcorn is an academic, a historian, one of the great gossips. I'd have counted him out but for something that Sophie came across in Athens." Yanni glanced at Sophie, who smiled.

"Ah, yes. He came to see Helena Spetsos while she was doing a somewhat risqué painting of Ariadne," she said. "He said he was there on behalf of the British Council, but frankly I didn't believe him. I wondered then if Helena had some kind of hold over him. I still wonder."

"Such a hold that she might tell him to murder somebody and he might do it?" asked Yanni.

"Well, put like that it sounds far-fetched, but if she was the killer he might have been an accomplice, and it's a possibility we should bear in mind," said Forrester. "He does seem to have helped her persuade Durrell to add Hydros to his itinerary. And had that not happened, of course, neither would the attack."

"What about your friend David Venables?" asked Sophie. "After all, he was the one who began the expedition that ended with them coming here."

"Venables is a tough egg," said Forrester. "I've known him for a long time and I know he's cynical and ambitious. But as you heard tonight he's a man of the left. The last thing he'd want to do is kill Ari and prevent him taking command of ELAS."

"What if Venables was trying to kill Giorgios?" said Sophie. "For some reason we don't know yet."

"Perhaps because the colonel was trying to persuade the General not to go over to the communists?" said Yanni.

Forrester considered. "Possible. But if Stephanides was trying to do that, I'm certain Venables wouldn't have tried to do away with him in a way that would have endangered Alexandros: that would be totally counterproductive. So for the time being I'm putting Venables fairly low on the list of suspects. But let's not forget his friend Keith Beamish. We know he was in the glade earlier in the day."

"But he called us over and talked to us," said Sophie. "If he'd been there to set some kind of booby trap he'd hardly have let us see him, would he?"

"Unless that was to throw us off the scent," said Forrester. "A sketchbook is a pretty good cover."

"I find it hard to believe though," said Sophie. "He's a nice man and a good artist."

Forrester laughed. "And good artists can't be criminals?" he said. "What about Caravaggio?"

"What did he do, boss?" said Yanni.

"Well, if you'd been in Rome in 1606 you might have come across him strolling through the city with a bunch of armed retainers looking for trouble," said Forrester. "He killed at least one man there and probably others in Naples and Milan. Even the Pope issued a death warrant for him."

"You're not seriously telling me Keith Beamish was some kind of Caravaggio, are you? I mean – he does watercolours," said Sophie.

"I'd forgotten that, my love," said Forrester. "The use of watercolours alone, of course, should prove his innocence." He ducked away as she swiped at him, but as he peered into the mist ahead he saw nothing but a jumble of faces each competing for his attention: Durrell, Venables, Beamish, Runcorn, Helena Spetsos, Ariadne, Penelope. Even a jealous Alexandros himself if Stephanides had been the intended victim. He closed his eyes and let the images fade away, and by the time the sun had fully risen the sea was as still as if it had been painted and they were approaching the headland at the mouth of the bay of Limani Sangri.

With a conscious effort he put the murder attempt out of his mind and concentrated on the German.

"It's a good thing we're coming by sea, but we have to face up to the fact that as soon as we round the headland and enter the inlet, Kretzmer may well recognise the boat."

"I can't see much way round that," said Sophie, but just before the headland, on the outer coast of the island, Forrester spotted a tiny cove not more than fifty yards wide.

"Can you take us in there, Yanni," he said, "and put me ashore?"

"Put *us* ashore," said Sophie.

"Sure, boss," said Yanni, "but what's the idea?"

"I want to take your binoculars up to the top and have

a look at the village before you go around the headland," said Forrester. "Before there's any chance of him knowing we're coming."

Half an hour later Forrester and Sophie were squirming upwards through the thyme-scented brush that covered the promontory, and the caïque, hundreds of feet below them in the cove, looked like a child's toy. Once they had reached the top they wormed themselves into a position where they could look down the length of the inlet towards the village. Forrester took out the binoculars and, making sure the lenses didn't catch the glare of the sun, concentrated his gaze on the tiny settlement at the head of the inlet. He began to note people moving about, fishermen tending to their boats on the shore and smoke rising from chimneys.

"Totally different from yesterday," he whispered to Sophie. "It looks back to normal."

"Does that mean he's already gone?" asked Sophie. Forrester let the binoculars move steadily over the hills to the left of the village, and then the right.

And then back again. For a long moment he remained still, staring at one particular spot.

"What?" asked Sophie. "Have you seen something?"

"It had to be there," said Forrester softly. "Of course, it had to be there."

"I don't understand," said Sophie, but Forrester motioned her to silence and shifted the binoculars slightly.

After a long moment he handed them to her.

Sophie adjusted the eyepiece and concentrated as the tiny, distant little world swam into focus. An old woman was loading two panniers of fruit onto a donkey. An old man sat smoking on a rock. A small child walked up a hill path leading away from the village.

A small child.

"Do you see the basket that the little girl is carrying?" asked Forrester.

"Yes. Perhaps she's taking some shepherd his lunch."

Forrester said nothing.

"What?"

"Move the binoculars ahead of her and then to the right."

Sophie did as he asked.

"Can you see the shadow at the top of the cliff?"

Sophie concentrated. "And?"

"The Germans had to have a gun emplacement to defend a landing place like this," said Forrester. "I think that's where she's going."

Sophie looked through the binoculars again. "You think she's taking food to Kretzmer?"

"The emplacement would be the ideal place to hole up if he's shifted out of the village but stayed in the area," said Forrester. "The perfect defensible vantage point."

"But surely as soon as he wasn't an immediate threat the villagers would have sent word over to Drakonaris?"

"Unless Kretzmer's still got a hostage with him. Which would also explain why the child is taking him food."

Sophie considered this. "And as soon as we sail into

the bay he'll know we're coming and threaten to kill the hostage unless we back off."

"Yes," said Forrester, "I think that's exactly what he'll do."

Before he had left the caïque, Forrester had already sketched out a plan of attack if the view from the headland confirmed his theory. He had discussed the options with Yanni and arranged to signal by mirror. This he now did, and as soon as Yanni had acknowledged his signal, Forrester and Sophie began to make their way around the bay from the headland towards the village – making sure, as they walked, that they were always hidden from the sightlines of the gun emplacement by the folds of the landscape.

Once they disturbed a flock of sheep guarded by a sleeping shepherd boy, and hid themselves as the animals ran from them, bleating. They watched nervously, expecting the boy to wake up at any moment and seek the source of the disturbance, but in the event he slept on and the sheep gradually calmed down and resumed grazing.

When they reached the outskirts of the village they climbed higher into the hills, circling around the houses to avoid being seen. They came to the path leading down to the waterfront, made sure no one was coming up or down it, crossed it swiftly and disappeared once more into the brush. As Forrester looked out over the bay he saw, as scheduled, Yanni's caïque coming around the headland and puttering into the bay, leaving a long white wake behind it in the deep blue of the water. Around them they heard the murmur of bees methodically looting the nectar from the flowers.

"What if he tries to leave?" asked Sophie. "Once he sees the caïque?"

"That's exactly what I'm hoping," said Forrester.

But as the caïque came closer and closer to Limani Sangri, there was no sign of anyone attempting to leave the gun emplacement. For perhaps five minutes, as they toiled up the same hill up which the child had hauled the basket, they were in a blind spot where the emplacement was out of their field of vision, but then suddenly they were pushing through a half-collapsed perimeter fence and into a concrete trench. Forrester took out the Luger and gestured to Sophie to stay behind him.

There was a rusted metal door hanging crookedly where the trench led into the gun complex itself, but fortunately the child who had been bringing the food must have left it half open and they were able to squeeze around it without setting off the telltale squeak of its hinges. Then they were in the semi-darkness of a dank concrete tunnel, with doorways leading off to abandoned ammunition bunkers and guard rooms. Swiftly Forrester ducked into the first, gun in hand in case Kretzmer was waiting for them, but it was empty, and though he performed the same exercise at every door, the result was the same every time.

Then they were in the final stretch, with the gun turret itself dead ahead of them, the light coming in through the slit through which the barrels of the German artillery pieces had once protruded. Once again, thought Forrester, he was about to face the Minotaur in his lair. But this time, he knew the Minotaur already had a victim with him.

"Kretzmer," called Forrester, his voice echoing from the concrete. "It's Forrester. Come out with your hands up."

There was no reply. Then he heard a child cry out.

"If you hurt her, Kretzmer, you're a dead man," he said, and the child cried out again. His bluff had been called: he had no option now.

He stepped into the turret and flung himself to the left, simultaneously ranging the Luger across the dark space to find Kretzmer.

There was no Kretzmer – just two frightened children roped to a stanchion. The basket the child had brought was on the floor, empty, as if the German, having eaten as much as he could, had stuffed the rest in his pockets before making his escape.

"Damn," said Forrester. "He must have slipped out while we were on the blind spot." Then Sophie was in the turret with him, untying the knots that held the children, and then Forrester was racing outside to look for any sign of his quarry. And sure enough, silhouetted against the sky at the top of the hill was the figure of a man, and Forrester began to race up the slope, his heart pounding, the sweat running into his eyes so that at first he thought that was the reason there were suddenly two Kretzmers on the skyline.

And then three.

And four.

But as he reached the crest he realised it wasn't Kretzmer at all; it was Lawrence Durrell, and with him were Charles

Runcorn, David Venables, Helena Spetsos, Ariadne Patrou, Prince Constantine Atreides and Keith Beamish.

"Hello, old chap," said Durrell. "So you want to have a look at Runcorn's castle too? I'm sure you'll enjoy it."

19

THE LEGEND OF COUNT BOHEMOND

As they waited for Sophie to join them, Forrester explained about Kretzmer. "I don't suppose any of you saw someone heading in this direction while I was coming up?"

"Actually I think I did," said Keith Beamish. "Not necessarily your chap but someone carrying something and moving oddly, as if he was limping. But it might just have been one of the islanders."

"I saw him too," said Ariadne, "over Keith's shoulder." She smiled at Forrester. "We were talking about vanishing points," she added, and Forrester noted the dark look that flashed across Helena Spetsos's face. "In paintings." She turned to Helena. "You never told me about them, did you?"

"Only about a dozen times," said Helena, "but you never listened."

"Which way was he going?" Forrester cut in, and when Beamish and Ariadne pointed westward Runcorn looked oddly gratified.

"So it seems as if he wants to visit Bohemond's castle too.

Perhaps he's interested in the Crusaders as well as the Minoans."

"I have to warn you Kretzmer is very dangerous," said Forrester. "He's armed and he's desperate. In fact if he's going to your castle I'd advise you all to give up the idea of an expedition there right now."

"You think I am afraid of the Germans?" asked Helena. "After what Ari and I went through together?"

"I must say, old chap," said Beamish, "I appreciate the warning, but I don't think we should let one fugitive Hun frighten us off. Does anybody else?" he said, turning to the rest of the party.

"And if Keith is not afraid," said Ariadne, "neither am I." Keith looked slightly embarrassed: it was clear Ariadne had decided this was her morning to make Helena jealous.

"Everybody else can do what they like," said Runcorn, "but I have no intention of letting some fugitive Teuton stop me visiting one of the most interesting sites in the Aegean."

Constantine Atreides looked doubtful, but there was a murmur of agreement from everyone else. "Well, whoever sees him first," said Forrester, "don't try anything on your own, call the rest of us. And keep your eyes peeled as we walk: he could well be waiting in ambush." There were no dissenting voices, and they set off again across the plateau, heading northwest.

Durrell fell into step beside Forrester. "What about your other quest, Duncan," he said conversationally, "to find out who brought down that shrine on the gallant colonel?"

"Still working on it," said Forrester briefly. "All I've established so far is that whoever did it used Nobel 808 and a ten-minute timer, which suggests he was pretty much in the vicinity when it happened."

"Was it the almond smell?" said Durrell. "Was that how you identified it?"

Forrester nodded.

"Almond smell?" said Keith Beamish. "What almond smell?"

"From the explosive that was used up at the grove," said Durrell. "You can always recognise plastique 808 by that particular odour, and Duncan here apparently got a good whiff of it on the pillars that were brought down."

"Does that help identify the culprit?" said Runcorn.

"Not really," said Forrester, "but it narrows things down a bit. The shepherd boy brought the decoy message to Alexandros at about three – the one asking him to meet me at the shrine. The rendezvous itself was for one hour later, at four, but according to Ari, the shepherd boy came from the far side of the island, which meant that whoever told him to deliver the message had to have left the *kastello* around noon, to give him time to find the boy, tell him what to do, and then get back to the grove to plant the explosive before Alexandros got there."

"He could have planted the explosive earlier," said Venables.

"He could have planted the explosive, but he couldn't have set the timer. So whoever committed the crime left *kastello* around noon yesterday and didn't return until some time after four, probably four-thirty. What I want to do this evening is to sit down with everybody and see if we can identify anybody that applies to."

"The problem is, old chap, we were all going about our own business," said Venables. "I for one wasn't keeping track of other people's movements."

"Me neither," said Atreides, "and I was down at the harbour for some of the time you speak of."

"Of course," said Forrester. "It's just a way of eliminating people who couldn't possibly have done it. But let's put it aside for now. Runcorn wants to concentrate on Count Bohemond, and I want to concentrate on Oberleutnant Kretzmer. Alright?"

Sophie caught up with Helena as they were passing a small cairn. "I was impressed by your reflexes," she said, "last night. I'm not sure I'd have ducked as quickly as you did."

"The woman is mad," said Helena. "I know how to deal with madwomen."

"Although the island's history would suggest they are dangerous to ignore," said Durrell, mischievously. "The maenads, you know."

"And to be fair, old girl," said Venables, "Mrs. Alexandros has every reason to be thoroughly annoyed with you. You came to this island to steal her husband. What did you expect her to do? Welcome you with open arms? Especially after you made such a fiasco of the reconciliation ceremony."

"I did not intend to damage the *ikons*," said Helena Spetsos. "I merely became unexpectedly unconscious."

Forrester kept a straight face.

"I wonder whether they'll attempt the ceremony again while we're here?" said Charles Runcorn. "It promised to be quite fascinating."

"They would be very foolish to try again," said Helena darkly. "The accident was a bad omen."

"I don't believe in omens," said Ariadne. "There is no reason why they shouldn't try again, provided somebody keeps tight hold of Helena. The General has come back to his wife and now they can live happily ever after."

Helena shot her a look that would have felled a horse. "You know nothing about it," she said. "Once something is broken it cannot be mended. The marriage is finished and all the *ikons* in the world won't change that."

"Particularly if they're broken," said Beamish.

"Well, there it is," said Runcorn, and the party stopped.

A mile away across the central plateau was the brooding bulk of the Crusader castle.

"Magnificent," said Atreides.

"Very impressive," said Venables.

"Who was this Bohemond, exactly?" asked Helena. "I have never heard of him."

"Well, this is a splendid opportunity for you then, because his story is one of the most intriguing mysteries of the entire Crusades."

"I thought Crusaders just killed Muslims," said Helena. "That is not very mysterious to me."

"Killing Muslims was what Count Bohemond went to the Holy Land *for*, dear lady," said Atreides. "It was his religious duty."

"And a pleasure, I'm sure," said Helena.

"Like you and the Germans," said Ariadne.

"It's true he played a fairly heroic role in the capture

of Jerusalem," said Charles Runcorn before Helena could respond. "It seems that as a result of single-handedly dispatching eight Mohammedans when he fought his way over the walls of the city, he was elected a founding member of the Holy Order of the Knights of St. James."

"I haven't heard of them," said Beamish.

"Were they like the Templars?" asked Venables.

"In a way," said Runcorn, "but whereas the Templars were dedicated to protecting *pilgrims* on their way to the Holy Land, the Knights of St. James were sworn to find and preserve its holiest *places*, which meant they did as much archaeology as fighting. For example they were one of the earliest groups to search for the room in which the Last Supper had taken place."

"The Cenacle," said Forrester, despite himself.

"Exactly. Most members of the Order concentrated on the sites linked with Jesus's time in the city, but Bohemond had a personal cleric named Michael of Cahors, who was reputed to be a mystic. He persuaded Bohemond to seek out relics mentioned in the Old Testament."

"Don't tell me he went after the Ark of the Covenant?" said Durrell.

"I believe he did actually," said Runcorn, "but as far as I know that search only led him to some caves above the Jordan Valley, which proved to be empty. But they struck lucky in another quest – for the Urim and the Thummim."

They were climbing an undulating patch of land now, and for a moment the castle was hidden from view. There was the scent of lavender on the breeze.

"What on earth were the Urim and the Thummim?" demanded Helena. "I have never heard of them, either."

"They're almost as fascinating as the Ark itself," said Lawrence Durrell quickly. "You'll forgive me for jumping in here, Runcorn, but I've just been reading up on them and it's an extraordinary story."

"My dear chap," said Runcorn, waving his acquiescence with a slightly forced smile. Lawrence Durrell, it had to be said, knew how to hold an audience.

There was a little chapel ahead of them and to their right, and Forrester's attention was split between Durrell's narrative and the possibility that Kretzmer was hiding there. He was beginning to worry that despite his words of warning the party still regarded the expedition to the castle as a holiday jaunt.

"The Urim and the Thummim appear in the Bible during the Exodus from Egypt," Durrell was saying, "around the same time as the Ark does."

Forrester sped up so he reached the chapel before them, stepped into its tiny porch and thrust open the creaking door. He remained motionless and at an oblique angle until his eyes accustomed themselves to the light, but when they did there was nothing there except a faded painting of a round-eyed Virgin slumbering in the cool, incense-scented darkness.

He rejoined the group as they walked on. Durrell was still in full flow and Forrester detected a slight grimace of annoyance on Runcorn's face. "The Urim and the Thummim," Durrell was saying, "seem to have been some kind of device used by the Jewish high priest to communicate with God. You'll remember at this point in Exodus the Israelites were only surviving because the Lord was providing them with manna. They had to keep in close touch with him to make sure he continued to supply what they needed."

"They're described in Exodus and Numbers," said Runcorn, as Durrell paused to take breath, "with a rather strange phrase: 'lights and perfections'."

"Lights and perfections?" said Sophie. "I don't understand. Is this a common phrase?"

"Common enough *words*," said Runcorn, "but not commonly used in combination. We believe they were worn by the high priest."

"The high priest," said Helena contemptuously, for no particular reason Forrester could discern.

"According to the historian Josephus," interjected the irrepressible Durrell, "the lights and perfections incorporated twelve brightly coloured jewels."

"I love jewels," said Ariadne, "but nobody ever buys me any," and she glanced roguishly at Keith Beamish, who blushed, as Runcorn stepped neatly back into the narrative.

"Josephus says these jewels shone with incredibly bright rays when God was present," he said quickly, "and depending on the *order* in which they shone, the priest could understand what God was telling him."

"Like using a radio to contact base when one was on a mission," said Venables. "You'd be familiar with that, Forrester?"

"We Greeks had very few radios in the mountains," said Helena, bitterly, "and the British ones never worked."

"Anyway," said Runcorn doggedly, "by the time the Crusaders got to the Holy Land the Urim and the Thummim hadn't been seen for a thousand years. So it was quite an achievement when Bohemond and Michael of Cahors found them."

"Where?" asked Atreides.

"Unfortunately," said Runcorn, "those pages of the court records have been destroyed."

"Court records? What court records?"

Runcorn paused, as if courteously giving Durrell the chance to show off again, but it was clear that this was part of the story into which the enthusiastic author could not insert himself.

"The court proceedings took place in the year 1112," Runcorn continued, "when Bohemond was tried in absentia, expelled from the Order and condemned to death."

"What on earth for?" said Venables. "I thought he was a hero."

They were crossing a little stream now, where bright green watercress trailed dreamily in the sparking water, shaded by a sycamore tree. Frogs began to croak in protest as they made their way over the stepping stones, and Ariadne scooped up a handful of water, splashed it on her face and then playfully at Helena.

"Do that again," said Helena, "and I will throw you in the stream." Ariadne immediately did it again and taking Keith Beamish's hand scrambled quickly to the other bank before Helena could fulfil her threat.

"He was expelled for *stealing* the Urim and the

Thummim," said Runcorn, ignoring these antics and helping Sophie onto the opposite bank.

"Stealing them?" said Sophie, shocked. "Surely not the action of a heroic crusading knight?"

"It seems so, I'm afraid. On the eleventh day of the eleventh month of the year 1111 Bohemond and his household left his palace in Jerusalem in great secrecy and boarded a ship at Acre – reportedly carrying chests full of treasure."

"But why on earth did he do it?" said Keith Beamish. "He'd be breaking an oath, wouldn't he? Risking eternal damnation, all that sort of thing?"

"Very much so," said Runcorn. "My instinct is that Michael had convinced Bohemond that he could, like the ancient Israelites, use the device to talk to God."

"And that fleeing with the treasures was what God wanted them to do," said Sophie.

"I can easily imagine it," said Runcorn. "Anyway it's from those court records that we get the best indication of what the Urim and the Thummim looked like, because the Order created a kind of watch list, which we still have."

The castle was less than a quarter of a mile away now. Forrester could see no sign of movement, but he felt a strange certainty that Kretzmer had concealed himself in the ruins. They certainly provided the best cover in that bare landscape. The others, however, seemed to have forgotten all about him, so caught up were they in Runcorn's story. "The device seems to have been some kind of breastplate sitting over the shoulders like part of a suit of armour. Interestingly, though this is not indicated in the Bible, there seem to have been two of them, perhaps one for the high priest and one for his acolyte."

"Put on the armour of God, so that you may stand with him against the devil," said Venables – and then, turning to the others, said apologetically, "Ephesians six. My father was a vicar. So did the Knights of St. James ever track Bohemond down?"

"At first no, despite an extensive search. In fact for many years he and his retinue, having set off in winter, well outside the sailing season in the Mediterranean, were believed to have perished in a shipwreck. The ironic thing was they *had* been shipwrecked, but on an island none of their pursuers had visited."

"Hydros," said Helena.

"Hydros," said Runcorn. "And it seems that Bohemond and most of his household must have survived the wreck, because they were strong enough to oblige the islanders to build the castle."

"Typical of the British," said Helena.

"Bohemond was from Normandy," said Keith Beamish. "Which is in France."

"I know where Normandy is," hissed Helena. "French, British, they are all the same."

"No, they aren't," said Ariadne. "The French are much more aristocratic and have better food."

"Stop talking nonsense," said Helena, "you know nothing about it."

"I knew a French countess once," said Ariadne. "She was lovely."

"The local people call the castle," said Runcorn with just enough volume to bring this dialogue to an end, "*Kastrosorasis*."

If Runcorn had been planning his disquisition in advance he could not have reached this point with better timing. They were now at the bottom of a long slope at the top of which, on the edge of the cliffs and silhouetted against the glittering sea, were the ruins of Bohemond's castle. Three quarters of the outer walls were still there, part of an inner keep and a curious broken tower on the far side, right next to the cliffs. A Greek windmill, obviously built with stones taken from the ruins, stood nearby, its white canvas sails turning lazily in the breeze from the sea. Someone had planted an olive grove, which ran right up to the castle walls, and there were the remains of an orchard on the eastern side.

"*Kastrosorasis*?" said David Venables. "What does that mean?"

"It sounds like a contraction of our Greek words for 'castle' and 'sight'," said Prince Atreides.

"Quite correct," said Runcorn. "'The Castle of Sight'. It's an eerie thought, isn't it, when we know that Michael of Cahors lived there, believing he had a direct line to heaven."

"Eerie indeed," said Beamish.

"Can you make out the tower on the cliff side of the castle? That's *Pyrgos Asteria* – the Tower of the Stars. Which is where, they say, Michael conducted his experiments."

"I wonder what the islanders made of it all," said Durrell, speculatively.

"I'm certain nobody asked them," Runcorn replied. "But there was one of them Bohemond must certainly have listened to. Her name was Demeter."

"The fertility goddess?" said Sophie.

"Well, an island woman named after the goddess. According to local lore she was also one of the local maenads."

"The bacchanalian women who tore men to pieces?" said Atreides.

"Only at certain times of year," said Runcorn.

"And when inspired to do so by the god," said Helena. "Meting out justice to men who deserved it."

"Somewhat rough justice," said Keith Beamish.

"What does it matter how rough it was?" asked Helena, glaring at him. "It was what the god wanted."

"Certainly Bohemond wasn't put off by Demeter's reputation," said Runcorn. "In fact he fell deeply in love, married her and was presented with a beautiful daughter called, inevitably, Persephone."

"How romantic," said Ariadne.

"Positively mythical," said Beamish.

"It *was* romantic," replied Runcorn, "and you could say it *became* mythical. It seems Bohemond loved Persephone dearly, and insisted that Michael taught her to read and write, though her mother never learned. Legend has it, father and daughter would often go hunting together through the woods."

"I've heard Bohemond's reign was a time of great prosperity for Hydros," said Atreides. "They say the olive groves flourished, the orchards were heavy with fruit, the cornfields rich with grain."

"All true," said Runcorn. "It was a golden time. And then the Holy Order of St. James caught up with him."

They were close to the castle now, and its grim walls were starting to block out the sun. Venables turned to Forrester. "There are so many parallels, aren't there? Bohemond fleeing here with the Urim and Thummim, and us pursuing another soldier who's made off with another precious artefact."

"True enough," said Forrester, "though I don't imagine Kretzmer has been using the stone to talk to the creator of the universe."

"Well, if he has," said Sophie, "let's hope that the creator of the universe has told him to give it up."

As the castle loomed over them Forrester reviewed the likelihood of Kretzmer hiding himself there. On one level the castle was a trap – a fortified enclave surrounded by walls – but it was so large, ruinous and complex it might also be the ideal place for the German to conceal himself in this bare, open landscape. However systematically they searched, Kretzmer would be able to move from hiding place to hiding place within the ruins, constantly staying ahead of them. Nor, thought Forrester, were there enough of them to surround the castle to prevent him leaving.

They were now beside a massive hole in the outer wall, and the tumbled rocks from the breach still lay in the courtyard beyond.

"I'm assuming that was the work of the Holy Order of St. James?" said Forrester.

"Almost certainly," said Runcorn. "When word of Bohemond's refuge finally reached them they sent a small army under the command of the head of the Order, Fulk of

Boulogne, who was under direct instructions from the Pope."

"The Pope?"

"Certainly. The Holy Father was determined to get his hands on the Urim and the Thummim."

"I suppose he didn't want any rival communicants with God," said Venables. "After all that was supposed to be his exclusive province."

"As a naturalist," said Beamish, turning to Venables, "have you ever come across any signs of religious belief among animals?"

"What a curious question," said Helena Spetsos.

"Not curious at all, dear lady," said Venables. "And the answer is no, which I think is because if there is a god why should we be the only species on Earth to be aware of the fact? And the truth is, Keith, I have never noticed any tiny hedgehog parish churches or miniature volish cathedrals."

"Not even an ancient shrine erected by pious foxes?" said Beamish.

Venables paused for a moment, as if searching his memory. "Not even an ancient shrine erected by foxes," he said at last. "And I think the reason is this: we humans invent religions to deal with our fear of death. Animals, not having the foresight to realise death is coming to them, have no need to create the myths needed to assuage their fear. Would you agree, Runcorn?"

"I am a member of the Church of England," said Runcorn, "and thus absolved of the necessity to even think about matters of religion, much less discuss them. Would you like me to continue with the story?" To which there was general assent.

"Well," said Runcorn, "Fulk and his army landed at Limani Sangri, marched overland to the Castle of Sight, and when Bohemond refused to surrender, laid siege. The siege went on for eight months, and during that time the island was laid waste, partly because any Crusader who ventured into the woods never returned. Not in one piece anyway."

"The maenads?" asked Helena.

"The maenads," said Runcorn.

"That," said Helena, "*would* be a good subject for a painting."

"Of course these ancient superstitions," said Atreides, fanning himself with his hat, "are never very far below the surface, even today."

"Why, Prince, do you think there are avenging maenads roaming the forests here right now?" asked Sophie.

"Why not?" said Helena. "We Greeks have been communing with the gods of these islands long before the Christians came."

Runcorn was clearly anxious to get the conversation back onto more historical lines. "I'm sure you have, dear lady," he said to Helena. "But of course Fulk had another reason for destroying the forests, which was to get the timber he needed to build a huge ballista."

"A giant Roman catapult, for those of you who haven't encountered one," said Durrell, helpfully.

Runcorn gave him a brief nod of acknowledgement. "When the ballista was completed the attackers began to hurl huge boulders into the castle walls until they finally made what is doubtless the breach we are looking at now."

He turned to Forrester. "Do you still think your fleeing German has taken refuge here?"

"It's a possibility," said Forrester. "Once again I'd urge you that we should end our visit here. He's held a whole village hostage for the past thirty-six hours and he won't hesitate to kill if he's cornered."

"Well in that case we'll make sure we don't corner him," said Runcorn, and began clambering over the fallen stones, with the rest of the party following him. Atreides hesitated when it came to the moment to scramble in, and Forrester saw his hesitation.

"Look, Connie," he said. "No false bravado. If you want to stay out of this place you should."

Atreides looked at him for a moment. "There is some nice shade in the orchard," he said. "I think I'll take advantage of it." And he strolled over to one of the lichened trees abutting the castle walls, sat down with his back against it and took out a cigar.

20

VANISHING POINT

Once in the shade of the remaining walls, it felt to Forrester as if they had stepped from the dazzling clear light of the Aegean into the gloom of the Middle Ages. In front of them was a stony, weed-infested space that had once doubtless been a courtyard teeming with men at arms. Beyond that were the ruins of the inner keep, itself partly battered down like the outer wall.

"When the Crusaders finally broke in," Runcorn was saying, "they faced the most ferocious defence any of them had ever encountered, led not just by Bohemond and Michael, but by Demeter and Persephone too."

Forrester could see in his mind's eye the small desperate band, their great swords flashing in the sun, their heavy chain mail armour weighing them down, but his eyes were constantly on the move, searching for any sign of life within the walls. He held out little hope of seeing anything, though: Kretzmer's best plan, if he had taken refuge in the castle, was to remain absolutely motionless.

Runcorn was halfway to the keep now. "The defenders disputed every inch of ground as they fell back, leaving the courtyard red with blood." They had reached the top of the rubble that must once have been the castle bailey.

"Would you mind pausing for a moment, Runcorn?" said Forrester. "This is a good vantage point and I'd just like to get everybody to choose one part of the castle and concentrate. Call out if you see any movement at all."

They did as Forrester asked, standing in silence for a long moment as their eyes ranged over the stones and shadows. Through the gap in the wall, at the top of a distant hill Forrester could see a figure coming down towards them. After a few seconds he realised it must be Yanni, and immediately felt better. It was always good to have Patrakis in the mix. One by one the observers reported on what they had seen, and each report was negative.

"If no one can see anything," said Runcorn, "may we continue the tour?"

"Of course," said Forrester. "I'm sorry to be spoiling the holiday atmosphere."

"On the contrary, my dear chap," said Runcorn. "You're adding an extra and entirely appropriate frisson of excitement." He led them across a grassy space towards a cylindrical building hard up against the sea wall. "We've now reached the foot of the Tower of Stars. It was here, where the stairs began, that Michael and Countess Demeter were slain."

"Michael and Demeter?" noted Sophie.

"Yes," said Runcorn. "It's an interesting combination,

isn't it? Bearing in mind that both of them, he through his mysticism and she through her Dionysian rites, may well have believed they communed with the gods."

Forrester glanced at Helena, but she said nothing.

"Indeed," went on Runcorn, "they may have become allies during Bohemond's stay on the island. I can easily imagine them exploring the woods together – perhaps even visiting the glade where poor Colonel Stephanides was nearly killed. At any rate they died here, fighting side by side. And their deaths gave Bohemond and his daughter the chance to escape to the top of the tower."

"Escape?" said Lawrence Durrell. "Wouldn't they be trapped up there?"

"So one would have thought," replied Runcorn. "But of course it's possible they had other plans – perhaps some idea of lowering themselves down the cliffs and escaping by boat."

"Surely not," said Durrell. "Isn't the famous *Roufichtra Medusa* very close to here?"

"The *Roufichtra Medusa* is immediately below the castle walls," said Runcorn with some satisfaction, like a man hearing the cue he has been waiting for. "Those with sufficiently good a head for heights will be able to see it quite shortly. But bear with me a moment. Where was I?"

"Father and daughter had fled into the tower," said Beamish.

"Ah, yes. Well, as soon as he knew the last two survivors were at the top, Fulk ordered the ballista to be trained on it, and by the time the Knights of St. James had fought their way up, the place was in ruins."

"And Bohemond and his daughter were dead?"

"Well, thereby hangs a tale. I think the besiegers had indeed expected to find them dead, but they had a surprise waiting for them." Runcorn began to scramble up the tumbled wreckage of the spiral staircase, but turned to speak as they started to follow him. "Be very careful here – it's all rather fragile. Make sure you don't dislodge the stones onto those coming up behind you."

It was a nervous climb, both because of the danger of causing the rest of the staircase to collapse and the claustrophobic narrowness of the stairwell. But at last, to Forrester's relief, they were at the top. It was a small platform, crowded once they were all on it, but the view was extraordinary. It seemed as if they could see the whole Aegean, dotted with islands and glittering in the afternoon sun. But it was the sea immediately below the castle walls that caught their attention, and suddenly everyone understood the meaning of the Greek phrase Durrell had used: *Roufichtra Medusa*.

Medusa's Whirlpool.

It was as if some infuriated goddess was spinning there, deep beneath the surface, her maw open, drawing anything that approached into the maelstrom. If there was ever an image of nature ready to seize and devour, this was it.

"My God," said Sophie, taking Forrester's arm and stepping away from the edge of the tower, "that is a terrible place."

"What on earth was Bohemond thinking, bringing his daughter up here?" asked Beamish, his face white.

"You must draw your own conclusions," said Runcorn.

"But this is what happened. When the Crusaders finally emerged from the stairwell, Bohemond and his daughter Persephone were ready for them – wearing the Urim and the Thummim."

"The breastplates," said Ariadne.

"Wearing them?"

"Yes, wearing them, like biblical priests."

"How terrible and splendid at the same time," said Sophie.

"As father and daughter swung their swords, according to Fulk's deathbed statement many years later, there emerged 'fierce beams of light, red, green and azure, blinding any who approached'. So effective was the defence put up by Bohemond and Persephone that the besiegers were actually being driven back – and Fulk ordered one more shot from the ballista. It might have killed his own men, of course, but Fulk wasn't the kind of man to care about that, and in fact he was lucky. The boulder smashed into Persephone, crushing her."

"Bastards," said Helena.

"Poor girl," said Sophie.

"And then the most extraordinary thing happened," said Runcorn.

"It's hard to imagine anything more extraordinary than what you've just told us," said David Venables.

"Well, listen to this," said Runcorn. "Bohemond took his dying daughter in his arms and climbed with her onto the battlements. Then he kissed her, whispered something in her ear, and leapt out over the maelstrom."

"Oh God," said Sophie. "So it swallowed them up."

"That's the fascinating part," said Runcorn. "Apparently not. As they fell, the two breastplates touched, and there was a flash of light so intense many of those who witnessed it did not recover their sight for days. And when the light died away, neither Bohemond nor his daughter were to be seen – not in the air, not in the sea and not on the rocks below the castle. They had vanished as if they had never been – and the Urim and the Thummim with them."

There was a silence as each of them saw, in their mind's eye, that final scene.

"What did Fulk do?" asked Forrester at last.

"What could he do?" said Runcorn. "He gathered his men together and left the island within the week. He went first to Rome to report to the Pope what had happened, and then resigned from the Order and retired to Melk Abbey in Austria. Much of what I've told you comes from the account he left there."

No one spoke for a while, imagining the last moments of Count Bohemond and his daughter, gazing at the extraordinary panorama spread before them before hurling themselves into – what? Heaven? Hell? Or another dimension of reality altogether?

"Sometimes I hate men," said Helena, half to herself.

Then there was a distant clatter of stones and Forrester looked down to see Yanni clambering in through the breach in the walls.

"Up here," he shouted, and waved.

Minutes later the Cretan had joined them on the tower.

"Is the bastard here, boss?" said Yanni as he emerged into the sunlight, breaking the mood created by the legend of Bohemond.

"It's a possibility," said Forrester. "There aren't many other places to hide around here. But none of us have seen him yet."

"So we go around the castle and flush him out," said Yanni. "Somebody staying up here to watch if he runs, then yelling to rest of us if they see him."

Forrester nodded. "Not a bad idea," he said. "If he *is* in residence. Perhaps the ladies would stay up here as watchers?"

"It's too hot to stay up here," said Helena. "I will join the hunt."

"Me too," said Ariadne. "Will you come with me, Keith? To look after me?" Again, Forrester saw Beamish blush like a schoolboy.

"When we search," said Forrester. "We search as a group. I'm not taking the risk of Kretzmer grabbing any one of us as a hostage. Sophie, would you stay here and be our spotter? We need someone with sharp eyes."

"Yes," said Sophie. "I need to sit down anyway," and she placed herself carefully on a fallen stone as far from the wall's edge as possible.

"Needless to say, if you see Kretzmer coming anywhere near the tower, yell bloody murder."

"You can rely on that," said Sophie, looking at him coolly. "I have no desire to be trapped here with that unhappy soul."

But it turned out that the sticking-together part of the

plan was easier said than done, because after they climbed back down to ground level and began to move steadily clockwise around the castle, the architecture of the place and the random nature of its ruination steadily broke the search party into units. As a result, quite often one or other of them was either alone or visible to just two or three other members of the search party. Forrester was acutely aware of the danger and kept stopping to herd them all back into a bunch, but for minutes at a time, he knew, they were horribly vulnerable. He wondered whether he was right to let them risk themselves like this, but the search, once begun, had a momentum of its own.

Besides, if he was honest with himself, the risk did not weigh more heavily with him than the prospect of finally laying his hands on the Minoan Rosetta Stone.

The first place they searched was the old guardroom. Forrester's initial instinct was that a glance would suffice to show it was empty, but when they went inside he realised the upper part of the walls were broken and provided innumerable hiding places, each of which had to be checked. And each of which proved to be empty.

Next came a series of tiny rooms, probably storage places and closets. In each one – nothing.

It was an eerie feeling as they entered the tall chamber that must have been the main hall of the castle. Forrester could imagine Bohemond and his consort presiding over his loyal retainers here, wondering when his former brothers in the Order of St. James would catch up with him, perhaps eyeing Michael doubtfully and wondering whether he had made the right decision in making off with the precious artefacts. And then perhaps looking at the beautiful Greek woman beside him, and the beloved daughter they had produced together – and concluding that whatever happened, this was the place he was destined to be.

They scrambled up a stairway onto the fighting platform that ran below the crenellations, with heart-stopping views out over the island and enough piles of rubble for Kretzmer to have secreted himself several times over. But he did not manifest himself. Every few minutes Forrester glanced over at Sophie on the tower. Each time she indicated with a shake of her head that she had seen nothing. Forrester also kept glancing at the spiral stairs to reassure himself that Kretzmer was not trying to get up there after her.

Finally they came to a point where the fighting platform was broken beyond repair and there was no way across the gap, and as the chapel was immediately below on their left, they decided to climb down and make it their next area of search.

The nave of the church was in a particular state of ruination, as if Fulk and his invading Crusaders had taken special pleasure in smashing up the renegades' place of worship, but it was still possible to make out, carved into the walls what looked like bas-reliefs of moons and stars. Images, Forrester thought, which would have been more appropriate in an astronomer's observatory than a Christian church. Low down in one corner was a Latin inscription that must have escaped the iconoclastic hands of Fulk's men.

ET CONCEDENTE PERFECTIONES LUMINA ET
LOCUTUS EST SUPER CAELOS CAELORUM.
ET QUI SUPER CAELO. ALIUS PRAETER
SAECULA SAECULORUM.

"'The lights and perfections have spoken'," said Lawrence Durrell, translating.

"'And vouchsafed that there is a heaven beyond the heavens.' What on earth does that mean?"

"And a heaven beyond that," read Forrester. "And another beyond that, for all eternity."

"An infinity of universes," said Durrell. "How very vertigo-making." He peered closer. "*Cave ne absorbeat et in tenebras lucem*," he read. "'Beware of the darkness lest it swallow up the light.' Not a very cheerful thought, is it?"

At which point the chapel darkened, there was a scraping noise directly above, and a rectangle of grey granite slid into view in a hole in the chapel roof.

"Scatter!" yelled Forrester, as a massive block of stone plunged down at them, hit the chapel floor and exploded with the force of its descent. Had they remained where they were for a second longer at least one of them would have been dead.

Forrester raced outside, but by the time he got there the chapel roof was empty.

"There he is!" shouted Sophie from the tower, pointing towards the ramparts, and Forrester looked up there at the very moment a figure vanished into a doorway. Suddenly people were scrambling from all directions to go after him.

In vain Forrester yelled at them to regroup, stay together, but the madness of the chase was on them and after the near miss in the chapel each one of them felt they had something to avenge.

Then a woman on horseback appeared on the brow of the hill directly in front of the castle, and spurred the animal to gallop furiously down towards it. As she rode, Forrester recognised her.

It was Penelope Alexandros.

And then Keith Beamish appeared, silhouetted against the sky on the castle ramparts, and shouted something as a gunshot rang out and he toppled slowly backwards into the sea. Forrester reached the spot where he had fallen just in time to see his body circle twice around the vortex before being sucked, forever, into its depths.

21

AFTERMATH

Forrester, almost overwhelmed by guilt and anger, could scarcely remember the journey back across the island, and it was only when they were back in their room in the *kastello* and he lay on the bed, his hands behind his head, staring up at the ceiling, that Sophie was able to speak to him directly.

"It wasn't your fault," she said.

"The hell it wasn't. The only reason Kretzmer was here on this island was because of me. And I let them follow him into the castle – if I'd stopped them he would still be alive."

"But we don't know it *was* Kretzmer who shot him," said Sophie.

"Of course it was Kretzmer," said Forrester. "Who else could it have been? Besides, you saw him yourself after he shoved the stone down through the chapel roof."

"That's what I wanted to tell you," said Sophie. "I'm not sure I did. All I know for certain is that there was somebody scrambling from the chapel onto the walls. I just assumed it was him."

"It had to be," said Forrester. "Everybody else was in the nave with me."

"Constantine Atreides wasn't," said Sophie. "Penelope Alexandros wasn't. And can you be absolutely certain all the people in our party came into the chapel with you in the first place?" Forrester stared at her bleakly, but it was a moment before he replied. The truth was he couldn't be totally sure who had been peering down at the inscription with him. And once he had rushed out of the place to go after Kretzmer he had no real idea who had gone where.

"But that still doesn't get around the fact that nobody had any motive to kill Keith," he said, "apart from Kretzmer."

"Kretzmer had no motive either," said Sophie, reasonably. "He might have killed him because he'd felt trapped, but apart from that…"

"Apart from that," said Forrester, "who else had any reason to murder Keith? Nobody."

"What about Helena Spetsos?" said Sophie. "After the way Ariadne was flirting with him on the walk."

"It would be a pretty extreme reaction to shoot somebody because of that," said Forrester.

"But we know Helena Spetsos *is* a woman given to extreme reactions, don't we?"

"Well – yes," said Forrester. "But all the same—"

"She's just finished three years guerrilla fighting in the mountains, killing anything or anyone that threatened her. And she's just met a major setback in her campaign to get Ari Alexandros back. Not a good time for young Keith to get in her way."

"But does she really care about Ariadne enough to kill for her?"

"I don't know," said Sophie. "Do you?"

Forrester had to admit he did not. He did not even bother to raise the question of whether Helena had actually had a gun with her at the castle. There was no reason to suppose she couldn't have laid her hands on one if she'd wanted to, and in the chaos after Beamish had been killed she could easily have concealed it. And even if they had the murder weapon there was no way of linking it directly to Beamish's death.

"I'd like to think it wasn't Kretzmer," said Forrester. "Keith was a nice kid. He didn't deserve to die."

"He didn't," said Sophie, "and I don't believe it was your fault he did."

It was several long moments before Forrester spoke again. "What should I do about Kretzmer? Assuming he's still at large?"

"I don't know," said Sophie, "but I don't want you going looking for him again. If there's one lesson from today, it's that. Do you agree?"

Forrester sighed. "I suppose so," he said.

"Good," said Sophie. "Then let's go down and join the others."

"You go first," said Forrester. "I need to speak to Ari."

He found Alexandros on the terrace, pacing up and down, smoking furiously.

"So, it goes on," said Forrester, declining the proffered packet.

"It goes on," said Alexandros, half to himself. "On my island."

"We'll get the bastard," said Forrester. "Whoever it is. And speaking of that, did you find out anything about who sent that decoy message yesterday?"

"I tracked down the family of the shepherd boy," said Alexandros.

"And what did they have to say?"

"They told me he has left the island."

"Left the island? What do you mean?"

"I mean he has gone to see his uncle on Antikythera."

"Damn!" said Forrester. "Is this just chance or did somebody get him out of here?"

"The parents say they know the uncle and he does sometimes visit Hydros in his caïque."

"They didn't see who spoke to their son, did they? When he was given the message for you."

"No, but they heard him speaking to someone outside the cottage just before he went off."

"Man or woman?"

"A man apparently."

"Speaking English or Greek?"

"It would have to be Greek, because the boy doesn't speak English. They didn't say it sounded like a foreigner, though."

"So it could have been somebody from the island?"

"Yes, my friend, it could," said Alexandros heavily. "So we are no better off for all my inquiries. What have you discovered?"

"I went back to the grove this morning," said Forrester.

"They used Nobel 808 and a timer."

"808? The British explosive."

"Plenty of that in these islands since the war. Anybody could have got hold of it."

"How long a timer?"

"Ten minutes."

"Ten..." said Alexandros. "They can't have been far away when..."

"By the way, while I was looking for the timer somebody took a pot-shot at me. Chased him, didn't catch him, so we're no better off there. How's Giorgios doing?"

Alexandros met his eyes briefly. "He is conscious again, in some pain, and very angry," he said. "As he has every right to be."

It was a shocked-looking group that gathered in the *kastello* dining room that night. Penelope presided over it with grim efficiency, as if determined by her very presence to instil a kind of normality. If she was amazed that after the events of the previous evening Helena Spetsos had the gall to show her face in the house, she hid the fact. The servants tiptoed in and out of the room with each course as if they were walking along the rim of a volcano.

"What is happening on my island?" said Alexandros as he finished his first glass of wine. "First the *ikons* are smashed—" he looked quickly at Helena, forestalling an interjection "—which I accept was an accident." Penelope snorted, but her husband ignored her. "Then the shrine is destroyed and my best friend is almost killed, and finally today, one of my guests is shot and plunges to his death in the *Roufichtra Medusa*." He glared round at them. "What is going on?" he demanded.

"Surely poor Beamish was killed by Forrester's Nazi?" said Lawrence Durrell. "Perhaps that same Nazi was responsible for the attack on Colonel Stephanides too?"

"I think I can absolve Kretzmer of that," said Forrester. "I know for a fact he was holed up at Limani Sangri when the colonel was injured."

"But you think he killed Mr. Beamish?" said Alexandros.

"It's possible," said Forrester. "But I simply don't know."

"What we should be asking ourselves," said Sophie, "is whether anyone else here had a reason to do it."

Everyone stared at her, and to Forrester's surprise he saw the colour rise in Penelope Alexandros's cheeks – but it was Ariadne who spoke.

"I'm sure Helena had nothing to do with it," she blurted out. "She knew it was just harmless flirting. I mean, with Keith and me."

"Shut up, you little fool," said Helena. "Nobody imagines I gave enough of a damn about that stupid Englishman to bother killing him."

"I hadn't, until this moment," said David Venables, "but that 'stupid Englishman' was my friend, so let me ask you, point blank, Miss Spetsos, did you kill him?"

"You are a fool to even ask," spat back Helena.

"I may be a fool," said Venables, "but I did ask and you haven't answered."

"The question does not deserve an answer," said Helena, and then, sensing the hostile looks focused on her from around the table, added quickly, "but still I will give you one. No, I did not kill your friend. I did not care about him enough to kill him."

"I appreciate your sympathy," said David Venables, looking her in the eyes. "I will bear it in mind." Without warning he turned his gaze on Constantine. "Do you mind me asking you, Prince, where you were when Keith was killed?"

"Why do you ask me?" replied Atreides with apparently genuine surprise. "I stayed outside the castle until the end – you know that."

"But you'd come back by the time Keith was killed."

"*After* he was killed," said Atreides firmly. "I had nothing to do with his death. Why would I want to kill that sweet young man? He was an artist. I have nothing but respect for artists."

Forrester stepped in before Venables could renew the interrogation and turned to Penelope.

"Mrs. Alexandros," he said, "perhaps you can shed some light on what happened. After all, you had the outsider's perspective. Did you see anything as you rode down the hill towards the castle?"

But Venables was not to be deflected so easily. "In fact, why were you coming to the castle at all?" he demanded.

"I live on this island," said Penelope sharply. "I do not have to account for my movements." She turned to Forrester. "To answer your question, Captain Forrester, as I rode down the hill I simply saw lots of people scattered about the castle.

I saw Sophie up on the tower. I saw another figure on the battlements – which must have been Mr. Beamish. And I saw Prince Atreides climbing in over the rubble."

"Before or after the shot?" asked Forrester. Again, he was certain, the colour rose in her cheeks. He saw Venables staring hard at her.

"Before."

Forrester felt the ripple of reaction that ran around the table.

"No!" said Atreides. "After!"

"Is it possible you're mistaken, Mrs. Alexandros?" said Durrell. "After all, you were galloping downhill at the time, and there was a lot going on."

"And we mustn't forget that sound travels considerably slower than light," said Runcorn.

"All this is true," said Penelope. "But you asked me what I saw, and I told you."

"This discussion is foolish," said Atreides. "Whether I went into the castle before or after the shot, it was not I who fired it. Surely it's obvious that the killer was the German soldier."

"Speaking of whom," said Durrell, "what are we going to do about him? I'm assuming, General, you don't really want him roaming about the island?"

"I notified the authorities in Lemnos about the murder," said Alexandros. "This group of islands is governed from there. I have also told them about the attempted murder of Colonel Stephanides and the presence of the fugitive, and I've suggested they send a police detective to deal with one and soldiers to track down the other."

"And when will they arrive?" asked Runcorn.

"That's the problem," said Alexandros. "Neither a detective nor any army unit is stationed in this part of the Aegean at present. Lemnos will have to send to Athens, and it may be some days before either policemen or soldiers arrive."

"So if you want to catch your Nazi, Forrester, and get your Minoan rock back, you'll have to organise another expedition," said Durrell.

"Not on the cards at present," said Forrester. "I blame myself for what happened to Keith Beamish today, and I'm not putting anyone else's life at risk. If the man gets away with the stone, he gets away with it. I think we should all stay close to the *kastello* until the soldiers arrive. Do you agree, Ari?"

"I do," said Alexandros.

"Even if one of us is a murderer?" asked Venables. "Because if it wasn't Kretzmer who shot Keith and tried to kill Colonel Stephanides, it was almost certainly someone here. And if so, they might well try again."

"In the name of God," said Penelope Alexandros, "can you stop talking about murder? I've had enough of it, more than enough. Will you please all leave it alone?"

"Of course, Mrs. Alexandros," said Runcorn. "In fact, dear lady, and General Alexandros, I rather wonder if we shouldn't all get out of your hair. You provided a wonderful, indeed literal port in the storm for us, but you've had nothing but trouble since we arrived. Durrell and I have been talking it over and it seems to us the best thing might be for us all to leave the island as soon as possible."

"Needless to say," said Forrester, "the same offer applies to us."

"I appreciate your consideration," said Alexandros, "but the authorities on Lemnos specifically asked me to ensure you remain here until they can send someone. I'm sorry, but it seems we are stuck with each other for the next few days."

There was a silence around the table.

22

INTO THE WOODS

Once again, as the moon rose, Forrester, Yanni and Sophie met on the quayside below the *kastello*.

"What do you think, Yanni?" said Forrester. "Do you think Kretzmer killed Keith Beamish?"

"He could have done, boss, but it could have just as easy been one of the others. Nobody knowing where they all were when gun was fired."

"We may be able to work it out though," said Forrester. He reached into his jacket pocket and took out a small leather-bound volume with three sheets of tracing paper tucked in it. "I found this in Ari's library. It's a nineteenth-century antiquarian's description of the castle, including a site plan."

He opened the book at the page marked with the tracing paper and showed them the thickly inked diagram of the castle's layout. Then he took a pencil and a sheet of the semi-transparent paper and made a tracing of the diagram. "That's the sea wall from which he fell after the shot," he said, passing the page to Yanni. As Patrakis took the tracing between his weathered fingers, Forrester began a second tracing, speaking to Yanni as he worked. "Who did you see near there?"

The Greek thought for a long moment and then jabbed his finger at the page. "Angry woman was here, English professor there, blond writer there, and dead man's friend there."

"Helena, Runcorn, Durrell and Venables," said Forrester, marking their positions on the map. "Were they going in the same direction as you or running away?"

"I know not, boss," said Yanni, "I was in big hurry."

"Never mind," said Forrester. "Let's put each one down with an arrow for which way you think they *might* have been going, and a question mark if you're *really* not sure."

Yanni complied, and the tracing paper began to fill up with annotations. Then Forrester turned to Sophie and went through the same exercise with her on the second tracing. In some cases she was able to corroborate Yanni's account, in others modify it, and in yet others to give Forrester the whereabouts of people Yanni had not seen. When she had finished Forrester made a third tracing and put down his own recollections of where everyone had been. Finally he put all three pieces of paper on top of one another and studied the results.

"Helena is still a possibility, isn't she?" he said at last. "All three of us put her where she was close enough to have done it."

"I know I was the one who was insisting we consider her a suspect," said Sophie, "but in the cold light of day

I find it very hard to believe she could really hate Keith Beamish that much. She knows Ariadne is a total flirt, and her whole goal is to get Alexandros back, not to cling to her little playmate. Besides, it was obvious Ariadne was just cosying up to Keith to annoy Helena. He was pretty much the innocent party."

"Up to a point," said Forrester, "but remember he told us up at the grove that he'd had his eye on Ariadne since Athens – and so Helena Spetsos could have been getting more and more steamed up about him for some time." He looked at the diagram again. "What about Runcorn? None of what we've got down here rules him out, does it?"

"And he was absolutely determined to get us to the castle even after you warned everybody that Kretzmer might be there," said Sophie. "If he'd wanted to kill Keith he must have realised that was the ideal opportunity."

"The problem is," said Forrester, "I can't think of any reason why he *would* want to. As far as I know he and Beamish scarcely knew each other. They were only introduced a few days ago in Athens through Venables."

"As far as you *know*," said Sophie. "Might they have met each other in England? During the war? Might Keith have been one of Runcorn's students, or a researcher?"

"And then there's the possibility that Helena Spetsos has some kind of hold over him, based on what you saw at her house in Athens," said Forrester. "Runcorn does seem to have been one of the voices urging Durrell to visit Hydros – that could have been on Helena's orders."

"What about your friend David Venables?" asked

Sophie. "Did he have any reason to kill Keith?"

"On the contrary," said Forrester. "Keith was his collaborator on the book he's writing. Without his illustrations the whole project may fall to pieces. Besides, they were friends."

"And you yourself have known Venables for years, haven't you?"

"I have. He's a passionate, opinionated man and outspoken on most subjects under the sun, but I've never noticed any murderous inclinations. He was a naturalist before he was a broadcaster. You know, studying voles and foxes and things."

"Really?" said Sophie. "It's hard to imagine him sitting in a hide waiting for hedgehogs to mate."

"Well, I'm not sure he did much of that. He made his name with a lot of very witty broadcasts for the BBC, making the animals sound like human beings."

"Which they're not," said Sophie.

"I think he knew that. But it went down well with audiences when everyone was so worried about the war."

"I remember you saying he was rather cynical."

"Yes. He may not have seen animals as human beings, but I think he *does* see human beings as animals."

"Perhaps that's what makes him a man of the left, as he always reminds us. What about Lawrence Durrell?"

"Again, I can't think of any reason why he would have anything against Keith Beamish. Plus, he's the one person we all seem to believe was well away from the place where Keith was shot. I distinctly remember him beside me in the chapel as we were reading those rather eerie inscriptions."

Sophie took the tracings from him. "So the wild card is Constantine Atreides, isn't it? He's the one none of us are sure of."

Forrester looked at the pages over her shoulder. "Connie did make rather a point of staying outside the castle when everyone else went in."

"And Penelope Alexandros said she saw him go into the castle *before* the gunshot," said Sophie.

"She did," said Forrester.

"In fact," Sophie went on, "why is he here on the island at all? Why is he one of the party?"

"I must ask Venables about that. Venables was the one who instigated the trip to Rhodes to see Lawrence Durrell and I think Atreides just tagged along."

"And once they were en route, he and Helena Spetsos persuaded Lawrence to include Hydros in his itinerary."

"I've discussed that with Larry, and interestingly it seems most of the persuading came from Charles Runcorn, because of his Bohemond obsession."

"Although Runcorn could have been acting for Helena Spetsos, after their little *mise en scène* in Athens."

"Quite possibly. But let's not get distracted from Connie Atreides. He's absolutely desperate that Alexandros doesn't throw his lot in with the communists, because if the General joins ELAS and they win a civil war, there'll be no chance of King George coming back to Greece."

"So he's probably here to put pressure on Alexandros not to do that?" said Sophie.

"I think he may well be," said Forrester.

"But what good is killing your English artist?" said Yanni. "That not helping Atreides persuade the General to say no to the Reds."

Forrester looked at him. "Not as such," he said. "But…"

"But what?" asked Sophie.

"I'm thinking back to the attack on Giorgios Stephanides," said Forrester. "Who were the witnesses?"

"You and me," said Sophie. "After all, we practically walked in on it."

"But there was one other person in the grove that day, wasn't there?" said Forrester.

Sophie looked at him, puzzled – and then realised. "You mean, in the morning, when we went through the first time."

"Who?" said Yanni.

Forrester turned to him. "Keith Beamish," he said.

For a moment all three sat there, digesting this.

Sophie was the first to speak. "You're thinking he might have seen something, something that implicated Constantine Atreides. Something that showed Atreides was behind what happened to Giorgios Stephanides."

"But Atreides was not trying to stop the *colonel* going to the communists," said Yanni. "It is the *General* who matters."

"True enough," said Forrester. "Giorgios is just a loyal lieutenant. But what if Connie had been going for Ari, and accidentally got Giorgios?"

"With plastique?" asked Sophie. "Does Atreides even know how to use plastique?"

"I don't know, someone might have taught him. And of course it didn't go as planned, did it? Anyway, if Keith

Beamish had got some clue he was involved, Atreides would have a motive to shut him up."

"What clue might Keith have got?" said Sophie. Forrester looked at her, realising.

"Remember what he said on the walk to the castle. About how he liked drawing things glimpsed through the trees? He may have been thinking about something he'd seen in the grove."

"Oh my God," said Sophie. "Of course."

"Something he drew," said Forrester slowly. "Something he drew in that sketchbook of his."

"And he didn't realise the significance of what he'd drawn, until I started talking about the killer's movements."

"And Atreides had to kill him before he spoke out," said Sophie.

"We have to find sketchbook, boss," said Yanni.

"The problem is," said Forrester, "if whoever killed Beamish, whether Atreides or anyone else, did so because he knew there was a clue in the sketchbook, he would've taken the sketchbook as well – or at least the relevant page. We might find it but we certainly wouldn't find the drawing with the clue, whatever it was."

"Perhaps Atreides still has the page on him, or hidden somewhere," said Sophie.

"I can't see why he would," said Forrester. "He would have destroyed it right away. And let's not forget we're building on very slender foundations in assuming it was Atreides behind either the original attack or Keith's murder."

"Except that Atreides is the one person whose

movements we can't be sure of before Keith was killed," said Sophie.

"Which isn't much to go on, is it?" said Forrester.

As Forrester slipped into sleep that night, the dreams rose up to engulf him. There was Kretzmer, as tall as a house, walking across the rooftops of Athens and hurling the head of Jason Michaelaides across the gulf that separated them. There were Alexandros and Helena Spetsos, Thompson submachine guns cradled in their arms, racing across an Olympian mountainside, firing at a pursuing German patrol. But as the Germans came closer Forrester saw, beneath their helmets, his own face, Sophie's, and that of Charles Runcorn. And then the whole party was all together on Yanni's boat in the middle of the storm, and Penelope and Ariadne were throwing icons overboard whilst Atreides lifted something wrapped in sacking out of the hold and held it aloft. As the wrappings blew away in the wind Forrester found himself looking into the reproachful face of Keith Beamish, the flesh melting from his bones, leaving behind only a gleaming skull.

Forrester's eyes snapped open in fear and for a long moment he felt himself hovering between consciousness and sleep, until he heard Sophie's soft breathing beside him and remembered where he was. For a moment he gazed at her sleeping face and felt profoundly reassured she was with him in the midst of all the madness. But his body was thick with sweat now and his mind in such turmoil he knew there was no prospect of sleep. Slowly, determined not to wake her, he eased himself out of bed and got dressed. At first he just intended to sit by the window looking out over the sleeping village, but his thoughts were racing so fast he knew he had to get out.

The house itself was in the grip of the peculiar silence of a crowded building where everyone is asleep. Beneath his feet the tiles were cool and smooth; when he stopped to listen he could hear the ticking of a distant clock. He looked into the main room and even in the darkness it felt as if the eyes of Ari's pirate ancestors were observing him from the portraits. He ran his fingers over the leather-bound spines of the books on the shelves and the pin-pricked map on the wall.

The Peloponnesian current. None of this would be happening if it had not been for the Peloponnesian current.

The Peloponnesian current and the storm.

Or, more accurately, it would have been happening, in some slightly altered form, but he would not have been here to be part of it.

Then he was outside and looking down the steep village street towards the moonlit sea. But instead of walking down towards the bay he turned left, uphill, away from the *kastello*, towards the pinewoods on the hills above.

He heard the voices as soon as he entered the shadow of the trees. The whispered words were indecipherable at first, and appeared to come from everywhere at once. It seemed to Forrester that he was listening to a language that had been spoken long before even the classic age of Greece, words from the time when the gods themselves were young. He stood for a long moment, trying to identify the direction from which they came – and then began walking deeper into the wood.

He peered into the shadows of the tree trunks, trying to make out who was speaking, but it seemed as if the voices were retreating before him. At last he stopped again, and suddenly he could see two figures close to one another less than thirty feet away, a man and a woman. Forrester was slightly uphill from them, looking down at them through the trees, and they were silhouetted against the relative lightness of the sea.

"I understand," he heard the man say, and then "your duty," followed by a string of angry, bitter words from the woman that were too low to make out – except for "… will die. I promise you." The man seemed tall enough to be Ari Alexandros, but the slope made it hard to judge. And the woman: could it be Helena Spetsos? Or Penelope Alexandros? He couldn't be sure. He had to be sure.

But as he stepped down the hill towards them, a twig snapped under his foot and instantly the two figures melted into the darkness. By the time he reached the place where they had been there was no one in sight in any direction, just the silent bay.

He stepped out onto the path, hesitated for a second and turned left, in the direction of the monastery, the direction he believed they'd gone. But ten minutes later he was sure he had made the wrong choice, because there was no sign of either the man or the woman, and he was standing on an empty grassy patch looking down on the monastery's sleeping walls.

Uncertain what to do, he lay down on the grass at the edge of the trees, thinking of Stephanides lying in its infirmary. For a long time he watched, arranging and rearranging the pieces of the puzzle in his mind. Who had he seen on the fringes of the wood? Had Alexandros been trying to kill Stephanides when he found him beside the fallen shrine? Had Helena killed Keith Beamish to protect her lover? Was she blackmailing Alexandros with what she knew? Or was it the other way round? And who had the woman promised would die next?

But gradually, Forrester's eyelids began to droop and long before the puzzle had resolved itself into any satisfactory shape he had fallen asleep in the grass.

23

THE FIELD TELEPHONE

Sophie woke within minutes of Forrester leaving the house, conscious even in her sleep that he had gone. She lay there for a while and then, uneasy when he did not return, rose and went downstairs. But instead of simply glancing into the main room as he had done, she went in and sat in one of the deep armchairs, considering his absence. How long she sat there she could not be sure, and perhaps she dozed because when she opened her eyes a woman was standing directly in front of her, looking down. Sophie suppressed a jolt of fear and then made out, in the darkness, the woman's face. It was Penelope.

"I couldn't sleep," said Sophie, "and Duncan seems to have gone for a walk."

"I need to walk too," said Penelope. "Will you come with me?"

Moments later, Sophie, dressed now and with her bag over her shoulder, was beside Penelope as they passed like two ghosts through the narrow lanes of the village.

They crossed a hump-backed bridge over a little stream that chuckled beneath them in the darkness, and then they were out of the village and walking along a narrow path cut into the face of the cliff. Finally they reached a little balconied belvedere tucked into the rock and sat down on a lichened stone bench. In one direction Sophie could look back towards Kastello Drakonaris, and in the other along the coast, where the nearby islands emerged from the dark sea like a pod of dolphins frozen in place as they leapt.

"I used to come here to think during the war," said Penelope. "Just to get away."

"It must have been a terrible strain, keeping the islanders safe from the Germans."

"No one was safe from the Germans," said Penelope. "But I did my best."

"I have some idea what that must have been like," said Sophie. "I had an estate in Norway when we were occupied and I had to try and shield my people from those bastards. There was a lot of smiling through gritted teeth."

Penelope gave her a long look. "Gritted teeth," she said. "Yes, I know all about the gritting of the teeth."

Both women sat in silence for a while, looking out over the night.

"Do you think your husband understands what it was like for you?" asked Sophie.

"Of course not. When he saw Germans, he killed them. He could never know what it was like to live with them."

Off to her right Sophie heard the scrape of stone on stone and felt suddenly certain they were no longer alone.

Whether Penelope felt it too, she could not be sure, but she knew, without doubt, that the tension on the balcony had suddenly increased. As if to break it she spoke again. "I felt so bad for you, about the ceremony. If I had been you I would have wanted to kill Helena Spetsos on the spot."

"If I had had a gun in my hand at that moment," said Penelope, "she would have been dead before she hit the floor. Fortunately I did not have a gun in my hand." She paused. "Or perhaps not so fortunately."

"You mean because she's still here," said Sophie, "and still trying to take your husband away?"

"She will never take my husband away," said Penelope. "Do you think for one moment I am going to let her have everything I sacrificed so much to save?"

Sophie looked at her and as she did she was sure there was something Penelope was not telling her, some shape in her narrative that was being deliberately shrouded.

"Sacrifices," said Sophie. And then went on, with sudden intuition, "Men don't know what sacrifices women have to make in times of war."

Penelope glanced at her and Sophie suddenly knew there was something this woman would kill for – and it was not to prevent Helena Spetsos stealing her husband.

"Who do you think killed Keith Beamish?" she asked. "Do you have any idea?"

There was a long pause before Penelope Alexandros spoke again. "All I know is that whatever Constantine Atreides said, I saw him going into the castle before I heard the shot."

"But why?" said Sophie. "Why would Prince Atreides

want to kill that young man?"

"I have no idea," said Penelope, flatly. "I just know what I saw and heard."

She stood up. "It's getting cold. We should get back."

Sophie got to her feet too. "We should. If Duncan finds me gone when he returns, he'll be worried."

"Yes," said Penelope. "The island has become a dangerous place again. Perhaps that is its natural state."

Forrester was woken by the monastery bell, chiming for the first service of the day. He got to his feet as the rising sun began to warm the grass, and then walked down towards the monastery's massive walls. The first small door he tried was open and he found himself inside the shady courtyard, savouring its coolness. He listened as the voices of the chanting monks rose from the chapel and, drawn by the sound, slipped into its dim, incense-scented interior, where Abbot Vasilios Spyridon was leading the monks in prayer.

"*As eucharistísoume ton evergetikó kai filéfsplachno Theó, ton Patéra tou Kyríou mas, ton Theo kai Sotíra, ton Iisoú Christó...*"

Forrester was not a believer, but the words flowed over him like balm, as if, despite his lack of faith, the belief of others, nurtured here for two thousand years, was nurturing him now. He certainly felt in need of nurture. At the end of the service he remained seated as the monks filed out, until he and Abbot Spyridon were the only two there. The Abbot came to sit beside him. "My son," he said. "You are troubled."

"I am troubled," said Forrester. "You have heard how the young British artist was killed at Bohemond's castle. If it was done by the German I seek, the German who has stolen the Cretan stone, I feel responsible. But I don't know if that is what happened, and I must find out."

"And you think I can help you?" said the Abbot, looking at Forrester from under bushy brows.

"Perhaps," said Forrester. "For example, I understand you grew up here on Hydros with Ari and Giorgios."

"I did," said the Abbot.

"And that they were boyhood friends, and both were close to Penelope."

"That is also true. When we were all children this island was our world. We were poor, but Giorgios was rich in imagination, and through his dreams, it became a paradise. You know the lake in the middle of the island? It was our magic ocean. We built our own Venetian galley there, you know, and went fishing for *karavída*."

"Crayfish?"

"Only we called them dragons, and Penelope was the island's goddess, and when we gave them to her she turned them back into crayfish, and we cooked and ate them by the lakeshore. That was when Penelope and Giorgios married."

"They married?"

"They were only ten. It was all make-believe, part of our game. We were crusading knights that day, I think. I married them: I was the Archbishop of Athens, if I recall rightly."

"I have heard that people expected Penelope to marry Giorgios for real when they grew up."

"They did. I amongst them. But Giorgios went to Athens to write his book and became famous, being pictured in the papers with film stars, and Penelope thought he had grown beyond her. Ari took advantage of his absence. He too loved Penelope, of course, but when Giorgios was there he was overshadowed. Only when Giorgios seemed to have forgotten Hydros and Penelope too was Ari able to win her heart. Thus emboldened, he joined the army and became a great man in his own right. A hero, such as we imagined ourselves to be when we were children."

"I have heard that Penelope and Giorgios remain very close to this day."

"We all four remain very close," said the Abbot guardedly. "We have been through much together."

"Let me be frank," said Forrester. "I found Ari bending over Giorgios at the fallen shrine. At the time I assumed he was trying to help him, but since then I have asked myself if he was trying to kill him."

"That is a grave accusation."

"It's not an accusation at this point. It is a speculation. But do you think it's possible? That it was in revenge for some sort of liaison between Giorgios and Penelope?"

The Abbot looked away. "Such a thought would not occur to me," he said at last – but Forrester sensed he had touched a nerve, just not the nerve he had been probing for. He tried again.

"Of course both Ari and Giorgios have been away from the island for a long time," he said. "Penelope has had years to think about them both."

"She has," said the Abbot. "But during that time she

had to think principally about how to protect the people of Hydros from the Germans."

"And I gather she succeeded," said Forrester. "There were no atrocities here during the war."

"There were not."

"And you credit that chiefly to her leadership?"

"I do," said the Abbot. "I too perhaps played some small part, but she bore the brunt of it."

Forrester waited for more, but nothing came. "What were the German commandants like? Many of those sent to the islands were beasts, I know, but some could be quite decent men."

This time, despite the gloom of the chapel, Forrester saw the Abbot's eyes flick toward him.

"We had three altogether," he said. "And one of them was a Prussian. But all were finally persuaded to behave like decent men, and few islanders were badly treated."

Forrester was about to ask how this had been achieved when the Abbot took his turn to ask a question.

"Where is your German now?" he asked. "The fugitive who may have killed the young artist? Is he still in Bohemond's castle?"

Forrester met the old man's shrewd eyes: it was a good question. "Probably not," he said. "If I were him I would have moved on. Whether or not he killed Keith Beamish, he knows we are aware of the castle as a possible hiding place and we could come back at any time."

He was about to return to the question of just how the German commandants had been persuaded to treat the islanders leniently when the Abbot said, "Have you heard the story of our field telephone?"

"Field telephone?" asked Forrester, puzzled.

"When the Germans were here they had an outpost on the island of Paxa, which is so close you can see it from here. It is very small but it was important because it gave them a lookout over the shipping lanes. The outpost was connected to us by a field telephone. They laid a cable across the bottom of the sea and put the receiving post in this very monastery. Perhaps you would like to see it?"

Forrester could not see the point of this unexpected offer but judged it polite to show interest. "Certainly," he said.

The Abbot gathered up his robes and led him down the length of the chapel, behind the altar, and through a small door in the wall. On the other side of the door was a steep, narrow stone staircase, which wound up to the top of a tower and ended in a tiny room. When Forrester was inside the Abbot closed the door carefully behind them. The windows of the room looked down on the monastery and the sea beyond, but it was what was in the centre that held his attention. It was a simple wooden table with a single chair beside it. On the table was a Wehrmacht field telephone.

"One night towards the end of the war a party of British commandos came ashore on Paxa in rubber boats and attacked the German outpost. As soon as they realised they were under attack, the oberleutnant called his superiors on this telephone. The German commandant was summoned and took the call. The line remained open throughout the attack."

"What happened?"

"The fight was very fierce. There was no question of quarter on either side. As the commandant listened on the telephone you see here, he heard machine-gun fire, then grenades, and finally the screams of men being killed with knives and bayonets. That was less clear, of course, but in the end, all six German defenders were dead."

"How macabre," said Forrester.

The Abbot nodded. "The garrison was never replaced," he said, "because it was too late in the war, and Paxa remained deserted. But no one ever dismantled the field telephone."

Forrester looked at the instrument. "So I could call the island if I wished to?" he said.

"You could," said the Abbot, meeting his eyes, "but if you did all you would hear would be the sound of dying men."

"You're saying it's haunted."

"It is. I have listened many times. If you lift the instrument and wind the handle, you will hear it for yourself."

"Why are you telling me this?"

The Abbot smiled enigmatically. "There are many mysteries on this island," he replied. "Perhaps your German fugitive has become one of them."

Before he left the monastery Forrester went to see Giorgios Stephanides. The colonel lay in the monks' infirmary, pale, heavily splinted and bandaged, but able to speak. Forrester sat down beside the bed and after the usual preliminaries said, "Ari asked me to help him find out who might have tried to kill you."

"That was very thoughtful of him," said Stephanides.

"Who do you think it was?" said Forrester.

Stephanides closed his eyes. "That is impossible for me to say."

"Let me be frank with you," said Forrester. "I have wondered if Ari himself might have wanted to kill you because you were too close to his wife. Do you think that is possible?"

There was a long silence. "Penelope and I were meant to be together," said Stephanides. "We were meant to be together from the day we were born. All I cared about then was her. All Ari cared about was himself. But she and I quarrelled and I went away to Athens, where I wrote my novel about the pain she had caused me, and tried to impress her by going out with film stars. And while I was making a fool of myself and getting my picture in the papers, Ari put on an army uniform and swept her off her feet. By the time I got back it was too late."

With an effort he turned his head and his dark eyes flashed as they met Forrester's. "All through the war, even as I fought alongside him, I wanted to kill the bastard."

"Why didn't you?" asked Forrester.

"Because he is a hero and a great man, and also my friend. But that does not stop me hating him."

"It almost sounds as though you might have been trying to kill *him* instead of the other way around," said Forrester.

"If I had been going to kill him, there were plenty of opportunities during the war. I would not have needed to use some sort of booby trap."

"Then I return to the question," said Forrester. "Was he trying to kill you? Perhaps because he thought you stood in the way of his reconciliation with Penelope?"

"I cannot believe he would think such a thing or do such a thing," said Stephanides. "I am his friend."

"You said he is your friend, too – and yet you hate him."

"Life is strange that way," said Stephanides, and closed his eyes. "I wish to sleep now."

Forrester walked to the door and opened it to leave. "One last question," he said. "Was the General standing between you and the shrine when the explosion went off, or was he on your far side?"

There was a long pause before the injured man answered. "He was on my far side," he said.

"Thank you," said Forrester.

24

THE MAN FROM ATHENS

Halfway down the path from the monastery to the *kastello* Forrester found Venables sitting on a tree trunk, staring out over the dazzling blue sea and smoking a cigarette. Companionably he shifted his canvas manuscript bag and moved along the bench so Forrester could sit down beside him.

"You don't use these, do you?" he asked, holding up the cigarette case, and then said, "I would have put you down as more of a pipe man, but you don't smoke a pipe either."

"Never felt the need," said Forrester.

"Not even to soothe your nerves, as the advertisements used to promise?"

"I have to admit," said Forrester, "my nerves are being sorely tried at present. As yours must be."

Venables nodded. "He was a bloody good chap. He didn't deserve to die. Oh, Christ, how banal that is. We all deserve to die. We all deserve to live. I just didn't expect to be robbed of his company so soon."

"Or his talent."

"Or indeed his talent." He turned to face Forrester. "Have you made any progress? Do you have any evidence that it was one of us and not your bloody Nazi?"

"No evidence," said Forrester. "Just possibilities."

"Such as?"

"That Keith saw something in the grove, possibly even sketched it, and he later realised the sketch pointed the finger at whoever tried to kill Giorgios Stephanides. Which led the murderer to take advantage of the situation at the castle to put him out of the way before he told anybody."

"Good God," said Venables. "Then we have to look at his sketchbooks right away."

"I think it's too late for that," said Forrester. "Whoever killed him will have already destroyed the evidence."

"Not necessarily," said Venables. "They certainly haven't got rid of all his sketchbooks: we were sharing a room and I saw them only this morning."

"Well, I suppose we should look at them," said Forrester, "but I don't expect to find anything now."

"Perhaps not," said Venables. "But we should go and see."

As Forrester stood up he staggered a little, dizzy, and Venables took his arm to steady him.

"Are you all right?" said Venables.

"I'm fine. I've just been up since the early hours." And as he said these words the image of the man and woman in the wood flashed with extraordinary vividness into his mind.

"What is it?" said Venables. "You look as if someone has just walked over your grave."

"I was up there last night," said Forrester, gesturing

towards the trees, "just wandering about because I couldn't sleep. I saw a man and a woman talking. Whispering. Conspiring. She promised someone would die."

"Who?"

"I don't know. At first I thought it was Alexandros and Helena."

"Jesus. You think Alexandros and that lesbian bitch got together to kill Keith? I'll fucking kill them – both of them."

It was Forrester's turn to put a hand on the other man's arm. "Don't be ridiculous. I saw two people among the trees, talking. I heard a few broken words. They could bear any number of interpretations. For example if it was Helena she could have been saying that it was Penelope who had to die. The woman might have been Ariadne. It might have been Penelope. When I moved towards them they heard me coming and slipped away."

"Penelope?"

"Well, that would make sense, wouldn't it? Helena wants Alexandros for herself, Penelope stands in the way; why wouldn't she want to kill her?"

"This place is a madhouse," said Venables.

"There's also the possibility," said Forrester, relentlessly, determined to divert Venables from some rash act, "that Alexandros himself was trying to kill Stephanides in the grove that day."

"But why?"

"Because Stephanides was trying to take Penelope away from him. She and Stephanides were childhood sweethearts – did you know that?"

"I did not," said Venables, looking at him with angry, almost wounded eyes, as if this complexity was too much for him. "All I know is that some swine shot my friend to save their own neck and I want to make sure they suffer for it. So let's go and look at those bloody sketchbooks." But as they reached the point on the path where the harbour came into view, they stopped dead, staring.

Fifteen Greek soldiers were marching down the gangplank of a Greek naval vessel moored beside the quay and forming up in a neat line under the eye of a sergeant. No sooner had they disembarked than a diminutive figure in a raincoat and fedora appeared at the top of the gangplank, and though he was too far away for Forrester to see his face, he knew instantly it was Inspector Kostopoulos.

Then the soldiers and their sergeant snapped to attention and saluted as a tall, commanding figure came down the harbour steps to greet them. It was General Aristotle Alexandros.

Half an hour later Inspector Kostopoulos was seated in the big armchair in the main room of the *kastello* under the portrait of a pirate chief, regarding the assembled company with a satisfaction that would not have been out of place if they had been brought there to celebrate his birthday. It was quite a crowd, including not only the servants but Abbot Spyridon and the devoted Chrystomatos.

"Is so good to seeing you all again," said Kostopoulos, "plus those not known to me yet but which acquaintanceship will make a very pleasant. I am speaking in English for benefit of those not knowing Greek, but also practising for when Scotland Yard calling me home." He waited for a response and when none came slapped the arm of his chair impatiently. "Was joke," he said. "British joke. Nobody here having sense of humour, obvious."

He sat up straighter in the chair and glared round at them. "My studying of Athens death of great poet Michaelaides still ongoing. But now is complicated, natural, by half crushing of Colonel Stephanides, and by shooting of English artist Beaming."

"Beamish," said Venables.

"Exactly," said Kostopoulos. "He is your friend?"

"Was," said Venables.

"So was you who shot him?" said Kostopoulos.

"What the hell are you talking about? Didn't you hear what I just said? He was my friend."

"Calming down, calming down," said the policeman. "Friends is shooting friends, sometimes, just like husbands and wives, everybody knowing that. No stone will be kicked about in this investigation. Nobody too important to accuse. Remembering that, please. Now, Kostopoulos fully aware of tin man roaming Hydros with stolen stone, Greek heritage at stake etcetera. So already Sergeant Bogdolu Pyrolithos and men are searching whole place and all can be resting assured stealer and stone together will be found."

He settled himself more comfortably in the armchair. "Now I explain my methods. Simple methods but always working for me. I will have a long talk with each person one by one, while all other persons staying nearby to be convenient. Everybody will tell the truth, of course, except the murderer, and when all stories are compared side by side murderer's lies will stand out like written in blood."

"What if the murderer is Oberleutnant Kretzmer?" said Lawrence Durrell. "Who is not here for you to talk to?"

"Then all can relax," said Kostopoulos, "because the next time anybody seeing tin man he will be lying on door."

He looked at them triumphantly – and saw their incomprehension. "By which I am meaning lying dead on door after Sergeant Pyrolithos and his men are shooting him and putting him on the door to bring him back here." No one responded, and suddenly Inspector Kostopoulos was angry.

"Is obvious what I mean," he barked. "Anybody ever seeing cowboy movie knowing what I am talking about. Dead outlaws always put on doors after shootout. Always. Anyway, totally beside point. I have seen enough of you. My initial impression have been made, which is good for some, not so good for others. Now I am telling everybody to get out excepting for General Alexandros. General Alexandros I am questioning first."

And one by one they stood up, avoiding each other's eyes, and left the room.

Forrester, however, stayed behind. "I was wondering how your investigations into Michaelaides's death were progressing? Did you find out what poison was used?"

Kostopoulos looked shifty. "Germans was pigs," he said. "Everything smashed before they leaving."

It was a moment before Forrester understood. "Including the police laboratory?"

"Also, best police doctor gone to communists. Disaster!"

"So you don't know what poison killed him?"

"Heart condition," said Kostopoulos, shrugging. "His own doctor saying he had heart condition. Maybe he dying natural, after all."

"It didn't look like a heart attack. You yourself said it was poison."

Kostopoulos squared his shoulders. "Michaelaides is old investigation," he said. "New investigation is what is counting. Please not to obstruct, Mist Forrest."

And that was that.

As soon as they were dismissed, Venables led Forrester and Sophie to the room he had been sharing with Keith Beamish. Beamish's backpack lay on his bed, and his sketchbooks were inside it. Without much hope Forrester sat down on the other bed with Venables and Sophie on either side and began to go through them from the beginning. The first pages showed scenes of Athens: the Acropolis, the market stalls, the Archbishop's palace and the café in Anafiotika where they had all dined the night Michaelaides was killed. There was even a rough sketch of the table with all of them around it, eating, drinking, talking in the moments before disaster struck. For some reason the light caught Constantine Atreides's distinctive panama hat so that it glowed with comic elegance in one corner.

Forrester flicked the pages back and looked again at the sketch of the Archbishop's reception. There was

Stephanides, Alexandros and Venables beside the kouros, there was Michaelaides, declaiming, his hand raised as if in benediction, about to descend on the statue's carved locks.

Venables handed him the second sketchbook. "Here we are on the way from Piraeus," he said, "with Runcorn and Helena and the rest of the gang."

Then there were pictures of the ancient harbour at Rhodes, and the whole group breakfasting at a table outside the tiny house there that Durrell had leased in the eucalyptus-shaded garden of an old Turkish mosque. Incongruously, everybody seemed to be eating Kellogg's Cornflakes.

The third sketchbook covered their voyage through the islands as Durrell visited his correspondents. There were any number of picturesque fishing villages, picturesque Greek peasants and picturesque children leading picturesque and heavily laden donkeys. Among the drawings created on the minesweeper itself, one showed Runcorn in close consultation with Helena; another, Venables and Prince Atreides looking out over the stern, their heads bent towards each other.

Then came Hydros, with a view of Drakonaris from the harbour, and a sketch, clearly drawn from memory, of the scene in the *kastello* when the Abbot and his acolyte had brought in the *ikons* on that fateful night, with Helena lying sprawled on the floor among the debris. The next pages were the ones Forrester and Sophie had seen Beamish drawing in the grove: both the wider views of Maia's shrine and the close-ups of the water trickling from the stone amphora. All three peered at them closely: none of the images seemed to contain any clue about who had planted the explosives that had brought the pillars down just hours later. Then Forrester held the sketchbook close to his eyes and peered at the join where the pages were bound.

"It's pretty much as I thought," he said. He handed the book to Venables, who examined it, cursed and passed it to Sophie. "You can see that someone has taken out a page," said Forrester.

Sophie pursed her lips. "So the question is," she said, "who had access to it?"

"Well, obviously me," said Venables. "I've been looking at Keith's sketchbooks since Athens to make sure I was gathering the right copy to go with his pictures. As it happens, I hadn't looked at what he'd drawn since we got to Hydros, and I hadn't looked at what he'd sketched of the shrine because it was no particular concern of mine until somebody shot him."

Forrester stood up and examined the door to the room. "And there's no lock," he said, "so pretty much anybody could have come in and looked at the sketchbooks."

"So what do we do now?" said Sophie.

"I suppose it's our duty to report this to Inspector Kostopoulos," said Forrester, "though I have to say I don't have high hopes of that gentleman's effectiveness."

"We should search for the missing page," said Venables. "If we find who has it, we have our man."

"Only if he was stupid enough not to destroy it," said Forrester. "Which seems to me highly unlikely."

* * *

Afterwards Forrester and Sophie went out onto the terrace and spoke quietly as they looked out over the harbour, and he told her about his conversations with Abbot Spyridon and Giorgios Stephanides.

"Penelope and Giorgios were lovers? Ah, that explains so much."

"I don't know that they were literally lovers," said Forrester. "They were childhood sweethearts, all three of them, but Giorgios went away to Athens to write his masterpiece and Ari put on a smart uniform and got in first."

"Perhaps that's what Penelope meant when she talked about sacrifices," said Sophie, and relayed her early-morning conversation with the chatelaine of the *kastello*.

Forrester considered. "But it sounds to me as if she was talking about sacrifices she had to make to keep the island safe during the war."

"Possibly," said Sophie, "although her main point was that Constantine Atreides went into the castle just before Keith Beamish was shot."

"She was clear about that, was she?"

"She was. But there's something else. A feeling I had as we were talking."

"Which was?"

"That someone was listening to everything we said, and Penelope knew it."

Forrester considered. "So it's possible that she told you what she told you for someone else's benefit?"

"Yes," said Sophie. "I'm almost certain that was exactly what was going on."

* * *

Forrester was lying down in his room, staring at the ceiling when Yanni found him.

"Well, boss," he said. "So the soldiers have come to find thy German for thee?"

"Here's the funny thing," said Forrester. "I had no problem hunting him myself. I feel a bit strange thinking of him being hunted down by other people."

"You English!" said Yanni. "Sentimentals, all."

"Both sentimental and hypocritical," said Forrester. "Despite those qualms I wouldn't really mind seeing him being carried in on Inspector Kostopoulos's proverbial door, provided the stone was still with him."

"What if thou couldst get the stone off him without him being placed on the door?"

Forrester looked at him, surprised. "Do you have any idea how that could be done?"

Yanni took a long drag on his cigarette and stared out over the bay. "Remember the windmill? Near the castle? I have been thinking about it, and if I was the German that's where I would have gone."

"Oh, my God," said Forrester. "Of course. The castle was the obvious place, but if he went to the windmill he could have watched us from there all along. Why the hell didn't we search it?"

"Distracted by murder," said Yanni, "right?"

"But if Kretzmer wasn't in the castle, who was it threw the rock down from the chapel roof?"

"Whoever killed Mr. Beamish," said Yanni, simply.

Suddenly Forrester was on his feet. "I have to go there. I have to go and check out that mill."

"If he's still there," said Yanni. "Plenty of time to escape since then."

"But where has he got to escape to? He needs a boat to get off the island. The only boats of any size are here. If I were him I would have waited until things settled down before coming to Drakonaris, wouldn't you?"

"But Kostopoulos says everyone must stay in *kastello*, right?"

"Screw Kostopoulos," said Forrester. "I'm going to the mill."

"Together," said Yanni.

Forrester shook his head. "No, I appreciate it. But I think this is something I should do on my own."

"The countess will want to come with thee."

"I know," said Forrester. "That's why I'm not going to tell her I'm going. And neither are you."

25

THE WINDMILL

Setting out for the mill unobserved proved to be easier said than done. Kostopoulos had taken the precaution of keeping two of the soldiers back from the search to make sure that no one left the *kastello* until he had spoken to the suspects. Having reconnoitred the front door and the kitchen door and discovered there was no easy way out there, Forrester decided that his best plan was to slip over the terrace balcony and drop a dozen feet down into the vegetable garden of the house immediately below.

From here he took one of the alleys that wound its way uphill through the whitewashed houses of the village, then hurried across the path that led to the monastery until he found himself once more in the silence of the woods. He stood still, listened for Sergeant Pyrolithos and his men, and heard nothing.

Ten minutes later he was passing through the grove, glancing briefly at the ruined shrine, and fifteen minutes after that was out on the open central plateau under the wide blue bowl of the sky. From here he could see the soldiers, in line in the distance, moving methodically across the island, but none of them looked up. The crickets were still chirping in the undergrowth and the scent of thyme still rose on the sun-warmed air.

For a mile or two he followed the path he and Sophie had taken on their way to Limani Sangri, but then, at the lake where he had been reminded of 'Morte d'Arthur', he branched off in the direction of Bohemond's castle.

This time when he reached the little chapel where he had searched for Kretzmer, he stepped inside with a different purpose. Sitting in its cool darkness, he considered his options. From now on, as he approached the mill, he would be easy to spot and his only hope of concealing himself was to go down flat in the heather and worm his way forwards on his belly. Then, when he was close to the mill, he could rise to his feet and make a dash for the door before Kretzmer had time to take action.

Even as he laid out this scenario, he knew it would be a mistake. Kretzmer would undoubtedly react violently to the sudden attack and their encounter would end in a shootout. Even if Forrester prevailed he would probably have to kill the German, and for some reason the idea now distressed him. Before leaving the chapel, without quite knowing why, he whispered a short prayer to the faded image of the Virgin on the far wall.

As a result of his deliberations, when he stepped out of the chapel he made no effort to conceal himself, walking steadily towards the windmill in full view of anyone who lay concealed within it. The closer he got the more vividly he was aware that though this method of approach might indeed reassure Kretzmer, it would also give him the perfect opportunity to pick him off at a distance. From long experience Forrester knew that the effective range of the Luger pistol Kretzmer had used in the cave was about one hundred and sixty feet: he came to a halt in front of the mill at two hundred.

Not far away now, the sea glittered glassily beyond Bohemond's castle. For a moment he had a vivid image of father and daughter leaping from the battlements with the Urim and the Thummim strapped to their bodies and bursting into celestial light in mid-air, and with it a gust of pity swept through him.

"Kretzmer!" he shouted. "I know you're in there." He did not know it, of course, but if he was wrong there would be no one there to contradict him. "Listen! There's a detachment of soldiers combing the island for you. Before long they'll find you and the chances are they'll kill you. I'd like to talk. Will you talk?"

There was no answer. The mill's canvas sails creaked gently in the breeze. Crickets chirped and bees buzzed. Not far away Forrester could hear the stream trickling lazily over its stony bed.

He took out the Luger and held it up by the barrel. "I am armed," he said, "as you are. But I'd like to resolve this without shooting. If you don't want to do that, fire a warning shot. Otherwise I'll assume you're ready to talk."

Forrester waited a long moment and then, still holding

the Luger by the barrel, began to move slowly forward until he was around a hundred and sixty feet from the mill.

In range.

He stood, unmoving, ready to dive into the heather at the first crack of a pistol.

Nothing happened. He walked another ten yards towards the mill and stopped again. This time, knowing that Kretzmer could now pick him off easily, it was harder to make himself wait. But he did.

"Kretzmer! Can you hear me? I'm coming into the mill. I mean you no harm. Hold your fire."

Again nothing. Now Forrester walked briskly, heading straight for the mill door. The paint was cracked and ancient; the mill's sun-bleached canvas sails went round right above his head, making just enough noise to stop him hearing if anyone was moving about inside the building. He pushed open the door.

"I'm coming in."

For a moment, as he left the bright sunlight and entered the dim dustiness of the interior, he was blinded, and if Kretzmer had been there, waiting for him, the crack of the Luger would have been the last thing he heard. But then his eyes became accustomed to the darkness, and he saw the huge toothed wooden wheel turning as it connected with the cogs that revolved the millstone. A dusty shaft of sunlight trickled lazily through a hole in the floor above.

"Kretzmer!"

Still no reply. Forrester walked around the circular interior of the mill – nothing. He came to the rough wooden ladder that led up through the trapdoor into the sail-loft.

"Kretzmer, I'm coming up."

He jammed the gun into his belt to free both hands for the ladder and began to climb. If Kretzmer was waiting for the moment of maximum vulnerability, this was it. He made himself draw deep, steady breaths as he climbed towards the trapdoor. Then his head and shoulders rose into the upper floor.

He paused then, but there was no need to look around for the German. Kretzmer lay huddled on a pile of sacking, shivering violently as he tried to keep his gun steady. His torn jacket was draped over him as a makeshift blanket. He had taken off his mask but the sight of his mangled face no longer horrified Forrester.

"Jesus," said Forrester softly. "You're in a bad way."

"*Verpiss dich*," said Kretzmer.

"Fuck off to you," said Forrester and hauled himself up into the loft.

"You are not taking the stone," said Kretzmer.

"Never mind the stone," said Forrester. "You need a doctor."

"You'll need an undertaker if you come any closer," said Kretzmer. "Stay away. *Ich lasse es fallen.*" *I will let it fall.*

It was a second or two before Forrester realised what the German was talking about – and then he saw the stone balanced on the edge of the hole in the floor.

"If it goes down it will smash on *der Mühlstein*."

The millstone: of course.

"You wouldn't do that," said Forrester.

"You want to find out?" said Kretzmer.

No, Forrester did not want to find out. He looked at the man's pale clammy skin, the thick drops of sweat gathered on what remained of his forehead like condensation on a windowpane.

"What happened? How did you get like this?"

Kretzmer made a noise that sounded like the ghost of a laugh. The ghost of something, anyway.

"Cracked ribs when the boat hit," he said, wheezing. "Maybe also something hurt inside."

"You probably punctured a lung," said Forrester. "You look as if you've got pneumonia."

Kretzmer stared at him balefully. "*Warum sollten Sie darauf?*"

"Good question. I don't know that I do care. But I don't want to see you shot down like a dog by the soldiers from Athens."

Kretzmer said nothing.

"They arrived a few hours ago and they're scouring the island for you right now. They've been told you're probably a murderer as well as a thief."

"I am neither. I have taken the stone, and pointed my gun at some people, but I have not killed anybody. Here, anyway."

"I'm inclined to believe you," said Forrester. "But if the soldiers find you they won't need much excuse to write a report saying 'Shot while trying to escape.'"

"Again, what matters it to you, English? You have been trying to kill me yourself ever since Crete."

Forrester thought about this. "Perhaps I've seen one pointless death too many," he said at last.

"Maybe you have. But you still won't talk me into giving you the stone. And if you try to take it I'll smash it to smithereens."

"The stone doesn't belong to you, Kretzmer. It doesn't belong to me either. And the truth is neither of us wants or needs to *possess* the damn thing. We don't want to put it on the mantelpiece, for Christ's sake, do we? We want to know what it says. Am I right?"

"These are just words coming out of your mouth," said Kretzmer weakly. "They mean nothing."

"They mean this," said Forrester, realising it even as he spoke. "That we agree to work on the tablet together. To publish a joint paper on what we discover. What do you say to that?"

For a long moment Kretzmer simply stared at him. Then he closed his eye briefly and then opened it again to glare. Forrester noticed now how red and bloodshot it was. "Why should I believe you?" he said. "You can promise this now – and then when you have the stone you can do what you like, turn me over to the authorities, anything."

Forrester considered. "I won't take the stone," he said at last. "I'll leave it here with you. I'll divert the soldiers away from the mill and I'll help you get out of here. I don't know how yet, but I will. Do you believe me?"

For what seemed like eternity the two men regarded one another, and then Kretzmer said, "Do you have anything to eat?"

Forrester reached into his pocket and brought out a handful of nuts and raisins he had taken from the kitchens of the *kastello*. Slowly he tipped them onto the sacking. Not letting go of his gun, Kretzmer picked up one of the raisins with his free hand and pushed it painfully into his mouth.

Then another. And a third. Then he said: "Whose name will come first on the paper?"

"Mine, of course," said Forrester, "because *F* comes before *K* in the alphabet."

"You will make me do all the work," said Kretzmer, "and claim all the credit."

"I would naturally expect you to work harder than me because you are German," Forrester replied. "And I will claim as much credit as I can. But your strange appearance will undoubtedly appeal to the popular press, and you will therefore probably get most of the publicity, however little you deserve it." Forrester saw the ghost of a smile pass across Kretzmer's ruined face.

Then there was some shouting in the distance and Forrester peered through the gap in the stones through which Kretzmer had doubtless watched his own approach, and saw that the soldiers from Athens were about half a mile away, heading in their direction.

"I'm going to take your jacket," said Forrester, and when Kretzmer nodded, he reached in for it. "I will be going towards the cliffs, near the castle, and then I will turn back, pass the mill again and go towards the soldiers, to whom I will speak. But I am not going to betray you."

"If you do," said Kretzmer, "I will push the stone through the hole in the floor and it will be destroyed."

"I know," said Forrester.

Then he climbed back down the ladder, slipped out of the door and, keeping the mill between himself and the oncoming platoon so he was invisible to them, ran as fast as he could towards the castle and threw something over the edge of the cliffs.

When the soldiers finally saw him he was running towards them and waving his arms.

"Over here!" he shouted. "He ran when he saw me and fell. Come along, hurry!" He began to run towards the castle again and the soldiers almost automatically fell into step with him. By the time they reached the edge of the cliff, Kretzmer's jacket was being drawn inexorably towards *Roufichtra Medusa*.

"There he is!" said Forrester, pointing, and though it was only the jacket they could see, such was the power of suggestion that, had they been asked to testify in court, each of them would have sworn they had seen the German being sucked into the whirlpool.

"Should we climb down to the bottom of the cliff and see if we can swim out to retrieve the body?" asked Forrester. Sergeant Bogdolu Pyrolithos peered down the hundred feet of sheer rock that separated them from the water, and shook his head.

"I do not think that will be necessary," he said.

26

TRUTH AND CONSEQUENCES

An hour later, as Forrester and the platoon were coming through the pinewood above the *kastello*, he saw Sophie coming up towards him. He strode ahead of the others and as he reached her she threw her arms around him and held him close. "Thank God," she said. "When Yanni told me where you had gone I thought I'd never see you again."

"Yanni shouldn't have told you," said Forrester.

"And you shouldn't have gone," said Sophie.

"I had to," said Forrester, "but I'm sorry I didn't warn you first." Then, speaking softly and quickly before the soldiers caught up with them he said, "It worked out well. I found Kretzmer, we did a deal and the stone is safe."

"A deal? With that monster? God in heaven," said Sophie. "How did you manage that?"

Sergeant Pyrolithos and his men had almost caught up. "No time to tell you now," said Forrester. "I have to get Brother Thersites from the monastery."

"That may not be possible right away. Inspector

Kostopoulos has named the murderer."

"Has he, by God? And who does he say it is?"

"Prince Atreides. They followed up your idea about Keith's sketchbook and searched for the missing page, which turned up in the prince's room. It proved he'd been at the shrine."

"How?"

"Keith had sketched his panama hat, of all things, lying near the edge of the grove. He must have taken it off when he planted the explosive."

"And he didn't destroy it as soon as he had it?"

"Apparently not."

"That's incredible. But Kostopoulos decided it was conclusive?"

"Well, there was also Penelope's evidence that Constantine went into the castle just before Keith was shot – and Socrates testified that he had seen the prince carrying something that smelled of almonds, which from what you said must have been the explosive."

"Socrates?"

"The gardener. The little bent old man with the broken nose."

"How did Atreides respond?"

"With loud protestations of innocence. Inspector Kostopoulos is still trying to make him confess."

They heard a door slam below them in the village – and then a burst of gunfire.

"Jesus," said Forrester. "What methods is he using?"

The sergeant and his men began to run immediately, pushing ahead of Forrester and Sophie.

By the time they reached the *kastello* the platoon had clattered off down the village street, and the action had clearly shifted down towards the harbour. There were two shots off to the north, where a steep set of stairs led to the water, and then a fusillade of rifle fire somewhere beyond that. Forrester was hurrying past a little fountain surrounded by shocked-looking villagers when a tall, oddly stooped figure appeared from an alley, and he was about to ask him what was going on when the man stumbled and fell at his feet.

It was General Ari Alexandros.

Blood was soaking Alexandros's shirt as Forrester knelt beside him, searching for the wound to staunch the flow, but before he found it the General spoke.

"Shoulder wound," he said. "The bastard tried to kill me again. Didn't manage it. Get me up."

As Forrester did so there was another burst of gunfire from the harbour and then silence.

With his arm around Forrester's shoulder and a villager supporting him on the other side, Alexandros lurched painfully back up the street towards the *kastello*.

"What happened?" said Forrester.

"That idiot Kostopoulos let Atreides get hold of a gun. He shot his way out of the house and made a break for the harbour. Your friend Venables and I went after him from opposite ends of the street. Atreides must have seen his chance while I was reloading."

"He shot you?"

"And I shot back. The English fired at the same time, and now the bastard will cause no more trouble."

"He's dead?" said Forrester.

"Dead," said the General. "And I owe it to you, Duncan."

"Me?"

"You were the one who put us on to him. With the sketchbook and the smell of almonds."

Penelope, Euripides and some of the other servants reached them and Penelope took over and organised them to get the wounded man up to the house. Brother Thersites had already been called and within minutes the General was lying on the dining-room table having the bullet removed.

"Well, well," said Charles Runcorn, as they gathered in the main room to hear the results of the operation. "Perhaps it was just his panama hat, but I have to admit the prince gave the impression of being such a harmless little chap."

"As harmless as those fascist swine ever are," said David Venables, coming in from the street. The left side of his face was covered in blood.

"What on earth happened to you?" said Durrell.

"Oh, this is nothing," said Venables, reaching a hand up to his torn scalp. "One of that little bastard's bullets sent a stone splinter my way. A couple of stitches will see me right."

"You should get it done as soon as General Alexandros has been helped," said Ariadne. "Here, let me clean it for you."

As she began her work, Inspector Kostopoulos came in, beaming. "Well," he said, "murderer found and murderer punished, all in one day. Is what newspapers will be calling Kostopoulos touch."

"Did Atreides admit his guilt when you were questioning him?" said Forrester. "Did he say why he'd killed Michaelaides and Beamish before he stole your gun and escaped?"

"Was no need," said Kostopoulos, looking slightly offended at the reference to the loss of his weapon. "Is obvious. Atreides trying to poison General in Athens, maybe with kouros, maybe not, fails, kills Michaelaides by accidental. Comes here, tries to bring down shrine on General, gets Stephanides instead. As proved by Socrates smelling him with dynamite and Englishman's stolen drawing showing panama hat near shrine, as always worn by Atreides. Later of course he is stealing drawing, but must have realised Englishman had seen it, so killing him at castle, as proved by General's lady seeing him sneak through walls just before English was shot. Altogether, he knew his goat was cooked, which is why he terrified to be questioned by Kostopoulos. Then, natural, shot while trying to escape," he added, with some satisfaction.

"But why did Prince Atreides want to kill General Alexandros in the first place?" said Ariadne, returning with a cloth and a bowl of water to attend to Venables's head.

"To stop him joining the communists, you little fool," said Helena Spetsos. "Ari is the best fighter in Greece. The people love him for what he did during the war against the Germans. Young men would flock to his banner. If Ari joins ELAS and there is a civil war, ELAS will win."

"And that would have meant Prince Atreides's precious King George would never have regained the throne," said Runcorn.

"So he was prepared to do anything to stop Alexandros leading ELAS," said Lawrence Durrell.

"Including killing my friend because he just happened to get in the way," said Venables bitterly. "If it wasn't Ari's bullet that killed him, Kostopoulos, I very much hope it was mine."

As Forrester was explaining to Kostopoulos that both Kretzmer and the stone had gone over the cliffs at Bohemond's castle and the search could now be called off, Brother Thersites emerged to announce that the bullet had been successfully removed from Alexandros's shoulder and he had retired to his room to sleep. Venables went in to have the wound in his scalp stitched, and when he had been patched up Forrester accompanied Thersites back to the monastery and explained that his labours were not yet over.

There was a wounded German to be looked after.

Before the monk would agree to treat Kretzmer, however, he insisted they consult the Abbot, and it was only after a long conversation that Vasilios agreed that Forrester's decision had been the right one. Instead of trying to tend to the German in his hiding place, however, he sent a party of monks with a stretcher to bring him to the monastery, where he was secreted, late that night, in the same infirmary where Giorgios Stephanides was still recuperating.

As a result it was not until just after midnight that an exhausted Forrester returned to the *kastello*. He was at the front door when he saw a tall, lean figure disappearing, with an awkward gait, down the street in the direction of the harbour, carrying a suitcase.

It was a matter of seconds before he realised who it was, and then, despite his own weariness, he was hurrying after him as fast as he could go.

Alexandros was bent over the engine compartment of his caïque as Forrester approached the waterfront, and by the time he reached the boat itself the engine had burst into life.

"You can cast off for me, if you like," said Alexandros, entering the wheelhouse. But Forrester ignored the suggestion.

"What the hell do you think you're doing?"

"I'm going to take up my command," said Alexandros.

"With ELAS?"

"Who else?"

"You're going to start a civil war because some pathetic little royalist tried to kill you?"

"That pathetic little royalist killed the best poet in Greece. He nearly killed my best friend and he killed the young Englishman everyone was so fond of. He would have finally got rid of me this afternoon if he had been a better shot."

"But he's dead," said Forrester. "He paid for what he did and it's over."

"You think he acted alone?" said Alexandros. "Don't be a fool, Duncan. Who do you think sent him here? The royalists, obviously. His cousin the king. The generals who surrendered to the Nazis instead of fighting one. And the damned politicians who were turning this country into a fascist state in the 1930s and just want to get on with the job."

A DUNCAN FORRESTER MYSTERY

"You've no proof of that."

"Duncan, you helped provide the proof yourself. You worked out that Michaelaides's death was because they were trying to poison me in Athens. You identified the explosive Atreides used. You saw that the artist was killed because his drawings proved who had planted the explosive. And my own wife saw Atreides go into the castle before the Englishman was shot. Don't try to unmake your case because I'm not doing what you expected me to do."

"If you decide to lead ELAS, Ari, there'll be civil war, and thousands of people will die as a result. Tens of thousands."

Alexandros cast off the last rope; now only the power of the engine kept the caïque against the quay.

"There'll be civil war anyway, Duncan, you know that, and thousands of people will die anyway, and if I'm not in the fight the wrong side will win."

"And the communists are the right side? Some of them are as big a bunch of bastards as the right. You know that as well as I do."

"Which means it's better if I'm in control instead of one of the bastards. Duncan, you may not see it now, but this whole campaign to get rid of me has made everything clear. I was wavering before, not sure where my duty lay, but I now see it clearly, for me and for Greece. You helped me to do that, my friend, so I thank you. I will see you when the war is over."

And with a brief salute, Alexandros spun the wheel and headed the caïque out to sea.

27

THE AFFAIR

When Forrester woke the next morning the bed beside him was empty and the sun was high.

He was still lying there, looking up at the pattern of light on the ceiling and letting the tumultuous events of the previous day run through his mind, when Sophie appeared with breakfast on a tray. He smiled, took a deep gulp of the strong, milky coffee, and listened as she told him what was going on in the rest of the house.

She herself had been awoken by a cry of distress from the main bedroom and had gone in to find Penelope Alexandros almost literally tearing out her hair, a note from her husband crumpled on the bed. Sophie had tried in vain to calm her but Penelope had rushed out of the house, gazed in anguish down at the harbour, and then rushed up the path into the woods.

Then as the news of Alexandros's departure reached the monastery, Giorgios Stephanides appeared, still heavily bandaged, and it was clear the General's defection had shaken him to the core. Pulling a rucksack over his shoulder, he went into the woods after Penelope.

Inspector Kostopoulos denounced the General angrily, claimed that his departure was a slur on his, Kostopoulos's honour, and promptly departed for Athens on the boat that had brought him and his military escort.

Durrell had been almost equally appalled at Alexandros's departure. The British government had a strong interest in Greece remaining a democracy and the news of Alexandros's decision to join the communists had to be conveyed to London as soon as possible. Forrester and Sophie reached the quayside as Runcorn and Durrell made the boat ready and Helena Spetsos chivvied them impatiently.

"Are we going to wait all day? Or are we going to go after him?"

"We can go after him as soon as you like," said Ariadne Patrou, "but we will not catch him if he does not want to be caught, and I don't think he does." Venables was already on the bridge, and gave Forrester an ironic, slightly melancholy salute as he caught his eye.

"Do you really think Alexandros is going to make such a difference?" said Forrester as he helped Durrell and Runcorn cast off the lines.

"I'm afraid so," said Durrell. "I very much fear that what's happened on this little island in the last few days is the beginning of a terrible disaster for millions of people."

And with that, the last line was cast off and the minesweeper curved out into the bay.

* * *

Sophie wanted to go to look for Penelope, but Giorgios Stephanides came down to the *kastello* later that morning to say he had found her and she did not want to see anyone. From the hints he dropped it seemed she was roaming through the woods, maddened by her loss, and as soon as he had gathered some supplies he was going back to be with her until calm had returned. Forrester could not help thinking she had become one of the maenads of old, and felt a secret relief that he and Sophie did not have to try to calm the distraught woman.

Convincing Yanni Patrakis that the hunt for Kretzmer was over and the issue between them resolved took some time, and it was not until the Cretan had personally visited the monastery infirmary and inspected the pale, weak German for himself that he was convinced Forrester and Sophie were finally safe from their enemy. He said very little to Kretzmer but examined the stone with great interest.

Yanni did not leave the island straightaway, however: it seemed that amidst all the events of the past few days, he had come across a comely widow from Limani Sangri, and decided to stay on for a while to see how things developed. Besides, he told Forrester, the fishing in that vicinity was very good, and with few boats around the size of his, there was very little competition.

For the next few days Forrester and Sophie spent most of their time at the monastery, Sophie assisting Brother Thersites in nursing Kretzmer back to health, and Forrester working with him on their first tentative attempts to relate the hieroglyphs on one face of the stone with the mysterious Minoan script on the other.

Not entirely to his surprise, Forrester found the German's almost feverish intensity both stimulating and challenging. It was as if the physical battle between them had been transformed into a mental contest in which the enemy now was those ancient and impenetrable symbols.

But absorbing and satisfying though this was, Forrester was troubled. It was not just the fact that as a result of Atreides being identified as the killer Alexandros had given his backing to a cause Forrester believed would be disastrous not just for Greece but for all southern Europe. It was also the fact that his instincts told him there was something deeply flawed about the evidence that had convicted the royal cousin.

To calm his mind, and as a respite from the intense intellectual effort on the stone, Forrester took long walks across the island. He passed through the grove many times and examined the fallen shrine again and again. He went back to Bohemond's castle with the diagrams that he, Yanni and Sophie had created, and retraced his steps on the day that Keith Beamish was shot. None of this activity proved that Atreides could not have been behind both the collapse of the shrine or the shooting at the castle, but all of it reinforced his growing conviction that there was something very skewed about the official verdict.

Several times as he walked the island, trying to tug aside this mental curtain, he had sensed the presence of someone watching him, and was almost certain it was Penelope Alexandros. But he had as little appetite for meeting her as she apparently had for meeting him.

And then came Kretzmer's bombshell. He did not intend it as a bombshell. The remark came quite casually, as they were taking a break from considering a Minoan symbol, and concerned a certain Major Heinz Baumann, whom Kretzmer had met on the Eastern Front.

The major had, he told Kretzmer in the midst of a particularly vicious bombardment, been the commandant of a small Greek island earlier in the war, where he had been persuaded to go easy on the islanders by a gravely beautiful woman of much local influence with whom he had had a torrid affair. Kretzmer did not know either the name of the island or the Greek seductress, but Sophie came into the room as he was finishing his story, and almost dropped the tray she was carrying.

Afterwards, as she and Forrester walked back to the *kastello*, she said, "That was what Penelope was talking about. That night when she talked to me at the lookout."

"What?" said Forrester. "I don't understand."

"She was talking about sacrifices," said Sophie. "Sacrifices women have to make during wars. Sacrifices she'd had to make to keep the islanders safe. Sacrifices men wouldn't understand."

"You think she was the woman Baumann was talking about?"

"I've no idea. It doesn't matter. But I'm sure she was referring to exactly the same situation."

"You mean that she slept with one of the German commandants here? To protect the island?"

"Yes, that's exactly what I mean. She wanted to talk about it, but she couldn't."

Forrester stared at her. "Blackmail," he said. "Somebody knew what had happened and was blackmailing her."

"I'm sure of it," said Sophie.

"Blackmailing her to say that Atreides had gone into the castle before Keith Beamish was shot."

"Yes."

They sat down on a patch of turf overlooking the village.

"What about Socrates?" said Forrester. "He testified that he smelt the explosive on Atreides. Why would he lie?"

"To protect her."

"Of course," said Forrester. "He must have known about her and the German commandant. Whoever was blackmailing Penelope approached him and said that unless he denounced Atreides, the truth about what had happened during the war would come out. And of course he would have done anything to make sure Alexandros didn't find out, whatever lies he had to tell."

Sophie's face darkened. "Does that mean whoever was doing the blackmailing was the killer?"

Forrester considered. "I think it does," he said at last.

28

THE CHOICE

Forrester looked balefully at the unshaven Greek peasant next to him, his head on the table, his sheepskin jacket reeking of sweat, his snores rattling the empty ouzo bottle that lay beside him. But in all truth, the man's stink was hard to distinguish in the general odour of unwashed humanity that filled the bar, stirred only when the door opened to admit another gang of stevedores rolling in from the dockside. Recorded bouzouki music thudded through the thick air, intensifying the headache that had been building behind Forrester's temples for an hour now.

He had been in this northern Greek port for three days, leaving word in all the most likely places that he needed a guide to take him towards the Yugoslav border to find ELAS. He had spoken to old wartime comrades, Turkish smugglers, shifty union officials, shady businessmen. Finally one of them, a scrap metal merchant out of Salonika, had agreed to meet him at this bar if he discovered anything.

But the man had not shown up, it was late in the evening,

the noise hammering off the low ceiling was increasingly intolerable, and the sheer mass of humanity in the place was claustrophobic. Forrester stood up to leave – as someone close beside him said, "I want you to try this, old chap, and tell me what you think."

David Venables slid onto the bench on the other side of the table and put a bottle and two glasses between them. Slowly, Forrester sat back down.

"You look as if you'd seen a ghost, Duncan. It can't be that much of a surprise, surely." Venables filled the glasses. "I haven't given up on the travel book, despite not having poor old Keith on the team, and my researches continue." He patted the familiar cavas manuscript bag. "Your health!" He raised his glass.

Forrester remained motionless.

"Suit yourself," said Venables, and drank. He wiped his lips and grinned at Forrester. "It's not poisoned, you know."

"Really?" said Forrester. "You surprise me."

"I don't quite take your meaning, old chap."

"Oh, I think you do," said Forrester. "You're quite a dab hand at poison, I think."

"Ah, you've already been drinking," said Venables equably. "And on that assumption I'll let it pass." He refilled his glass.

"Your assumption is wrong," said Forrester. "I'm not remotely drunk and the accusation is not made lightly. I believe you were responsible for the death of Jason Michaelaides."

"The poet? Why on earth would I want to kill Jason Michaelaides?"

"I don't think you did," said Forrester. "I think the real target was Ari Alexandros, and Michaelaides got in the way."

"Why on earth would I want to kill Ari Alexandros?"

"Again, I don't think you did," said Forrester. "I think you simply wanted Ari to *believe* someone was trying to kill him and Michaelaides was an unintended casualty. I'm assuming you put a bit of poisoned *tiropita* on Alexandros's plate at the Archbishop's party and Michaelaides ate it by mistake. It wouldn't even have killed him if he hadn't had a heart condition. So your little scheme didn't have the effect on Alexandros that you intended."

"And what in your disordered mind did I intend?" said Venables.

"You intended to make him think that the royalists were trying to kill him. If he believed that, it would almost certainly prompt him to join ELAS."

"Rubbish."

"Unfortunately for you," said Forrester, "Ari decided the best course was to retire to the comparative safety of Hydros and re-establish his relationship with his wife. Thus obliging you to follow him there."

"But as you know, Forrester," said Venables, filling his glass again, "I didn't follow him. I went to visit Lawrence Durrell in Rhodes."

"And took Constantine Atreides and Helena Spetsos with you. You knew that Durrell was planning a tour of inspection of that part of the Aegean, and you knew Helena would insist he visited Hydros. Her obsession with

Alexandros was the perfect cover. And Atreides the perfect fall guy for whatever you were able to pull off there."

"How did I know that Durrell was planning a tour of inspection? How could I possibly have a piece of information like that?"

"I'll get onto that later," said Forrester. "But first I want to look at your next attempt to convince Alexandros that the royalists were out to kill him."

"I made no such attempt," said Venables firmly.

"You planted the plastique at the shrine so that it would collapse as Alexandros was waiting for me in the grove. You may not have intended to injure Stephanides, but the fact that he turned up and took the brunt only helped. It made Alexandros even angrier, so that all you needed to do was to point the finger at Constantine Atreides and your job was done. Unfortunately for you, your friend Keith Beamish had been sketching up there that morning."

"And as you very well know, providing the proof that Atreides planted the explosive."

"That was your stroke of genius, of course," said Forrester. "But let's consider whether Keith Beamish might not have discovered who had planted the explosive in an entirely different way. Would you mind showing me your satchel?"

Venables stared at him, and then shrugged. "Why not?" he said, bringing it out onto the table. "It has the same contents as it did when you first met me under that pub table during the blitz." He emptied the bag. A few pens fell out, and an oilskin package. Venables opened the package to reveal a pile of manuscript pages.

Forrester picked up the empty oilskin pouch and pressed it to his nose. "Wonderful aroma," he said.

"Oilskin," said Venables. "It has quite a strong smell. And your point is?"

"That smell is what makes it the perfect thing for hiding the aroma of Nobel 808," said Forrester. "You could stay in the same room, even the same cabin with Keith Beamish and he'd never know that…" He pulled at a loose thread. "…there was a stick of 808 sewn away inside the bottom flap. Unless he looked inside."

"Keith was under strict instructions never to look at my manuscript," said Venables evenly. "I trusted him implicitly."

"Apparently unwisely," said Forrester. He gave the thread another tug and a little mouth appeared in the lining of the bottom of the bag. "My guess is that he wanted to know what you'd been writing about him and Ariadne, but it doesn't matter. What does matter is that he opened the satchel, looked through your manuscript – and smelt something odd."

"Rubbish," said Venables.

"Not being familiar with explosives, of course, he didn't know what that almond scent signified – until we were on the way to the castle and I happened to mention it."

"This is supposition on supposition, Forrester."

"I should have realised that he'd made the connection when he started talking to you about foxes and shrines, as we walked," said Forrester. "I didn't understand then it was an accusation. But you did, didn't you? You realised he was onto you. Which was why you killed him."

"Keith was my friend," said Venables. "And he was my collaborator. How could you even imagine I would kill someone who was so vital to me?"

"Your book was a cover from the beginning," said Forrester. "And you were perfectly prepared to sacrifice Keith Beamish for the cause, weren't you?"

"Keith was killed by Constantine Atreides," said Venables doggedly. "You saw the sketch he made that proved the bastard was in the grove that morning."

"I did see it," said Forrester. "It did indeed look conclusive. But unfortunately for you after you all left Countess Arnfeldt-Laurvig examined the page very closely – and do you know what she found? Pressure marks on every stroke delineating Atreides's hat."

"Meaning what?"

"Meaning that it had been added to the drawing by somebody using a piece of tracing paper. The hat in the drawing was identical to the drawing of the hat in the sketch Keith Beamish made that night in Anafiotika. You simply added it in. And of course that explains why Keith made no reference to having seen Atreides's hat in the grove that day: he hadn't."

"Bullshit. It was Atreides who killed Keith. You know damn well Alexandros's wife virtually saw him do it."

"Ah, Penelope Alexandros. That was another place where your excellent sources of information came in handy. You knew that she had been the mistress of at least one German commandant on Hydros during the war, didn't you? That was how she had made sure the islanders were spared the kind of atrocities that happened elsewhere. And you used that fact to blackmail her into saying what you wanted her to say."

"Unprovable," said Venables. "Did she tell you that I blackmailed her? I don't expect so."

"No," said Forrester, "you wouldn't expect her to identify you, would you, because you had taken the precaution of sending your demands in the form of notes, which she naturally destroyed."

"But Penelope Alexandros wasn't the only one pointing the finger at Atreides, was she?"

"No, you used the same method to blackmail the gardener into naming Atreides. He knew about Penelope Alexandros and the German commander, he knew why she had done it, and he would do anything to protect her. His evidence against Constantine seemed like the final nail in the coffin for Atreides, but in fact it was the final nail in yours."

"What do you mean?" said Venables.

"Because after Constantine was dead and you were all gone Socrates identified you as the man who blackmailed him."

"He couldn't have!" said Venables. "He never saw me."

Forrester said nothing, but simply stared.

"What I mean—" said Venables – but it was too late.

"What you mean," said Forrester, "is that you did it. You manipulated the entire situation to achieve your ends. You created the illusion that someone was trying to kill Ari Alexandros, when no one was trying to do so. In

Athens you wanted him to believe someone had tried to kill him with poison – no one had. On Hydros you wanted him to believe the sabotage of the shrine was aimed at him – it wasn't. And when Atreides tried to escape it was the perfect opportunity for you to take a shot at Alexandros and make it look as if it was Connie's last effort to fulfil his mission. Before, of course, you shot Atreides yourself to ensure the case against him would never be properly examined. I have to congratulate you, Venables, it was a brilliant campaign – and it succeeded. Alexandros finally snapped, decided he wasn't going to let the royalists or the right-wingers either frighten or eliminate him and went to join ELAS. Your masters must have been very pleased."

"My 'masters'," said Venables contemptuously. "I am not some lackey, like you, Forrester. I fight for what I believe in."

"And what do you believe in?" said Forrester.

Venables glanced around the room, then spat back: "The forces of history, the triumph of the proletariat. Everything that Karl Marx predicted in *Das Kapital*."

"And you were prepared to sacrifice your friend for that? Because he realised you were a murdering bastard? And Jason Michaelaides, who had never done you any harm? And Connie Atreides, who wouldn't hurt a fly? And Giorgios Stephanides, who was just an accidental casualty? And me, come to think of it, when you took a potshot at me in the wood that night. Together with anybody else who got in the way of the forces of history."

"Of course I was," said Venables, his face suddenly radiant, as if lit by an inner glow. "Unlike you, Duncan, I believe in something. And as a result of what I did the cause has received a powerful new recruit – one who'll change history."

"Unless he learns the truth about you and the Party," said Forrester. "Unless he learns that the reason you were able to blackmail his wife was because the Party gave you the information you needed. Because that was what happened, wasn't it? And he'll know the truth when he hears it."

"From you?" said Venables. "What makes you think you're going to get anywhere near him?"

"Oh, I'll reach him in the end," said Forrester. "I fought the Wehrmacht in these mountains, and it'll take more than someone like you to stop me. And by the way, if you're thinking of trying to bump me off here, I should warn you I already have a Luger pointed at your stomach under the table."

To Forrester's surprise Venables smiled. "Well, I don't have a gun," he said. "I have no need. I just want to take something out of my top pocket to show you. It's not a weapon – it's something I think you'll be quite interested in. Will you permit that?"

Forrester's eyes narrowed, but he nodded. Venables reached up and took out an envelope. From the envelope he took out a photograph. He pushed the photograph across the table to Forrester.

"Do you recognise him?"

Forrester stared at the picture. It was a black and white

prison photograph of a gaunt middle-aged man with wild, unfocused eyes. "I've never seen him before in my life," said Forrester, but at some deep subterranean level, he knew this was not entirely true.

"You may not know him personally, but a good friend of yours is very familiar with him," said Venables. "Countess Arnfeldt-Laurvig."

Forrester felt his mouth go dry.

"That is her husband, the count," said Venables.

"He's dead," said Forrester. "He died during the war."

"So the countess believed," said Venables. "Otherwise I'm sure she would never have betrayed him by becoming your lover. But the fact is he was captured, and through the complex convolutions of battle in the northern latitudes, ended up in a Russian prisoner-of-war camp. He is now about to be released. He is, of course, eager to return to his wife and estates."

"Why are you telling me this?"

"He is a degenerate, a drunkard – and is now a shell of a man, bitter, diseased and full of anger. It would be a tragedy for a woman like the countess to have him in her life again."

Forrester forced himself to speak. "And your point is?"

"As you have realised," said Venables, relaxing, "I am a member of the Communist Party. As a result of my achievements I am in very good standing with the Party. One word from me and the count will not be released back into the world, but will vanish harmlessly into the camps, where doubtless he will not survive for long, which will be a great blessing for you and the countess."

"In return for what?"

"In return for you giving up your hopeless quest to find General Alexandros and agreeing not to cast doubts in his mind about the rightness of his decision to lead ELAS to victory. If anyone asks, you have tried and you have failed. No one will ever know anything different apart from you and me."

"And if I refuse?"

"The count will be released and repatriated and you will be condemning the woman you love to many years of misery. You will be sacrificing her for some abstract political cause – exactly what you accused me of doing in relation to poor Keith and Michaelaides and the ridiculous Prince Atreides. Are you prepared to do that, Forrester?"

Forrester closed his eyes. Had Venables offered him the bribe as a means of securing his own happiness it would have been easy to refuse. But Venables had put Sophie on the altar of sacrifice, and handed Forrester the knife. Besides, wasn't he right? Alexandros had made his decision. What was the point in trying to change his mind?

He thought, for a long moment, of the years ahead with Sophie if the count remained in a Russian Gulag. Of the peace and contentment they could bring each other. Of the fact that he loved her and she brought a balm to his soul after years of drought.

He saw all that and he knew it could never be. If he told her that her husband was still alive, she would have to go to him. If he did not, the lie would poison everything.

"I'll make a deal with you," he said, "but it's not the one you've offered. If you agree to release the count into my custody, I'll agree to give up my quest to find Alexandros and tell him the truth."

Venables stared at him. "But that's ridiculous," he said. "All your efforts to incriminate me have been for nothing, and you lose a woman you clearly care about. Because she will take him back, you know that don't you? She will take him back like a wounded animal and look after him for years to come and you will lose her."

Forrester felt himself grow cold in the oppressive heat of the bar. Every word that Venables said was like a knife twisting in his heart. And yet he could do no other.

"That is as it may be," he said. "But that is my decision. Do we have a deal?"

Venables reached down to the table, repacked the manuscript in its oilskin pouch, returned it to the canvas bag, returned the photograph to his pocket, and buttoned his coat. "Very well," he said. "If you come with me now, we will make the necessary arrangements."

Forrester let out a long breath, picked up the glass that had lain untouched before him since Venables arrived, and drained it. Then, together, the two men walked out of the bar.

Nothing happened for a long moment after the door slammed behind them. Then the stinking drunken Greek peasant who had lain patiently with his head on the table throughout the conversation, as Forrester had asked him to, straightened up.

It was Colonel Giorgios Stephanides.

"Well played, my friend," he said to himself. "I will give your regards to the General when I make my report. But I am sorry about you losing your woman. She was a good woman, too. And they're not easy to find."

AFTERWORD

Greece did indeed erupt into civil war later that year, and ELAS came close to victory on several occasions. But General Ari Alexandros was not there to ensure that victory was complete. Ten days after the events described in this book, he unexpectedly left ELAS headquarters near the Yugoslav border and returned, in the company of Colonel Giorgios Stephanides, to Athens, where they were both given key commands in the Greek Army.

The long-awaited elections, held on 31 March 1946, put the royalists in power, and in a referendum in September 1946 the people of Greece voted for King George II to return.

The civil war finally ended, with the communists defeated, in September 1949.

But by that time Forrester was far away.

AUTHOR'S NOTE

Some of the Greek islands in the book, home to the local variants of the Greek myths expounded by my characters, do not appear on any map, and though there were several Bohemonds at large during the Crusades, mine and the knightly order to which he belonged escaped the attentions of all historians, just as my islands eluded even the most conscientious geographers. I hope, however, that the isle of Hydros and story of Bohemond and his family will now find a home in your imagination.

Thanks for their help to Athina Plakoudi and Shelly Papadopoulos and the Greek Heritage Society of Southern California. There were two books which I found particularly useful in conjuring up the atmosphere of Greece and its islands in 1946: Osbert Lancaster's *Classical Landscape with Figures* and Lawrence Durrell's *Reflections on a Marine Venus*, both of which are as enjoyable as they are informative. Any of my readers who wish to delve further into the world of *The Age of Olympus* would be well advised to start there.

ABOUT THE AUTHOR

Gavin Scott is a British Hollywood screenwriter, novelist and journalist, based in Santa Monica, California. He spent twenty years as a radio and television reporter for BBC and ITN, during which time he interviewed J.B. Priestley, Iris Murdoch and Christopher Isherwood, among many others. He is writer of the Emmy-winning mini-series *The Mists of Avalon*, he developed and scripted *The Young Indiana Jones Chronicles* for George Lucas, wrote the BAFTA-nominated *The Borrowers*, and worked with Stephen Spielberg on *Small Soldiers*. His first novel in the Duncan Forrester series, *The Age of Treachery*, was published in 2016.

THE AGE OF EXODUS

A DUNCAN FORRESTER MYSTERY

GAVIN SCOTT

It's 1947. As Britain's new Labour government struggles to cope with the break-up of Empire, there's a grisly murder in the British Museum, terrorists target British Foreign Secretary Ernest Bevin and Forrester boards the *Queen Mary* for a fateful voyage to New York.

PRAISE FOR THE SERIES

"A dashing new hero has been born"
Library Journal (starred review)

"A promising postwar series"
Booklist

"Fans of *Morse* will love it"
Mark Oldfield

AVAILABLE APRIL 2018